## About the Author

The only girl in the midst of four brothers, I spent my childhood hiding behind romance novels. Now the mother of four overly-energetic children, a Whimsy kitty and slobber-flinging Great Dane, fiction is still my refuge. Excessive caffeine fuels my typing, stiletto heels maintain my sass, and the splendors of Idaho alongside its gregarious people inspire my muse.

You can follow me on Twitter @_AngelNicholas.

Also by Angel Nicholas

*Sweet Deception*

# Dying for Love

## ANGEL NICHOLAS

A division of HarperCollins*Publishers*
www.harpercollins.co.uk

*Harper*
An imprint of HarperCollins*Publishers* Ltd
The News Building
1 London Bridge Street
London SE1 9GF

www.harpercollins.co.uk

A paperback original 2016
1

ISBN: 9780008194574

Set in Minion by Palimpsest Book Production Ltd, Falkirk, Stirlingshire

Printed and bound in Great Britain

**MIX**
Paper from
responsible sources
FSC
www.fsc.org
**FSC™ C007454**

*To Grace*

# PROLOGUE

*April 19, 1986*

Cassandra's knuckles whitened on the steering wheel. A wild hare hopped across the rusty train tracks and a gentle breeze blew through the open windows, mixing freshly bloomed jasmine with the smell of poverty.

She turned. Sober gazes met hers over the worn bench seat, her children's little faces pale in the unusual spring heat. Her sweet babies had learned early in life to be very, very quiet. If they managed to blend into the woodwork, Daddy might not notice them. Being noticed was never a good thing. Not in their home.

Sandra swallowed the sob threatening her tenuous calm and tore her gaze away.

Where was the train? Closing her eyes, she pictured the train schedule—and easy feat, thanks to her photographic memory—then glanced at the dusty clock set in the dashboard. Pointless, since it had stopped working two years ago on October 9. The night her youngest, Gracie, was born.

Hoss had flown into a rage when her water broke and soaked the car seat on the way home from a high-school football game. He insisted on going to every game even though their children weren't old enough to play and they didn't know anyone on the team. Reliving his long-gone glory days always put him in a foul mood.

"Don't you have any self-control, you pathetic cow?"

Spittle flew from his mouth and his big fist slammed into the dashboard clock. She shrank against her door and wrapped her arms protectively around her swollen belly.

"I'm sorry," she whispered. "I knew the baby was comin'. I just didn't want to interrupt the game for you."

Mollified, he swung the big boat of a car around. The county hospital was on the opposite side of the small, downtrodden town, a full thirty minutes from where their sagging trailer sat in the woods outside the town limits.

Hoss said they lived so far out because he liked his privacy, but Sandra knew better. He didn't want anyone to know what went on in their home. Like it was any secret. She'd seen the way folks looked at her and her ever-increasing brood of children, curious gazes lingering on shabby clothes and the dark bruises peeking from long sleeves before sliding away.

She knew better than to expect any help. People she'd grown up with, known since she was a baby, turned their backs on the obvious signs of abuse and neglect. They still thought of the man she'd married as a hero. They saw him or heard his name and got that look in their eyes.

The quarterback who'd put their small town on the map. Took the team all the way to the state championship and brought home the big trophy. Even with the evidence right in front of them, they didn't want to believe the good ol' Sathers boy would beat his pretty little wife and sweet babies. Or worse.

"Momma, I have to pee."

The soft whisper startled Sandra.

She stared down the tracks again, then sighed. "All right, Suzy."

Putting her shoulder into it, she shoved open the car door and stood. Her five-year-old scrambled over the front seat and out of the car. It had to be urgent or Suzy wouldn't have said a word.

"Hurry, baby." She glanced down the tracks again.

Suzy rushed to the side of the road and slipped behind a bush to take care of business. She'd been going to pee a lot lately. Sandra rubbed her arms, worried there might be a problem.

Suffocating guilt rose. Guilt was her constant companion. What kind of mother couldn't take care of her children? Take them to the doctor. Protect them. She tried to intervene. She always tried. Even if he beat her unconscious, it was worth it if he left her babies alone. She never succeeded, though.

The first time, their oldest was just two years old and on a crying jag from the pain of cutting a handful of teeth all at once. Sandra had seen the rage in his eyes and stepped in front of him when he reached for the baby. Hoss threw her across the room, bruising her entire backside black and blue and knocking her unconscious. But the worst had come after. When she'd opened her eyes again, hell had risen from the bowels of the earth and taken over her living room. The sight of him hurting their little girl was seared into her brain.

She wouldn't have to worry about her babies much longer. She glanced again at the tracks. From a long way off, a piercing whistle blew. Her nerves trembled—almost broke.

Squaring her shoulders and firming her chin, she took a deep breath.

Panic crawled up her throat, so she took another breath. She smiled through the open window at her little ones, sitting so quiet in the backseat. Gracie, her precious blue-eyed girl, sat on the farthest side of the car in her high-backed infant seat. There weren't enough seat belts, so as the littlest, she was the only one securely buckled in.

The train whistle blew again.

"Time to go, Suzy."

"Comin', Momma."

Suzy appeared a few seconds later, her dingy white shirt tucked neatly into her worn plaid skirt. She smoothed her neat braids as she climbed the side of the road. On impulse, Sandra knelt on the hard-packed dirt road and gathered Suzy into her arms. Tears she refused to shed burned her eyes.

"I love you so much. You know that, right?"

"Yes, Mama."

Sandra reluctantly released her and rose. "Go on, baby."

Suzy climbed across the seat and into the back. Legs trembling, Sandra stepped into the car and settled behind the big steering wheel. Driving had come back as easy as pie, despite not having done it for years. Her husband insisted on taking her and the children into town whenever they needed anything.

"Can't have my family wandering 'round without my protection now, can I?" An ugly grin twisted his lips, his dark-blue eyes hard.

They never went anywhere without him. Not since she'd made the painful mistake of talking to the sheriff about her husband's violent outbursts. The sheriff had heard her out with polite deference, then sent her home and gone straight to his old football buddy. The broken leg she suffered as a result had never seen medical attention. She'd walked with a limp ever since.

One last time, Sandra turned around. A smile trembled. She met the gaze of each of her babies, her heart overflowing with love.

They looked so pretty. She'd dressed them in their Sunday best, hand-me-downs and thrift-store finds, before leaving the house an hour ago. They were early, but she didn't want to risk missing the train. Besides, she couldn't stand being in the house another minute.

Her gaze lingered on the baby, still so tiny and fragile. Gracie's little arm was swollen and bruised, her face splotchy from the silent tears still trailing down her pale cheeks. Sandra recognized the signs of a broken bone. Her belly clenched and her hands fisted. The animal she'd married had finally gone too far.

The brilliant slash of blood on the baseball bat she'd used on his head flashed in her mind's eye. Nausea rose, but she choked it down. He was still breathing when she'd left.

How long before someone discovered what she'd done? People would be horrified, but they hadn't lived with her husband all these years. They hadn't seen what he'd done. How he'd stolen her babies' childhoods.

No, she was doing what was best. For all of them.

The car began to vibrate. A whimper sounded behind her. She looked out the window. The fast-moving freight train came around the curve in the tracks.

Finally. Her shoulders sagged and tears she'd held back for years stung her eyes.

Finally.

Dusk settled around them. The lead engine completed the turn and the blinding headlight lit the interior of the car. The whistle blew, long and hard. Metal brakes shrieked. Gracie began to cry, but Sandra shut out the sound. The train wouldn't be able to stop or slow down in time.

She'd planned their location well. With a 4.0 grade-point average throughout high school, her teachers had predicted a bright future for her. Such a shame she'd waited until now to apply her sharp intelligence. She'd had a beautiful life back then. Supportive home environment, loving parents. . . she missed them so much.

"I'll see you soon, Mom and Dad," she whispered. "You'll finally get to meet your grandbabies."

Sparks flew beneath the train as it roared toward them. The engineer pulled on the whistle; the high-pitched wail ear-piercing. Behind her, stifled sobs joined Gracie's and the handles clicked uselessly on doors rusted shut years ago. The car rocked with the force of the oncoming train. The lines of an old lullaby ran through her mind.

*Rock a bye, baby, in the treetop.*
*When the bough breaks, the cradle will fall.*
*Down will come baby, cradle and all.*

5

She resisted the urge for one more look at her babies. Not the time to be weak. She had to do this one thing for her girls. Be strong. There was no other choice. No other option.

*Dear God, I've been a miserable failure my whole life. I don't deserve any favors, but please. . . Please, take care of my babies.*

The brilliant white light grew in strength until it blocked out everything else.

"Momma?" a little voice whimpered.

# CHAPTER ONE

*Twenty-five years later*

"Sweet angels in heaven, I need coffee."

Grace Debry walked into her kitchen, hand outstretched for salvation in a coffeepot, and tripped. Her hip smacked into the granite counter and tears of pain blinded her. She righted herself, rubbing her hip, blinked her gaze clear and screamed.

Her kitchen had been ransacked. A sea of kitchen gadgets covered the pristine black counters. Kitchen towels were everywhere. Spatulas, a meat tenderizer, large spoons, and a collection of other utensils spilled from drawers. The oven door was wide open. Her entire collection of cookware covered the stovetop and sink.

"Purple dandelion blood."

She covered her mouth, her hand trembling. If only she hadn't given up swearing. Her foster mother had hated swearing with a passion. Always said it showed a severe lack of vocabulary. Pulse thundering in her ears, she stepped back and took in the rest of her condo at a glance. A well-executed swear word would make her feel so much better right now.

The peaceful serenity of her neat living room and cozy furniture arrangement made the carnage of her kitchen all the more bizarre. She wrapped her arms around her ribcage, trying to still her trembling. The front door and balcony slider were securely dead-bolted.

Maybe she'd woken in the middle of the night and trashed her kitchen? She shook her head. Sleepwalking wasn't part of her repertoire. She nibbled on her lip. No, not possible. She'd shared numerous bedrooms growing up—not to mention the occasional bed. She would know. Foster kids were not merciful creatures. Neither were jealous co-workers, come to think of it. She'd kept so much to herself since moving to the area, she didn't know anyone outside of work. Except the little elderly lady downstairs. She couldn't imagine her or anyone else she knew indulging in a little B&E for kicks and giggles. Or screams.

Swallowing to moisten her dry mouth, she braved the kitchen again. Her heavy marble rolling pin rested against the carpet edge at the entrance. So that was what she'd tripped over.

Grace focused on the pantry door.

A kernel of caution nudged her. The intruder could be behind that door. She snatched the marble rolling pin off the floor and faced off with her frosted-glass pantry door. Reaching for the gleaming silver handle, her tongue glued itself to the roof of her mouth.

Banging against her front door ripped another scream from her.

"Grace? Are you alright, *cher*?"

Hand pressed against her racing heart, Grace spun and leapt over the mess covering her floor. She glanced at the wall-mounted clock in her living room. They weren't carpooling today, which meant Lisette had heard her scream from across the hallway. Grace would be mortified about screaming later. Right now, she was grateful for a friend.

Grace looked through the peephole. Her petite Cajun neighbor from New Orleans bounced on the other side, anxiously twining her long hair around her fingertip. Grace unlocked and opened the door with hands that trembled.

Lisette burst through the opening. "*Mon amie*! What happened?"

Grace took her time shutting and locking the door. They'd

become instant friends when Grace had moved in six months ago, but a lifetime of keeping her own council gave her pause.

A hiss of breath sounded from across the room. Grace turned. Her neighbor stood in the arched entrance to her kitchen. She should have known the warm bundle of energy, otherwise known as Lisette de LaCroix, aka Lisie, wouldn't wait for an invitation.

"*Soc au' lait*! What happened?"

Grace sighed, some of her fear draining now that she wasn't alone. "I don't know. I found it like this when I walked in for my coffee."

Lisette's impossibly big brown eyes widened. "Surely you heard something?"

This had happened while she'd slept. Grace paused in the middle of the living room, light-headed at the realization that an intruder had ransacked her kitchen while she slept just a room away. Her knees trembled. She snapped her spine straight and sucked in a deep breath.

Joining her friend, she shook her head. "I wear noise-cancelling earbuds at night."

"Maybe it was done while you were at work yesterday?"

"No. . . "

Grace stared at the pantry door. She hadn't checked inside yet. Hefting the rolling pin she hadn't even thought to put down— latent terror, no doubt—she carefully maneuvered through the maze of kitchen gadgets. Her pulse skipped a beat.

"What're you doing, *cher*?"

With a shaky exhale and shakier smile, she glanced at Lisette. "I was just getting ready to check the pantry when you arrived."

"Check for. . .Oh!" Lisette's eyes narrowed. She quickly selected a copper-bottomed skillet, then nodded. "Ready."

Grace considered asking her to leave for half a beat. She'd feel awful if anything happened to the first real friend she'd made since high school. No way Lisette would go without a fight, though. Stomach clenched tighter than her hand around the marble rolling pin, Grace faced the pantry, yanked open the door and flipped on the light, ready to brain anything that moved.

Empty.

She sagged against the door frame. The floor was piled high with foodstuffs, miscellaneous kitchen tools and dishes, leaving the shelves bare. Her pantry hadn't escaped her uninvited visitor, but at least the culprit was gone.

Thumbnail caught between her teeth, she turned. "Why would someone break into my place only to mess up my kitchen?"

Lisette tapped the saucepan against her thigh, arched brows drawn together in a frown. "I don't know, but I don't like it."

The buzzer on the coffeepot went off. Grace jumped and slapped her hand over her mouth to smother a shriek. *Just the coffeepot, Grace. Get it together.* She glanced at her watch.

"Oh, crap. I'm gonna be late for work." Leaping over a saucepot, spatula and potato masher, she ran to the bedroom. "Crap, crap, crap."

At least her makeup and hair were done. Throwing on the outfit she laid out last night would take two minutes, racing down the three flights of stairs and along the sidewalk to her car two and a half, and the drive to the office ten—fifteen if traffic was snarled.

"You can't go to work. You have to call the police and report this."

Grace tugged her skirt over her hips and zipped it, frowning. "Why?"

Lisette blinked. "Because your home was broken into, *cher*. The police are here to protect you. Let them do their job."

She snorted and pulled her blouse over her head, muttering, "They wouldn't know how to do their job with a flashlight, map and CliffsNotes."

"Pardon?"

"I don't see the point."

Lips tightening, Lisette planted her hands on the generous

10

curves of her hips. "What's wrong with you? You act like it don' madda'! I'm a fixin' to do it myself."

Grace winced. Whenever Lisette's Louisiana drawl thickened, the poo was about to hit the fan. If she started spewing French, it was time to hit the deck. Grace slipped on her shoes and jewelry, stalling. The amount of faith she had in the police could be measured in a thimble, thanks to her childhood experiences.

"Lisie, you know how my boss is. I have a presentation this morning and I absolutely cannot be late. I'll call the police," she tried not to gag on the lie, "the moment I get home."

"Promise me."

"Cross my heart."

Lisette stepped out of the doorway and Grace flew past her. Flipped off the coffeepot, snatched up her purse and briefcase, and yanked the door open.

Lisette zapped her with a gimlet-eyed stare as she walked out. "I'm gonna be checking on you tonight."

Grace smiled. "Thank you."

Her friend disappeared into her own condo. Grace quickly locked her door, turned and froze. Back pressed to the door, she flicked her gaze up and down the open-air hallway. A stranger had likely stood in the very same spot before stealing inside her condo while she slept. Oblivious.

Tears stung her eyes. Her nails dug into her palm. She took a deep breath and blinked the moisture away. Life wouldn't wait while she had a meltdown.

Forcefully shoving away from the door, she jogged down the hall. She almost tripped on the stairs in her low heels and forced herself to slow down. A goose egg on her forehead would not be a good look in the board meeting scheduled for. . . a quick glance at her watch nearly made her trip again. Holy rosebuds. Twenty minutes to get her butt in her office and go over the monthly report on construction progress and actual cost versus estimates before her presentation to Matthew Duncan.

Having her boss's steely-eyed gaze focused solely on her for the space of ten minutes tried her nerves every time.

She refused to think about what it did to other parts of her body.

"Oh, Gracie. There you are."

Oh, no. Not now. She didn't have time. Not to mention her hands were still shaking.

Grace squeezed her eyes closed, reminded herself that she adored her neighbor, plastered on a smile and swung around. Mrs. Freeman's massive Great Dane strolled beside her, matching his regal walk to the old lady's shuffling gait.

"Mrs. Freeman." Grace scanned the area for strangers. No one else was in sight. Grace relaxed a little. "How are you?"

"Just fine, dear. Off to work?"

Apollo pranced, his tongue lolling and eager black eyes focused on Grace. He never once tugged on the leash anchoring him to Mrs. Freeman.

"Yes."

Grace sighed softly and surrendered, scratching Apollo's head. He heaved a big doggie sigh of pleasure and leaned into her.

"What are you up to today? Breakfast with your boyfriend?"

Mrs. Freeman glowed with pleasure. "Gracie, you know Roger isn't my boyfriend."

"Mr. Gray adores you, and you know it. He takes you out to breakfast as often as you let him, and he'd probably take you to lunch and dinner too. Last week he even took Apollo to his vet appointment when you weren't feeling well. If that isn't a sure sign of devotion, I don't know what is."

"Roger and I are just friends. He loved his wife, and he still grieves her passing. We fill a space in one another's life, that's all."

"If you say so." She rubbed Apollo's back. "We know better, don't we, Apollo?"

Mrs. Freeman chuckled. "You'd better skedaddle on to work,

dear. You don't want that ferocious boss of yours getting on your case first thing."

Grace pretended a shiver. "Heavens, no."

"Some men hide a big heart behind a tough demeanor. My George was that way." Mrs. Freeman's eyes went misty. "Tough as a pit bull on the outside, soft and affectionate as an old tabby cat on the inside. Your Mr. Duncan might just need a good woman to tame him."

"Maybe, but that good woman won't be me." Grace glanced at the parking lot then did a double-take. Her car wasn't in its usual spot. The pit of her stomach fell. "Where's my car?"

Mrs. Freeman edged her walker forward. "There it is, dear. Across the way."

Grace followed the direction of the old woman's trembling, wrinkled finger. Her brand- new tango-red Honda Accord Crosstour sat on the far side of the parking lot beneath a big tree. She blinked, her pulse skittering. Her lips tightened. What the hell?

Mrs. Freeman tutted. "The carport is safer than that old tree."

"Um-hmm."

She clutched the handle of her briefcase tight enough to leave finger imprints. No way had she parked there last night. She was never that tired. There'd better not be a single hairline scratch on the finish, or someone was going down. As a practical joke, the humor escaped her. As something more. . . She didn't want to think about anything more. She scanned their surroundings again.

Casual expression firmly in place, she glanced at the elderly woman. "Have you heard about any weird break-ins in the complex?"

Mrs. Freeman's smile disappeared and a little frown crinkled the white skin between her slim brows. "No, dear. Why? Is something wrong?"

Grace forced her stiff cheeks into a smile. "Goodness, no. Just something I overheard in the hallway the other day. I'm sure it's nothing. You know how kids are." Leaning down, she planted a

13

soft kiss on Mrs. Freeman's age-weathered cheek and patted Apollo. "Lovely to see you both. I'll be by to take Apollo for a walk when I get home."

She glanced back as she reached the parking lot. Mrs. Freeman's smile was troubled. Guilt bit hard. Grace waved at Roger Gray as he eased his big Lincoln to a stop near the curb. So he *was* taking Mrs. Freeman out for breakfast.

As she neared her car, the hair on her neck rose. She glanced around. No face peered from the bushes, no curtains twitched and nothing shifted in the cool morning air. Rubbing her neck with an unsteady hand, she circled the car. Not so much as a fingerprint marred the gleaming finish. She tried the handle. Locked. Rummaging in her purse for the keys, so jittery she may as well have drank the whole untouched pot of coffee, she glanced around again.

A chilly spring breeze ruffled the trees. Shadows skittered for cover.

Grace shivered and hit the remote button to unlock the Honda. With a quick look in the backseat, she tossed in her purse and briefcase, slid into the driver's seat, slammed the door shut and locked it. She wrapped trembling fingers around the leather steering wheel.

"No boogeyman is going to jump out from behind the tree." She glanced through the sunroof at the tree branches waving overhead. "Or out of the tree." The whole morning had her on edge, totally creeped out and talking to herself, which was friggin' fantastic.

Starting the car, she took a deep breath, focused on the smooth sound of the new engine and automatically checked the gas level. A paper covered the gauges.

**Nice car, slut**


*****

14

Matt Duncan peered through the door as Grace got off the elevator and walked down the hall toward her office. He snapped straight, shaking his head in disgust. Leering at an employee—he was such a pervert. In his defense, he'd been closing his door when the elevator pinged. The glimpse of Grace emerging froze him in place.

For six long months he'd worked hard to hide his attraction to her. Ever since she'd walked across his office for her interview. Marilyn Monroe couldn't have done that expanse of polished hardwood more justice. He'd instinctively checked to make sure his tongue wasn't hanging out. Miracle of miracles, no drool pooled on his desk either.

Her job performance, warm friendliness with the other staff, persistent charm, quick wit, and sharp intelligence had quickly made her an asset. And served to fuel and deepen his attraction. Admiration and respect rode hard alongside physical attraction.

He scrubbed a hand over his face and clicked the door shut. The day had barely begun and was already headed to hell in a handbasket. Breakfast with his mom and stepdad had rocked his world, and not in a good way. The cherry on top of his crappy morning? His receptionist reminding him of his brother's appointment.

"Mr. Duncan?"

Matt strode over to his desk and hit the intercom button. "Yes?"

"Your eight-thirty appointment is here."

Not what he wanted to deal with today. Especially since his mom hadn't shared her devastating diagnosis with Jeff yet. Cancer. Damn, she didn't deserve that. Not after all she'd been through with her ex-husband—his father—screwing around on her.

"Send him in."

Retrieving his coffee from the bar, he carried it to his desk. A large object between him and his brother was always beneficial. Jeff threw open the door and stomped in before Matt's butt hit leather. Great. Already sporting an attitude.

15

Matt leaned back, sipping cold coffee gone bitter. His brother flung himself into one of the hard chairs facing the big desk. His worn polo shirt pulled taut over his round belly. Prematurely thinning hair added to Jeff's general resentment of the world. In less charitable moments, Matt wondered how they came from the same parents.

"Hey, big bro." Jeff didn't make eye contact. "What's up?"

"You tell me. You're the one who asked to see me."

Jeff snorted, finally raising watery eyes to Matt. "Yeah, and I have to make an appointment with your stinkin' secretary to even get in the door."

"You said it was about business, and that's how a business is run. People make appointments with one another so they can schedule their day. Makes things easier on everyone."

"Or just you."

Matt gently set his cup on the desk and laced his fingers together in his lap. "How've you been?"

"Fine."

"How's your new job?"

Jeff laced and unlaced his fingers, straightened and slouched and then straightened again. Matt tensed. His brother cracked his neck.

"That's kinda what I wanted to talk to you about. Things didn't go so good. The supervisor was totally unreasonable when I forgot to come back from lunch last week."

"You forgot. . ." Matt pinched the bridge of his nose. ". . . to come back from lunch?"

"Yeah. I got distracted. So, I figured, ya know, to hell with it."

"Really." Matt wanted to close his eyes and pretend Jeff wasn't sitting there. That he hadn't just blown off this latest job. One Matt had gotten for him, calling in yet another favor. He couldn't wait to hear from the contractor. In fact, he was surprised he hadn't already.

"I was hoping you'd let me help out on the construction site again."

16

Matt bit back a sharp bark of laughter. "You think I should let you back on my job sites, where you took your buddies after-hours two months ago and let them take off with fifteen hundred dollars in materials and tools. Three months ago you almost killed a guy when you swung the crane around too fast and lost a load of lumber."

Jeff slunk lower. "No need to get bitchy about it, man."

"I've warned you before. No foul language in my office."

"Sh. . . Damn, dude. What's gotten into you?"

"During the ten years you blew off, roaming free and living off Dad, having a grand ol' time, I've worked my butt off building this business. I have a reputation for well-built structures and well-run construction sites. *All* of my employees behave in a professional manner at *all* times."

"I had my own business for a while, ya know."

Oh, Matt knew. He knew too much about that disaster. It had taken the whole family pooling their resources to drag Jeff's butt out of the sinkhole he'd created. Plus, a corporate lawyer, moving company and a psychiatrist. He didn't need to be reminded of that fiasco.

"I can't allow you on the job sites."

Jeff stared at the floor and shrugged his shoulders. Beneath the desk, Matt fisted his hand. This shadow of a man was all that was left of his brother. He had so many memories of growing up together, playing alongside each other and on the river, hunting and camping together and the stringers of fish they caught.

He sighed and scrubbed a hand over his face. "Would you like something to drink?"

"Nah. I gotta go."

Jeff rose but hesitated, studying the floor. Opened and closed his mouth. In the end, he just turned and walked out without another word. Matt stared after him. He had spent months working through his anger over his brother's betrayal, and Jeff never expressed an ounce of remorse.

His shoulders slumped and he fought the urge to lay his head on the desk.

An image of Grace flashed through his mind. The shock of his mom's news had brought the reality of life sharply into focus. Between his brother's behavior and his mom's illness, he didn't know how much more his family could take. Life was too damn short. He squared his shoulders. It was time to see if there was more to his attraction.

## CHAPTER TWO

"Grace, isn't that report due to Mr. Duncan. As of, like, five minutes ago."

"Yes. I'm on my way. I promise."

"He's in a real mood today, ya know." Sally shook her head and walked away.

Like her day didn't already suck. Getting fired on top of everything else would seriously suck. She'd snagged a position that a lot of people would kill for, in a firm recently listed in the top ten list of a local business publication. At twenty-seven, she was the youngest executive in the large construction firm.

Not to mention, the job enabled her to pay for her beautiful new car.

The low-grade headache thrumming at the base of her skull kicked up a notch. She wanted to drop her aching head into her hands and sob for a few minutes. Or hours. Something. . . anything to release the build-up of fear, stress and delayed shock. Instead, she straightened her shoulders.

Grace hit PRINT, swiveled around in her chair and snagged a binder from the storage cabinet. Mr. Duncan insisted reports be presented neatly and properly. Printed, bound, no factual errors and no typos.

In the six months she'd worked there, only two people had made the mistake of handing imperfect work to Mr. Duncan. They were no longer employed at the prestigious firm of Duncan Construction, Inc. Personally, she thought that was a bit over the top. Matthew Duncan might be hot sin walking, but he didn't have to act like the Devil incarnate.

Not that Mr. Duncan was interested in her opinion. Nor would she ever dare voice it. She liked her job and would very much like to keep it. Especially in this economy. A fabulous job she enjoyed was a bonus she didn't intend to waste by bandying about her opinions about.

She'd worked too hard, for too long to get where she was.

Neatly bound report in hand, she rushed out of her office. Sally, the first friend Grace had made at work, looked up from her desk and sent her a sympathetic smile as she held up two fingers crossed for luck. Grace blew out a breath and grinned.

The click-clack of her modest black pumps followed her down the tiled hallway. The rich cinnamon scent permeating the hall was supposed to be calming. She inhaled deeply.

Mr. Duncan wouldn't fly off the handle just because he requested this report be in his hands at 9:30 and it was now—she glanced at her watch and swallowed—9:44. Her stomach tightened and she started relaxation breathing.

"Better hurry, Grace," a masculine voice whispered in her ear.

Without thinking, she spun around and lightly whacked Luke in the gut. "Not funny."

Hitting her co-worker. Nice. Very professional. She winced. Too much time spent around too many boys growing up and too much. . . everything this morning.

Luke doubled over, groaning like she'd punched him. Lips twitching, Grace kept walking.

"Oh, man." He caught up and clapped a hand over his mouth. His cheeks bulged. "Ooh. . ." One hand pressed to his stomach, he staggered across her path and collapsed against the wall.

"Good grief, Luke." Grace rolled her eyes. "Get over yourself already."

He straightened, grinning. "Hey, just trying to keep your spirits up. Facing old man Duncan would terrify anyone. Especially with mediocre, late work in hand."

"Hey!"

Luke trotted off down the hall with a jaunty wave. The nerve. She did good work, no, *excellent* work, for this company. Mr. Duncan wouldn't can her because of one late report. He was a reasonable man. Well, sort of reasonable. In an anal-retentive, obsessive-compulsive kind of way.

She smiled at Nancy, Mr. Duncan's secretary. Outside Mr. Duncan's door, she took another deep breath. The stupid cinnamon was *so* not doing its job.

Grace stared at the dark mahogany door, straightened the hem of her short, fitted blazer, smoothed the back of her knee-length matching tweed skirt and, in general, procrastinated as only a terrified employee could. She'd just about, kind of, almost, worked up the nerve to knock.

"Fortifying yourself to beard the lion?" said a deep voice behind her.

She jumped and almost dropped the precious report. She squeezed her eyes shut and resisted the urge to bang her head against the door. Great. Caught dawdling like a student called into the principal's office. By her boss, nonetheless. Reminding herself to breathe, she turned.

"Why, yes." She forced a smile.

Mr. Duncan's bland expression betrayed none of the soft mockery she could have sworn his voice contained. Did his lips quirk, or was it a trick of the light? He was infamous for his non-existent sense of humor.

"Well, let's not delay a second longer." Reaching past her, he turned the knob and pushed open the door. "After you."

His nearness and masculine scent curled around her with wanton invitation. Imagined invitation, she sternly reminded herself, splashing cold water on her overactive hormones. Dredging up confidence she didn't feel, she smiled and strode past him into the cool interior of the immaculate office. The door closed quietly behind her.

"Mr—"

"Would you care for a drink, Miss Debry? A shot of Scotch, perhaps?"

She jerked her head up. Again with the dark humor. No, she had to be mistaken. Overwrought with stress and attraction to the point she was imagining things. Sad, really.

His back to her, he rummaged through the bar. From experience, she knew how well stocked it was.

"Um, no. I don't think a shot of anything would be a good idea at. . ." She glanced at her watch and winced. Well, no point putting off the inevitable. She cleared her throat. "Nine forty-eight in the morning."

"How terribly precise, Miss Debry. No, I don't suppose it would be appropriate to indulge so early."

He sighed. The unusual sign of humanity took her aback. He sounded tired. More than tired. Bone-deep weary.

"How about some coffee, then? Water? Juice?"

"Coffee would be nice. Thank you." Swallowing might prove an issue, but he was clearly determined she drink *something*.

"Cream and sugar, as I recall."

"Yes."

*Were you courteous to someone you were about to fire? A final liquid meal before kicking them out in the cold?* She failed to find any comfort in his hospitality. She eyed his broad shoulders, refusing to allow her gaze to dip lower, no matter how much it wanted to. Since when did he remember personal details about his employees, like how they drank coffee? The fact he'd taken note of her preferences was bewildering.

"I—"

"Please, have a seat. No need to stand when there are relatively comfortable chairs just waiting to be of use."

He turned from the bar, coffee cup in hand and she headed

for one of the chairs facing the massive desk dominating the space. An excellent place for intimidating employees.

"No, no. Not there."

Her eyebrows shot up at the impatience lacing his words. She always sat in one of those chairs during a meeting with him. Just like he always sat in his elegant black chair behind the large expanse of gleaming wood, maintaining the proper distance between a denizen of the construction world and his employees. *Always.*

"Yes, I know. I'm excessively full of what's proper, establishing my authority and all that crap. Come sit over here."

The conversation area he indicated faced the floor-to-ceiling windows overlooking the city. She glanced again at the low-backed chairs in front of his polished desk. Uncertainty sat low and uncomfortable in her belly. Her stomach rolled. Shoulders back, head erect, Grace walked over and sat in a comfortable chair.

She'd always assumed the hard chairs were intentional. A subtle hint that relaxing in his presence was unacceptable.

He placed the full coffee cup and saucer on the table between them, then settled in a neighboring chair. "Is that the report?"

"Yes." She handed the paperwork to him. "I'm sorry it's late, Mr. Duncan."

"Don't worry about it."

Eyes widening, she clenched her jaw to keep her mouth from dropping open.

He tossed the report on a little table. "I'm sure it won't happen again."

"No, sir."

He nodded, staring out the windows. It was a beautiful view. Neo-classic buildings sat with cheerful disregard amongst high-rise glass structures like theirs. The oldest had been there since the city's birth well over one hundred years ago.

The trees were still stark and barren despite the warmer weather. The river twisted like a dark ribbon through the midst of the city that had grown up around it. Hence the city's nickname, The City of Trees.

Mr. Duncan's dark gaze returned to her with uncomfortable intensity. She resisted the urge to squirm.

"Are you okay, sir? You don't quite seem yourself."

Like she knew him. She gnawed on the side of her lip, wishing she'd kept her big mouth shut. His reserve kept everyone at a distance, even higher-up executives who'd worked with him for years. She was a newbie, inexperienced in the ways of office politics and Mr. Duncan.

"Let's just say today hasn't turned out as expected." A grim smile twisted his lips.

"I apologize. I had no business prying."

Sighing, he ran a hand through his brown hair, leaving it ruffled. She'd never seen him anything but perfect. The glossy strands looked silky-soft all mussed and somehow made him more human and approachable. More masculine. Her fingers twitched with the desire to touch.

Grace threw the emergency brake on her thoughts and smoothed the wrinkles from her skirt. Time for a strategic retreat.

"If there's nothing else. . ." She started to rise.

"You haven't touched your coffee."

"Right."

Sinking back into the chair, she picked up the delicate china. The rich coffee aroma liquefied her resistance and she relaxed a little, sipping quietly. A dab of cream and a touch of sweetness. Why she was surprised to find the coffee just right, she didn't know. Mr. Duncan did everything to perfection. It was one of the reasons his company was so successful.

She glanced up. He was watching her. Something in his eyes made her cheeks heat, but his strained expression kept her butt planted firmly in the chair. He looked grievous. Lonely?

"So." Desperate, she searched for a safe topic of conversation.

She lifted the cup to her mouth, sipped and absently licked a stray drop of coffee from the rim. "Did you grow up in Boise?"

His gaze, which had been on her lips, returned to her eyes. She had a sudden urge for lip liner and glossy lipstick. Mr. Duncan settled back. He seemed relieved, as if he'd been afraid she would abandon him.

Wow. She totally needed to get a grip.

"Yes. What about you? I know you graduated from Purdue then worked in the Chicago area for several years before moving here. Did you grow up in Lafayette?"

She blinked. Did he pay such close attention to everyone he hired? Duh. Of course he did. No reason he'd pay special attention to her.

"I grew up in Northern Indiana by Lake Michigan. I lived in Michigan City for a while, then spent all of high school with a family that lived near the border of Michigan City and LaPorte."

"That's right. You grew up in foster care. Not an easy childhood."

Her eyes had to be as big as saucers. She shifted uncomfortably. "How did you know that?"

Amusement brightened his eyes. "You did consent to a full background check, Miss Debry."

"Well, yes. But I. . . that is. . ." She cleared her throat. "I didn't know the extent of what such a check would reveal. Or that you would remember it."

He inclined his head. "You interest me."

Grace blinked. Interested him like an insect squashed between two slides and pressed into the plate beneath a microscope lens? "No."

His eyebrows rose. "No?"

Her face heated. "No, it wasn't difficult growing up in foster care."

"Ah. Good."

She fiddled with her cup. That was a lie, but she didn't share

25

her past. Besides, her mind had gone completely and utterly blank. In a gulp, she finished her coffee and gently set the cup and saucer on the low table.

Mr. Duncan met her gaze. "What brought you to Boise? It's a long way from the Midwest."

"I got tired of the crowds. Chicago is a beautiful city, but it's congested and rundown. I wanted a change."

"Why Boise?" He leaned forward. "You could have gone anywhere. You have excellent references. You're young. The world is your oyster."

A slight smile revealed a dimple on his left cheek. Attraction zipped through her veins without permission.

Stomach tightening, Grace licked her lips. "I Googled it. Boise sounded small enough to offer room to roam, yet large enough to offer the amenities and shopping I enjoy. Plus, the athleticism of the area appealed to me. Skiing, cycling, hiking. The Greenbelt." She gestured toward the river. "I was able to find a great condo overlooking the Greenbelt and the Boise River, just past Katherine Albertson Park."

A great condo easily broken into. . . The scene in her kitchen flashed in her mind. Her hands shook and she tucked them beneath her legs, focusing on the here and now. She chewed on the corner of her lip. Reduced to rambling. Time to go. She didn't care how lonely he seemed. He was handsome and wealthy. No way was he lonely.

"I need to get back to work." Grabbing the cup and saucer, Grace rose and ducked behind the elaborate bar set-up. She washed her dishes and returned them to the sleek wall-mounted cabinets. Turning to leave, she abruptly backed into the cabinet. Mr. Duncan lounged against the granite counter.

She'd never realized how big he was. Other than his demand for perfection, she hadn't allowed herself to notice anything beyond his extravagant signature on her paychecks. Not his broad shoulders. Not his incredible eyes. Definitely not the way he moved, that somehow communicated "great in bed" to all her feminine transponders.

"Housekeeping takes care of dirty dishes." His disconcerting dimple winked into existence again.

"I know." She stepped closer, but he didn't budge. "Um, I need to sort through the bids for the Peterman Project and select the contractors for the interior."

He nodded, his gaze unwavering. There was more than enough space between him and the wall to get past. Still, her nerves stuttered and her breath hitched.

"Well, I'll just get back to work then." She edged past him.

He didn't move, but his brown eyes sparked with some emotion that made her long to further investigate this new side of her enigmatic boss.

Grace wasn't too proud to admit she all but ran. Confused and alarmed by the arousal humming through her, she hurried back to the safe walls of her office. The comfy custom chair embraced her. The bubbles floating across her monitor mesmerized her.

"So, how'd it go?"

She startled like a kid caught with her hand in the cookie jar. Luke hung halfway into her office, staring with obvious lust at her coveted corner office.

"How did what go?"

He frowned. "The meeting with Mr. Duncan. I heard your report was late."

"Oh, right. Well, uh, he wasn't happy. He said to make sure it didn't happen again."

His eyes narrowed. "That's it?"

"You needn't sound so disappointed."

Returned to his usual cheeky self in a blink, he grinned. "Hey, I fully intend to have my name on this door at some point."

She laughed and shook her head. "Well, I hate to disappoint you, but you'll have to wait until I either do something really stupid or get promoted."

"No doubt. You wanna get lunch?"

Pulling out the estimates for the Peterson Project, she started sorting them into categories. Plumbing, electric, flooring. "Not today. I was industrious and brought a healthy lunch from home."

"Far be it for me to compromise your lovely curves."

She glanced up and caught his lecherous grin. "Practicing for The Shakespeare Festival already?"

The grin transformed into a pout. "At least you could pretend, Grace. You're a beautiful woman. I'm a handsome man. Why not?"

"You don't need me to stroke your ego. It's perfectly healthy without my help. Besides, I adore you like the obnoxious brother I never had."

Something flickered in his brown eyes. She laughed at his disgruntled expression.

"That's revolting." He stomped away.

As much as Luke enjoyed playing the office Romeo, he wouldn't know what to do if she tried to play his Juliet. Body language was a hobby of hers and his screamed he wasn't attracted to her, no matter what he might claim.

Mr. Duncan's heated gaze filled her head. Now there was a man who didn't pretend. What had he meant, he was *interested* in her? Because she was a benefit to his company?

He certainly hadn't looked like he was thinking about business. The expression on his face, in his eyes. Well, he *looked* like he was thinking about soft sheets and sex. No, she must have misunderstood. Her foster mom always said she read too much into people.

The pang of loss throbbed. Laura had died a few months before Grace graduated from Purdue at the top of her class. She would have been so proud. If only breast cancer hadn't cut her life so short.

What would Laura have thought of Mr. Duncan? Probably too stiff and formal, too precise for her taste. Laura had learned to live with chaos, setting aside her need for neatness and order in favor of unquestioning love. The foster children she'd accepted into her home, with open arms, demanded that and more. Laura had surrendered everything she had with a gracious sweetness that, years later, still humbled Grace.

A co-worker's strong cologne drifted through her door. Gross. She wrinkled her nose. Mr. Duncan, on the other hand, smelled incredible.

# CHAPTER THREE

Matt had gritted his teeth as Grace bolted from his office. Discovering her hovering outside his door, bracing herself to meet the Big Bad Wolf in all his toothy glory, had not improved his mood. He liked that his employees were terrified of him. It kept them on their toes. But terrified was a world away from the emotion he wanted from Grace.

Hours later, he still couldn't get the disastrous meeting out of his head. The buzz of the intercom was a welcome distraction.

"A Mr. Whiles on the phone for you, Mr. Duncan. He's a bail bondsman."

Matt raised his eyebrows. "Put him through." The line clicked. "This is Duncan."

"Mr. Duncan, my name is William Whiles. I'm checking up on an employee of yours. Grace Debry. Can you confirm she's employed at your firm?"

Matt hesitated. "I'm sorry, I didn't catch your business."

"Bail bondsman. Protecting my investment, ya know?"

Leaning back, Matt absently picked up an ink pen. "Really?"

"Yes, sir. You can't be too careful nowadays, not even with a pretty little thing like her."

His jaw clenched at the overt familiarity. "Miss Debry is out on bail?"

"Yep, that's right."

Matt's gut tightened and he exhaled evenly. "What exactly was her offense?"

"Can't rightly say. Not my end of the problem."

She wouldn't be the first employee to have a problem with the law, but he wasn't buying it. "You don't mind if I put you on hold, do you?"

"Not at all. You can't be too safe nowadays. No sir'ey. You go right ahead. I'll wait."

"Thank you."

Matt dialed Grace's extension on another line and asked her to come to his office. From his company's initial investigation and working with her for six months, she didn't seem like the kind of woman to get into legal trouble. William Whiles, however. . .

Matt steepled his fingers beneath his chin. Why would someone call under false pretenses? Was Grace involved in something dangerous? Gambling? No. She'd bought a new car a few months ago. The dealership had called after hours to verify her employment and he'd personally taken the call. Drugs? No way. His protective instincts were warring against his usual level-headed approach, making him want to punch William Whiles in the face and ask questions later.

A soft knock, then the door pushed open and Grace peeked in.

"Please, come in and have a seat."

The gentle sway of her hips as she approached was mesmerizing. He swallowed with difficulty, thankful for the cover of the desk. She glided into one of the chairs facing his desk and crossed one well-shaped bare leg over the other. Lusting after an employee was making office life horny. . . thorny. Pants tight, Matt shifted.

"Mr. Duncan?"

*Right. Get a grip.* "I have. . ." He glanced at his phone lines. The blinking light had stopped blinking. ". . . *had* a William Whiles on hold. Do you know him?"

Grace frowned and he tried not to think how adorable she looked. "No, I don't. Why?"

31

"He claimed to be a bail bondsman and wanted to verify your employment."

The frown intensified. Her gaze snapped to his, fair skin flushing then washing free of color. Emerald eyes darkening, Grace's chin notched up. "I've never been arrested in my life."

Husky with anger, her voice lit his libido on fire. The way she walked and talked combined with the fire in her eyes. . . Maybe he should call his secretary to monitor the meeting before he lost control, went into caveman mode and alienated Grace. Not to mention got sued for everything he owned.

The simplicity of her response and obvious anger evaporated any doubt and confirmed his initial suspicion. Too bad he'd inadvertently given the guy the info he wanted. "He claimed you were out on bail. I think he was just looking for information. Unfortunately, he knows you work here now. I'm really sorry."

The tightness bracketing Grace's mouth relaxed, but worry lines puckered her brow instead. His skin prickled with guilt. Her hair was pulled back in some sort of complicated twist, emphasizing her frail beauty. Granted, he knew she was far from frail after countless board meetings and watching her butt heads with misogynistic contractors. Her inner strength drew him as much, if not more, than her looks.

Matt cleared his throat, annoyed with himself for mooning over her like a pubescent high-school freshman, frustrated with his inability to fix this, and concerned because she still looked too pale. "Miss Debry, is there something going on I can help with? Is someone bothering you?"

She glanced at him, then her gaze fell to her fingers, twisted together in her lap. Her lips parted and closed several times. Chest rising and falling on a silent exhalation, she smiled. "I'm fine, but thank you for your concern. I'd better get back to work."

She didn't look fine. Not knowing what else to say or how to convince her to confide in him, he let her go.

Halfway across the room, she turned back. "I'm sorry you

were. . ." she waved a slender hand vaguely, "disturbed on my behalf."

"It's not your fault."

Grace nodded, hesitated for another second then spun on her heel and left.

As soon as she closed the door, Matt picked up the phone and buzzed his secretary. "Nancy, was there a number for the last caller?"

"Just a second, I'll check."

Impatiently tapping his fingers on the desk, he stared out the window. What was going on with Grace? He wanted to help. Needed to in a way he couldn't describe. Cursing his helplessness, he flung the pen he'd been fiddling with onto the desk.

The line clicked open. "The number was blocked, Mr. Duncan."

"Damn."

"Can I help with something, sir?"

"I'd really like that last number."

"Shall I call security to see whether they can find anything?"

Matt hesitated and the line beeped.

"I need to pick up that call."

"Of course. Thank you."

The situation didn't sit well. He felt like he'd harmed Grace, and that was the last thing he ever wanted to do.

\*\*\*\*\*

Grace drummed her fingers on the steering wheel. She couldn't decide if she was happy to be going home or not. Discovering her kitchen trashed had left her more than a little freaked out. The weird phone call Mr. Duncan had received didn't help. She needed a dog. One with really big teeth.

She couldn't call the police. What would she say? *"Hi. Someone rearranged all of my kitchen stuff then moved my car to a different spot in the parking lot."*

Right. They'd think she was an escaped mental patient. Besides, her time as a foster child had painted an unfavorable picture of the police. They were sometimes called upon to deliver her from home to home. They could have been carting a cardboard box for all the interest they'd shown. Sitting in the backseat of a patrol car, throat tight, leg bouncing and separated from the uniformed officers by a cage, hadn't left the best impression.

Like a magnet, the paper lying on the passenger seat drew her gaze. So simple and unassuming. A stray scrap of paper. Could have been anything. Yet it felt like an oversized tarantula crouched on the seat, unmoving, creepy eyes following her every move.

"Just a prank. Some kids getting off on freaking me out."

Even spoken aloud, the words did little to reassure her. She pulled into her apartment complex and parked in her assigned space. Her car had better be in the same spot in the morning.

Trudging up the sixty-two steps to her condo—she'd counted—she hesitated outside her door. *Please, please, please. No more surprises.*

Grace unlocked the door and pushed. It swung inward, banging softly into the wall. Nothing stirred. She stepped inside and set down her purse, rubbing the back of her neck.

"Miss Debry?"

With a startled squeak of surprise, Grace swung around. "Mr. Duncan?"

"Are you okay?" He glanced inside, brow drawn tight.

"What are you doing here?" Leaving the door open behind her. *Way to be vigilant, Grace.*

His frown deepened, but when his gaze again met hers, his eyes were shuttered. "After today's call, I was worried about you."

"You were?"

"Is that really so hard to believe?"

"Well, yeah."

He didn't respond, just watched her with his unfathomable brown eyes. Heat climbed up her neck and settled in her cheeks. Okay, the polite thing would be to invite him in. She glanced through her lashes. His gaze was fastened on her breasts. Her nipples went pebble-hard in a heartbeat. Gnawing on the inside of her cheek, she gestured him in—not the most gracious invite ever.

"So." She shut the door and faced him. "You came here just to check on me?"

The setting sun speared through the glass balcony doors and outlined him, making him appear bigger. Harder. Grimmer. Which oddly made her feel safe.

"It's not often I have people call and lie about one of my employees, Grace."

Grace? What happened to Miss Debry?

"Uh. . ."

*Nice. Smooth, Grace. Way to fumble like a virgin in the backseat of a car with the quarterback.* It'd been a long day. The furnace kicked on and carried Mr. Duncan's cologne on a burst of warm air, further hobbling her brain.

She cleared her throat. "How about those Boise State Broncos?"

Mr. Duncan's lips twitched. "I wasn't aware they were playing."

"They're not?"

"No. It's March." The twitch spread to a smile and out sprang his dimple.

She crossed her arms. Stared at his mouth. Uncrossed her arms. Cleared her throat again. "Oh."

His smile slipped into obscurity. That wasn't disappointment making her sigh. Really.

"Why don't you tell me what's going on?"

The temporary haze of desire lifted and the reality of her morning flooded back. Her muscles clenched. She glanced at the kitchen.

"Grace." He walked like a cat. In a heartbeat he'd crossed the room and stood far too close, a breath away from invading her personal space. "Please."

His low voice, combined with a word she'd never heard from

him, turned her to mush. Totally unfair. She sighed and gestured toward the kitchen. "Have a look at my kitchen."

He turned without question and crossed the room.

Restless from the day's events and his presence in her space, she kicked off her shoes and curled into a corner of the couch. "I'm sure it's nothing. Just someone messing with me."

He turned, frowning. "Assuming you're normally neat here, like at work, this is more than someone messing with your stuff."

He'd noticed she was neat at work? "It's not a big deal."

The frown turned into a glare and she sighed.

"Fine, it is a big deal. Also, when I left for work this morning, my car had been moved across the parking lot."

Mr. Duncan's expression cleared, leaving him about as readable as a brick wall. "What did the police say?"

She bounced off the couch and paced to the sliding door that led onto her small balcony. "Nothing, since I didn't call them. What would I have said? Someone didn't like the placement of my baking tools and spaghetti noodles? My car drove itself across the parking lot? Oh, but nothing was taken, Officer. No, the car wasn't harmed. Of course I'm not on any medication. Oh, you'd like to take me down to the hospital for a psych evaluation? On the state's dime? How generous."

"Are you finished?"

"Yes." She crossed her arms.

"No damage done and nothing taken doesn't mitigate the situation. Someone broke into your home and your car."

"Nobody threatened me."

He strolled toward her. "You have to be hurt or confronted to get scared?"

"No, but nothing major happened." Her voice rose. She hated being backed into a corner, and that was exactly what he was doing. Deep breaths. Self-control. She refused to yell at her boss.

"Show some common sense. A crime was committed and you need to report it."

"I don't want to, Matt!"

Grace gasped and slapped a hand over her mouth. She'd yelled. Called him by his first name. Holy crap. He was not the friendly, easy-going kind of boss that promoted familiarity.

His eyes dark with intensity, he closed the distance between them and gently took her hand between his. "Sweetheart, I'm sorry it upsets you. I'm sure you have your reasons, but this is important."

*Sweetheart? What. . .* Gaze never leaving hers, he brushed his lips across the back of her knuckles.

Her knees turned to water. The look in his eyes was the same as when they had stood behind the bar in his office. Right before she'd bolted.

Nerves licked along her spine. She moistened her lips. "I do realize it's important. It's just. . . I don't like the police. My childhood. . . They aren't. . ." She bit back a groan and pressed her lips together, meeting his gaze. Noticed tiny flecks of light that seemed to dance in his brown eyes, enticing her closer. Fogging her brain. "I don't like the police," she finished softly.

His heat and cologne  were an intimate invitation her body was only too happy to accept. Sat up and begged to accept. She swallowed. His finger glided along the edge of her jaw, the coarse texture against her skin surprising and arousing. She glanced down. Rough calluses lined the inside of his hand and fingers. She'd never noticed his hands before; now they fascinated her.

"Call the police."

Minty-fresh breath washed over her face. Instinct as old as time brought her a step closer. Matt's eyes narrowed and his gaze dropped to her lips. His head lowered.

She jerked back and slammed into the glass door. Her face heating, she reached up to rub her abused head. Matt. . . *Mr. Duncan*, beat her to it. His strong fingers massaged her scalp. Her eyelids drifted shut. Angelic cherubs above, he knew how to use his fingers. Another, much lower, throb joined the first.

Firm, masculine lips feathered across hers. How she managed to remain upright and not melt into a puddle, she didn't know. Opening her eyes, she stared at Matt. Head cradled in his broad palm, his lips an inch from hers, she forgot how to breathe.

Regret flickered in the depths of his eyes, and he gently untangled his hand. Her happy bits whimpered in denial. Her conscience slapped them into silence—the one thing in her whole body staving off looming insanity.

Number-one mistake—fling with your boss.

"I'd say I'm sorry," Matt shrugged, "but. . ."

*I'm not,* was unsaid, but she heard it just the same. Matt's gaze lingered on her mouth.

She bit her tongue to stop herself from saying anything dumb. Or worse, licking her lips again.

"I'd better go."

Doorknob in hand, he paused and seemed to consider her. She tried to meld into the glass door, struggling to wrap her brain around what had just happened.

"Promise you'll call the police and have the locks changed, Grace. Please."

Her knees trembled. Two pleases in the space of fifteen minutes from her intractable employer. She nodded, releasing her tongue to gnaw on the inside of her cheek. The door closed behind him and silence descended. Relaxing in small increments, she slid to the floor.

A bouquet of flowers she'd received the other day drew her gaze. They'd shown up on her doorstep without a card. Glancing from them to her disaster zone of a kitchen, she narrowed her eyes. The coincidence was too much to ignore. She rose, snatched them out of the vase, yanked open the balcony door and tossed them over the railing.

"What the. . ." came a male voice from below.

Grace groaned and leaned over the balcony railing. Mr. Duncan straightened, a few of the discarded flowers in hand. Flower petals decorated his dark hair and the breadth of his shoulders. He glanced up.

Perfect. Could this day get any better? She smiled weakly.

He waved the flowers. "Friends of yours?"

"Not exactly. Sorry."

He grinned. Even three flights away, it decimated her. Sweet heaven, his smile should be illegal.

"No problem." He waved and walked away.

She was rooted to the spot. His athletic stride carried him around the side of the building. She groaned and dropped her head into her hands.

Perfect. Just. . . perfect. In the space of twenty-four hours, her life had gone from pleasantly simple to anxiety- and lust-ridden. She massaged her temples. Boring was so underappreciated.

- Freaked out by stranger invading her home. . . . . . . . . CHECK
- Ticked about stranger moving her precious car. . . . . . . . . CHECK
- Mysterious flowers messing with her head. . . . . . . . . CHECK
- Flirting & considering having a wild fling w/boss. . . . . . . . . CHECK
- Men in white coats arriving soon to cart her off. . . . . . . . . CHECK

Sweet baby cherubs, her life was ricocheting out of control. Grace dialed the police with a soft groan. World's Biggest Idiot should be stamped across her forehead.

An hour later, she ushered the uniformed police officer out and pressed cool palms to her hot cheeks as she stood in the doorway. Calmly dealing with the sanctimonious, condescending prick had taken every iota of self-control she possessed.

*"Probably just a prank, miss. We'll send a cruiser through the area on a regular basis, if it'll make you more comfortable."*

The only thing missing was a pat on the head.

Lisie's door cracked open and her friend's head popped out, her eyes big as saucers and swimming with worry when they met hers. Despite the circumstances, Grace couldn't help smiling and rolling her eyes at Her Royal Nosiness.

"You want some company, *cher*?"

"No, thanks. I think I'm going to turn in early."

"Alright." Lisie frowned. "Give me a call when you're ready to tackle that mess and I'll come help, you hear?"

"Bossy."

"Is that a yes?"

Grace brought her heels together and snapped a mock salute. "Yes, ma'am. Thank you, ma'am."

Lisie snorted a soft laugh and pointed a long-tipped finger at her. "I'm holdin' you to it."

Smiling, Grace closed her door and leaned back against it. A glance at her kitchen and her smile slipped away on a sigh and a shiver. There be creepers out there.

# CHAPTER FOUR

Matt steered the heavy bike into Julia Davis Park. Bright sunshine, blue skies, warm temperatures, and a cool breeze felt more like May than March. He idled to a stop at the side of the narrow road, near a large fountain in the center of the park.

People rode bicycles, children swarmed over the playground, old couples fed ducks and teenagers played with their dogs. Fresh-cut grass scented the air. His gaze swung back to one of the teenagers with a dog and he stiffened, blindly reaching to turn off the rumbling engine.

A big dog had a female teenager down on the grass and it looked like. . . He shot off the bike and was running before he'd completed the thought.

The closer he got, the bigger the dog became. It loomed, massive and fierce, over the girl on the ground. The dog raised its massive head, locked gazes with him and shifted to stand over the girl. The animal's protective stance slowed Matt. He stopped several yards away.

The girl lying on the grass tilted her head back. He didn't dare look away from the huge dog, but an inkling of suspicion trickled through him. From the corner of his eye, pink infused her cheeks and her eyes shone bright with laughter. He might have misjudged the situation.

"Apollo, down." The dog obeyed her firm command with the docility of a pussycat. Apollo's gaze didn't waver. The message came through loud and clear: watch his step or he'd be dog chow.

The girl rolled into a sitting position with fluid grace and tilted her head to the side as she contemplated him.

Daring to look away from the big dog, he met her eyes and rocked back on his heels. Hard. "Grace?"

She laughed and hugged her knees to her chest. Her cheeks were rosy from wrestling with the dog, she had grass in her dark hair and there was dog slobber on her pants. He couldn't remember a more appealing sight.

"Hello, Mr. Duncan."

She'd called him Matt at her apartment a few days ago.

He cleared his throat and shoved his hands in the pockets of his jeans. "I didn't know you had a dog."

"You mean your extensive background check missed something?" Her light, teasing tone stirred something in him. "I don't have a dog. Apollo belongs to my neighbor. I enjoy playing with him and take him out for walks whenever I can. There weren't any dogs in the foster homes I grew up in, and I always wanted one."

"Really?" Apollo lay panting on the grass, watching him. Must be a male neighbor. He couldn't imagine anyone else owning a dog like that. Jealousy sucker-punched him and he crossed his arms. "He doesn't give you any problems? He's awfully big."

She chuckled and stood, brushing grass off her jeans. "Now there's an understatement. He's an absolute teddy bear, though. Wouldn't hurt a flea. We were just wrestling when you came flying to the rescue." She gave a cheeky grin.

Unbelievably, heat washed over Matt's face. He didn't usually get embarrassed. Ever.

Grace's grin widened, displaying a playful side he hadn't seen in the office. "You're very sweet. It probably looked like he was mauling me, instead of playing. I don't know why, but his muzzle tickles and when I start laughing, it eggs him on."

He glanced at her jeans, enjoying the way they molded to her curves, and up to her fitted T-shirt. She filled out casual clothes very well. *Very* well. He'd like to find her ticklish spots.

His gaze returned to her face. Deep rose painted her cheekbones. The deepening shade of her green eyes reminded him of standing in her apartment, the soft curves of her body between the glass door and him. Their almost-kiss had fueled his fantasies all week.

Unfortunately, he still didn't know how to handle the situation. Pursuing an employee seemed unethical. Not to mention putting him at risk of a major sexual-harassment lawsuit. Plus, he wasn't great with personal relationships. Matt's gaze shifted to Apollo again, jealous heat burning his belly. "The dog's owner doesn't mind you borrowing him?"

"No. She's pushing eighty and is glad to have someone with a bit more energy to play with him."

"What's an old woman doing with a Great Dane?"

Her eyes narrowed and cooled. Well, shit. Grace's fondness for the dog must extend to the owner.

"He's very gentle and not at all demanding. I'm sure he'd be content to sit at home with her. He was doing exactly that before I moved in and he never appeared unhappy or neglected."

"Sorry. Didn't mean to imply anything bad about the dog or the lady."

She nodded. In his experience, women pouted, whined and gave him the cold shoulder. They did not, ever, forgive after a simple apology.

Grace sat and patted the ground. "Pull up a section of grass."

Only a fool would turn down an invitation to sit in the sunshine with a beautiful woman. He parked his butt.

"You look different than you do at work." He bit off a groan. Freakin' brilliant observation, Sherlock.

Grace laughed. "So do you."

She was watching some kids play across the park, leaving him to admire her profile. Desire thickened his cock and tongue. He shifted, focusing beyond the physical to tamp down his arousal. Like her funny, quirky personality, the impish mischievousness he sometimes saw in her eyes and her unfailing honesty—even when it didn't flatter her.

"So. . ." Matt searched for a conversational gambit to save his ass. "If you like dogs so much, why don't you get one of your own?"

She shrugged. "I work a lot and live in a condo with no yard, none of which sounds like the ideal life for a dog."

As much as he wanted to show up on her doorstep tomorrow with a puppy—and what the hell was that about?—her reasoning was sound. Since he couldn't exactly buy her a house, he tossed about for another topic. Something that didn't involve the sudden onset of a rapidly deteriorating mental state—his.

"Did you call the police?" He hadn't seen her at work to ask. Not wanting to come off as stalkerish, he hadn't sought her out either.

She nodded, wrinkling her nose. "Fat lot of good it did me."

He frowned. "Why?"

"They brushed the whole thing off as some sort of prank. No damage done." She glanced at him, then away again just as quickly. "Thank you for your help, though. It was sweet of you to be so concerned."

Mouth pulled tight, he straightened. "The police did nothing?"

"They took a report, patted me on the head and left." Grace plucked blades of grass, looking vulnerable as hell until she glanced up and grinned. "Just like I said they would."

Despite the annoyance riding him hard over the police, he couldn't resist her smile. "Yeah, yeah."

"May I ask you a personal question?"

Matt froze, a dozen unpleasant scenarios running through his mind. "Sure."

"The other day at work, you seemed off. What was wrong?"

Damn. Not as bad as he'd feared, but the last thing he wanted was to come across as a momma's boy. Still, he couldn't lie. Not to her. "My mom has breast cancer."

"Oh, Matt."

Her slender fingers brushed down his arm and settled on top of his hand. His work-roughened hands, thanks to time spent on job sites instead of sitting in the office. Her hands were baby-soft and pale. The contrast enhanced her femininity. Made him feel like a pheasant begging for the fair maiden. He grimaced. Yeah, he'd officially lost his mind.

"That's awful. I lost my foster mom to breast cancer several years ago. They're able to detect cancer so early, though. With treatment, your mom has excellent chances for recovery."

He blinked away a sheen of moisture and cleared his throat. The depth of her sympathy disarmed him. "I'm sorry about your foster mom. I sincerely hope you're right. My mom just remarried a few months ago. My stepdad will be devastated if anything happens to her."

"So will you."

"Yeah."

Grace wove her fingers through his and squeezed. He didn't want to think about his mom dying a slow, miserable death. Life pulsed and flowed around him, drawing him out of the gray pallor that clung to him every time he thought about his mom's illness.

With a final squeeze, Grace released his hand. He immediately missed the contact. Apollo nudged his blocky head onto Grace's lap. She stroked his head and envy clawed at Matt's gut. Jealous of a dog. He'd better keep a close eye out for the men in white coats.

Grace's gaze skimmed his heavy boots, worn blue jeans and black leather jacket over a T-shirt. He'd taken off his dark sunglasses and stuck the earpiece in the collar of his shirt. Her perusal sent his senses humming like a high-performance engine begging to be set loose.

"You aren't exactly dressed for a day at the park."

"I was riding through until I saw the dog on you." He wasn't about to admit he'd thought she was a teenage girl.

"You're riding a bicycle dressed like that?"

He chuckled. "Not exactly."

Matt pointed to his Harley parked at the curb. Her reaction didn't disappoint. Those gorgeous eyes widened and her mouth formed a little "O" of surprise. He wanted to explore those lips, taste them and learn their texture. The little brush days ago hadn't been nearly enough.

"Would you like a ride?"

Where had that come from?

Not that he regretted the invitation. The thought of her riding behind him on his bike had certain body parts growing out of proportion to the situation.

"I can't." Her lower lip jutted out in disappointment.

He barely managed to leash his primal urges. This wasn't the time to introduce her to Caveman Duncan.

"I have to take Apollo home." She grinned, impish and adorable. "Unless you're hiding a doggy side car somewhere."

"Uh, no."

Her smile slipped a little and her gaze drifted back to his motorcycle.

"You like motorcycles?"

"Oh, yeah."

The husky way she spoke had his body stomping with impatience at the gate. Damn. A glass of chipped ice would come in handy about now. . . to dump down the front of his pants. "How about I swing by your condo in an hour? We can go for a ride and grab dinner."

"I would love that. Thank you." She snagged Apollo's leash off the grass and scrambled to her feet. "I'd better run if I'm going to be ready on time. See you soon."

She waved and started across the expanse of grass. Matt stood rooted, mesmerized by the way her jeans cupped her swaying bottom. She turned and he jerked his gaze to her face, guilty as a horny teenager caught ogling a *Playboy* magazine.

"Do you remember where I live?"

He grinned.

"Right." She rolled her eyes. "You have a photographic memory."

With another jaunty wave, she spun on her heel. Putting his photographic memory to its best use in years, he memorized the way her hips rocked until she disappeared around a curve in the Greenbelt. Shaking off his hormone-induced stupor, Matt headed for his bike. He settled in the seat with a grimace.

Several hours of similar agony loomed in his future. With her wrapped around him like a second skin, riding behind him on the Harley, he didn't have a prayer of controlling his body. He didn't care. The pleasure of feeling her against him and the delight of her company would be worth it.

He straddled the bike, pulled his helmet on and gunned the engine. He had a few things to do before heading to Grace's condo.

## CHAPTER FIVE

Grace let herself into her condo, collapsed against the door then half a second later pushed upright and exited the condo again. She pounded her fist on Lisie's door, chewing on the inside of her lip, gaze repeatedly skipping toward the stairs Matt would soon climb.

The door jerked inward by a rather irate-looking Lisie, her fist planted on her hip and dark eyes blazing. "Where's da fire, sug?"

"I'm going out with my boss."

"Ooooh!" Lisie rubbed her hands together, shrugged out of her paint smock and followed Grace back to her place. "Watcha gonna wear?"

"Clothes?" Grace rushed into her bedroom, unbuttoning her jeans and yanking off her T-shirt. They landed in her hamper as she passed into the en suite bathroom.

The cool tile underfoot and the sea-green-and-blue color scheme calmed her. She'd spent her first weekend painting and decorating the condo. All her years moving to different foster homes had taught her how to quickly make a space feel like home. She had more resources these days, but the goal stayed the same.

She shook her head over the way she'd bolted as soon as she'd rounded the corner and escaped the heat of Matt's gaze. Good thing she stayed in shape, or she'd never have made it to her building. Apollo loped easily at her side for the entire three-quarter mile—show-off.

Not taking the time to visit with Mrs. Freeman when she

dropped him off made her feel guilty. She'd promised to stop by tomorrow after church to make up for it.

Grace splashed water on her cheeks. The cold sting helped. Exertion, desire, and anticipation hummed through her body.

"How long since ya been on a date?"

Frowning, she turned. Lisie lounged against the bathroom doorframe, examining her lethally long, meticulously manicured fingernails. "Is it a date?"

One eyebrow arched. "You tell me, *cher.*"

She pictured Matt standing in the park. Arms crossed, jacket straining across his broad shoulders, legs spread and denim hugging thick muscles. His casual clothes revealed a physique she never would have suspected lurked within his polite business suits. From the unapologetically masculine black leather to the gleaming chrome Harley beast, there'd been nothing polite about him today. Heaven help her, she got damp just thinking about it.

"If it isn't a date, someone should alert my hormones."

Lisie grinned. "Dere ya go. Is a date."

"Hmm. . ." It had to be politically incorrect to want to jump her boss, even if he'd indulged in a few carnal thoughts of his own. The strain on his poor zipper would have been obvious to a blind man. She deserved a medal for not staring.

Her shiver had nothing to do with cool tiles or chilly water. He was uber-delish, business savvy, street smart and had a wicked sense of humor. With the speed of a woman who'd worked in a beauty salon through college, she went from day-off to date-night in minutes. She amped up her makeup, brushed her hair, added a few curls, then spritzed with a yummy-smelling hairspray.

In her bedroom, she refreshed her deodorant and perfume. Then she hurried into the spacious walk-in closet. Her clothes lay scattered on the floor. The wood hangers dangled on the rod, empty. She blindly reached for the wall for support. Chills crawled over her skin. Not again.

49

Grace backed out and stared at her bedroom. Nothing looked out of place. Yet every scrap of clothing that had been hanging in her closet, organized by color and style with OCD precision, lay on the floor.

"*Cher*, wha's wrong?"

Trembling, she waved at her closet. Lisie scrambled off the middle of her bed, where she'd made herself comfy. Grace rubbed her arms and approached her dresser. She stared at the drawers, afraid to open them. *Fast, like a Band-Aid.* She yanked open the first drawer. Then the next and the next and the next.

The drawers were undisturbed. Her socks were still tucked in place, alongside her neatly folded panties. Each drawer was just as it had been when she'd left that morning. Staying a good five feet back, just in case, she peeked under the big bed.

Nothing. It didn't make any sense. Any more so than the incident on Tuesday.

"Saints above." Lisie crossed herself. "Ya best pack a valise and come stay with me."

Grace blinked. "A what?"

"A. . . suitcase, y'all call it."

She shook her head and walked through the rest of her condo. Running away wasn't an option. Her laptop sat in its usual place atop the pretty desk she'd picked up at an antique store several years ago. The flat-screen TV was untouched, as were her stereo and other components. Everything was fine. In its place, neat and orderly. The fan circled lazily overhead. Goose bumps broke out across her skin. Someone rapped on her front door and she jumped.

"Sweet baby cherubs."

She pressed a hand to her galloping heart then whipped around in search of a weapon. Throw pillows, delicate hand-blown glass bowl, dainty lamp. Damnit. Why hadn't she decorated with anything heavy? Or sharp and pointy? She grabbed her cordless handset and approached the door as another knock sounded.

Lisie wrapped an arm around her waist, patting her. "Calm down, sug. I don't think da bad man would knock. Is likely da hotness ya call 'boss.'"

"Grace?"

Holy crap. It was Matt. She glanced down at her bra and panties.

"Uh, just a sec."

Grace raced for her room on less-than-steady feet. She couldn't leave him standing outside while she dug through the pile of clothes, trying to find something to wear. Groaning, she snatched her robe off the bedpost and stuffed her trembling arms into the sleeves. Tying the sash with a sharp yank, she hurried out, ignored Lisie's squeak of alarm, and yanked open her door.

Matt's eyes widened and she glanced down. Greeting someone at her front door had been the last thing on her mind when she purchased the robe. Her face warmed. The burned-out velvet exposed as much as it covered.

Nothing left but to brazen it out, she smiled. No biggie. She greeted big, hunky men who just happened to pay her salary dressed like this *all* the time.

"I'm so sorry, Mr. Duncan. Come in, please. I'm not ready yet."

Lisie snickered. *Oh great, Grace. Nothing like stating the obvious.*

"Please don't apologize. I'll be reliving this moment for days." He strolled in, his woodsy cologne blanking her brain. "I prefer when you call me Matt. It might be kind of awkward if you call me Mr. Duncan all evening."

That answered one question. "Sure." She closed the door and indicated Lisie. "Meet my neighbor, Lisie. Can I get you a drink?"

"Nice to meet you, Lisie."

"The pleasure is all mine, dawlin'."

Matt didn't seem to notice her BFF's fawning. Instead, he stood stock still in the middle of her living room, staring at her legs. She yanked on the robe's hem, but no amount of tugging lengthened the damn thing. His gaze crawled up her body.

51

A firm believer in equality, Grace returned the perusal. Once again, he had his sunglasses tucked into the neckline of his shirt. Never before had she found that sexy, but hey, times changed. From the look of it, he wore a black silk T-shirt under his leather jacket. He looked scrumptious in black.

Lisie cleared her throat. When she glanced at her, she fanned her face, eyes wide. If it wouldn't have been obvious, Grace would have done the same.

"What do you have?"

"What?" She blinked and whipped her gaze back to Matt. Her female parts were begging to get up close and personal with his male parts, but she was fairly sure that wasn't what he meant. Especially not in front of her friend. She wasn't into that sort of thing.

His lips curved to reveal that tempting dimple. She didn't know what she'd do if he gave her a real smile. Probably melt into a puddle of undersexed hormones at his feet.

"You offered me a drink?"

"Oh. Right. Um. . . soda, iced tea, wine and water."

"A glass of ice water would be nice." The intensity of his gaze ratcheted up a few notches. "It's a bit warm in here."

She swallowed and hurried into her kitchen. Lisie followed close on her heels.

"Damn, sug!" Lisie hissed, eyes bugging a bit as she ogled Matt. "You could'a warned me."

Grace shrugged and stole glances at him over her shoulder as she grabbed a glass. He strolled over to the French doors that opened onto a nice-sized balcony overlooking the Boise River. Ice clinked loudly in the glass from the dispenser and he turned. Grace's face heated and she lowered her gaze, but couldn't resist sneaking another peek through her lashes.

"I'll leave you to it, *cher.*" Lisie winked at her before heading to the front door. "Hope to see you again soon, dawlin," she called to Matt. He nodded his head and waved, smiling at her.

Looking oddly at home in Grace's feminine room, he settled onto her couch. Except for his earlier visit, no men had been in her living room. In her condo, period. Not even a date in seven months. No wonder she was having a hormone overload. She wasn't used to being aware of her sexuality, much less someone else's.

Lifting a black boot to settle his ankle on his other knee, he rested a long arm on the back of the couch.

"Sorry I'm not ready." She thought about the mess in her closet and her knees weakened. "I found. . . I don't know what I found, actually. The clothes in my closet. . ." She bit the inside of her lip and walked into the living room. She didn't want to get into this with him again. "Never mind. I'll just be a few minutes."

He accepted the glass of ice water, frowning. "What did you find?"

"Matt." She sighed and surrendered to the inevitable. "The clothes in my closet are messed up."

"Show me." He rose.

Grace sighed again, but what difference did it make? She led him to the open closet door. He stood beside her, silent. She shivered. Clothes that had hung just so, neatly folded sweaters, her shoes—they were all scattered on the floor.

Matt wrapped an arm around her and pulled her snugly to his side. She hadn't expected it or wanted it, but sharing the moment helped. Diluted the impact somehow. The warmth of his body and the hard muscles wrapped around her melted the insulating layer of shock.

She leaned against him, struggling to resist hiding her face in his shirt. Hiding from the fear that had every muscle clenched to the point of pain. From the sense of violation churning her stomach. Hiding from the thought of a stranger in her home. Again.

"You need to call the police. I know it seemed like a waste of

53

time the first time, but you still need to file a report." His gaze held her fast. "This is the second time. In case anything else happens, and I'm not saying anything else will, but if it does, this will be factored into the equation."

Her head began to throb.

His eyebrow arched. "You didn't get your locks re-keyed, did you?"

Shoulders drooping, she shook her head. The urge to rest her head against his broad shoulders was strong. She resisted.

Matt's lips tightened, then he pressed a kiss to her forehead. "I'll call a locksmith while you get dressed."

She nodded, numb. He was taking this so seriously it made it hard to pass it off as some teenage prank. His arm tightened around her, then let go. The bedroom door shut behind him with a quiet click.

Grace allowed a moment to wallow, then straightened her shoulders and pulled on a pair of blue jeans. Reluctantly, she went into her closet and dug through the pile on the floor. Something was odd about some of the clothes.

The arm of a red sweater seemed too long, while a black skirt was oddly misshapen. She held them up and gasped. Hands trembling, she dug through the pile. About half of them were torn or ripped. Her lower lip quivered and she bit it, blinking back tears.

Sitting on her closet floor and having a good old-fashioned sob-fest sounded appealing, but her boss was waiting in the other room. They were moving into dating territory, and she didn't want to start out with puffy eyes and a red nose. Not attractive. She yanked a lightweight cashmere sweater off the floor.

A jagged-edged piece of paper fluttered to the floor. Her breath caught. The white square lay on top of the tweed skirt she'd worn to work a few days ago. Innocuous. Apprehension coiled inside. Not another one.

With the same cautious respect she would show a boa

constrictor, she picked it up. She took a breath. Squeezed her eyes shut and flipped the paper over. She opened one eye and peered at the paper.

Both eyes open, she sat back on her heels.

**_Think you're something special, don't you? A fancy job, big condo and expensive clothes won't change anything. You're nothing but trailer trash, slut._**

*Trailer trash?*

A shudder trembled the paper in her fingers. On the edge of hysteria, she rubbed her forehead. *Be rational. Deep breath.* Her chest rose and fell on a deep inhalation. *Okay, good. You're life hasn't been a bed of roses. You can cope without falling apart. It's just words on a piece of paper. Yes, someone was in your home. Someone damaged your clothes. No biggie. Clothes are replaceable. The important thing is, whoever was here is gone. Right now, there's a big, handsome man waiting in your living room. For you. Focus on that.*

Grace straightened her shoulders, wiped a stray tear from her cheek and stood. She set the paper on her bed and pulled the intact cashmere sweater over her head. Her thoughts ran in circles as she tugged on socks and tennis shoes. Looping a strand of hair round her finger, she stared at the paper. What she wouldn't give to crumple it into a ball and toss it. Instead, she grabbed the scrap and headed into the living room, resigned to the inevitable.

Matt glanced up from where he sat on her floral couch, her cordless phone and the phone book in hand. Her lips twitched. Like a physical caress, his gaze moved over her. Appreciation gleamed in the dark depths. His eyes narrowed on the paper in her hand.

"What's that?"

"I found it on the floor mixed in with the clothes—most of which have been slashed." She placed it face up on the coffee table. Matt leaned forward.

"Trailer trash?"

She settled on the couch beside him. "I've never even lived in a trailer."

"I don't like this, Grace. The note makes it more personal."

She bit her lip, not wanting to mention the other note. The one she'd found in her car. A stress headache bloomed into life right behind her eyes. He picked up her cordless from the coffee table and handed it to her. "Call the police."

"You know you're incredibly bossy, right?"

"Hazard of *being* the boss, I guess."

He leaned back against her pillows. He didn't even appear offended. Relaxed and comfortable came to mind, despite the frown drawing his dark brows together and the tight set of his lips. Sprawled on her couch, he also looked entirely too sexy for her peace of mind.

His gaze dropped to the phone lying in her limp hand, then back up to her face, with a lift of his brow.

"Bossy," but still she dialed. Bossy, yes. But right too. At least he provided a distraction from her fear.

## CHAPTER SIX

Matt settled into the booth across from Grace. Sharing her side of the table held more appeal, but that would probably be pressing his luck. Besides, he'd been patient for six of the longest months of his life, admiring her intelligence, spirit, fire and beauty from afar. He could be patient a while longer.

Dusky rose spread across her cheeks. To his amusement, she avoided eye contact, perusing her menu with great interest. The past week had shown she wasn't immune to him. Before that, she hadn't revealed the slightest awareness of him as a man. He had started to worry.

He wasn't worried anymore.

He glanced at the menu. Angell's Bar & Grill tended to be fairly quiet, even during the dinner rush. Classy, great food and they weren't too fussy about how their customers dressed.

They placed their orders and he rested his arms on the table. If he wasn't mistaken, Grace had enjoyed riding on his bike. He'd certainly gotten a rise out of her riding behind him. Literally and figuratively. She'd wrapped herself around him in a way that went beyond the mere physical.

He sipped his water, searching for a safe topic of conversation. Something to keep her mind off the creep breaking into her place. "Have you made it out of the city yet?"

"I went to McCall. The Winter Carnival was fun, and the ice sculptures were amazing."

"They're different every year too. I try not to miss it." He grinned. "They can get pretty goofy. There was a toilet one year."

"You're kidding."

Matt shrugged, laughing. Grace chuckled, but a few seconds later her gaze drifted to the window. She had to be pretty upset about what happened at her condo. A woman living alone. . . He didn't like her vulnerability with some freak on the loose. May as well address the elephant in the room.

"Is there anyone you've met since moving here that seemed off?"

Her expression didn't so much as flicker, which told him her mind had been in the same place. She shook her head.

"I've been searching my brain. No one comes to mind. Nothing out of the ordinary has happened. No creepy vibes. No strange men following me." She shrugged.

"All you can do at this point is be extra vigilant." He wished he could offer her something more tangible.

"You're right. It's just so. . . I don't know. Out of left field. I haven't even lived here that long. This kind of stuff happens in the movies, to other people."

Their food arrived and Grace poked at her steak, swirled the tines of fork in her mashed potatoes, stabbed a piece of lettuce, then set the fork down without taking a bite. He hated not knowing what to do and longed to find a way to comfort and reassure her. He'd dreamt about having her all to himself for months, and while he'd take it any way he could get it, knowing she was upset dimmed his pleasure. His mother had taught him that most women preferred a sympathetic ear to Mr. Fix It, but it was a difficult urge to resist.

Grace rubbed the back of her neck, cast him a soft smile, and began eating her meal. His shoulders relaxed.

Man, he had it bad.

Grace glanced up. "What made you get into construction?"

"My father was in the business, so I grew up around it. Starting

58

up my own business was a natural extension. I just grew it bigger and better."

Grace laughed. "Nothing wrong with your ego."

"Hey, I won't lie." He grinned. "I'm proud of the company I've built from the ground up."

"You have every reason to be proud of your accomplishments. What's it feel like, when you're driving around and look at a restaurant, a store, or someone's home, and know you made that happen? You've left your fingerprint on this valley. That's gotta feel good."

He shrugged. No one had ever put it like that. She made him sound like more than he was, which felt damn good.

"I don't think about it."

Her eyes widened and she leaned forward. The low neck of her sweater gaped and no force on earth could have stopped him from enjoying the view. Beautiful, smooth skin the color of fresh cream. The lace at the top of her bra was just visible. He jerked his gaze back to her face and shifted the napkin in his lap a little higher.

"How is that possible?"

"I guess when I see the buildings my crews have put up, I'm still looking at them with a critical eye. Either that, or they blend into the landscape. It's just business."

Obviously unable to comprehend his lack of emotional depth, she shook her head. Great. Now she was probably rating him alongside a caveman. Desperate to save her opinion of him, he racked his brain. And came up empty. He frowned. Was he really that lame?

"Well, I have no room to talk." She sighed. "I've never created anything. I still think it's awesome, being able to leave your mark on the world like you do. I'd love to be able to do that."

Relief flowed. Admiration laced her voice. She sure made an impact with him, but he doubted she'd been referring to that kind of mark.

"You're part of the machine that puts those buildings in the ground, you know."

She tilted her head and stared at him. Having her undivided attention made his hands clammy. How could one woman make him feel like an awkward teenage boy? He could handle a room full of businessmen, the wealthy couple who thought they could have the world at a bargain and the contract gone bad, with ease. Sit a black-haired, green-eyed woman in front of him and his nerve went out the nearest window.

When it came to romancing a woman, he didn't have a clue. If a woman wanted him, he'd never had to work for it. If she didn't, why bother? It was the twenty-first century. Women were aggressive; they went after what they wanted.

Grace shrugged. "I may be a small part—very small, but it's not the same. Still, I appreciate you saying so."

"If you want to leave a mark, have an impact, why are you working behind the scenes? Why not go for something more? There has to be something you love, some other desire behind that statement."

She flushed and dropped her gaze. So there was something.

"Not really."

"That's a yes. You just haven't decided whether to pursue it. Life is short, Grace. Go for your dreams."

"You make it sound so easy. So simple. It's not."

"Why? Because it's something that scares you? Chasing your dreams can be terrifying. The thrill of catching them is worth it."

She stared.

He shifted in his seat. "What?"

"You have the soul of a poet, Matt."

A slow smile bloomed and sparkled in her eyes, tugging at his very non-poetic soul. He swallowed. Just because he admired her, cared for her and wanted her, didn't mean forever. Hell, she hadn't even seen him as anything but her boss until recently.

"However. . ."

"Ah." Matt grinned. "There's always a *however.*"

"I've never been exactly 'normal.'" She made air quotes. "Not many foster kids are. Heck, I don't even know who my parents are."

"That's rough."

She shrugged. "I survived. After being shuffled from home to home for years, I landed on Laura's doorstep. She was a great foster mom. Taught me how to open up to people and shaped me into who I am today."

"Sounds like she was an amazing woman. I'm glad you found someone to nurture you, sweetheart."

Grace glanced up, eyes widening, and he cursed his slip. He wasn't a teenager. He knew better than to wear his heart on his sleeve.

He cleared his throat. "Would you like dessert?"

"No thank you. This was plenty. I'm stuffed. I can't believe I ate that much."

He grinned and lifted a finger for the check.

His hand on the small of her back, he escorted her out of the restaurant. He leaned a fraction closer, dropped his chin and inhaled. She smelled like heaven. A sweet musky scent that was pure woman. She turned and smiled, her hair brushing across the back of his hand like strands of silk.

"Thank you for dinner. And for the ride." Her gaze went to his Harley. A woman after his own heart, lusting after power and a rumbling engine. He could get into that.

*Down, boy.*

Handing her the spare helmet, he threw a leg over and settled on the low seat. He pulled on his helmet and started the bike, then held out his hand to help her on. He turned to make sure she got on safely. Grace grinned like a kid in a candy store, her eyes glinting behind the visor.

She climbed on like an old pro, hands clutching his sides while she settled. Her legs came to rest alongside his, her arms wrapped around him, and he revved the motor. The bike vibrated between his legs, and he could have sworn Grace moaned. Her arms tightened around him.

She did things to him he wouldn't have thought possible. He'd perfected self-control. Or so he'd thought, until she came into his life.

Matt eased away from the curb, Grace clinging to him like a second skin. About as close to heaven as a guy could get. He rumbled to a stop at a red light and glanced back.

Grace raised her head and met his eyes. Cheeks pink, lids half-closed and moist lips parted, she was the picture of a woman on the verge of an orgasm. He bit back a groan. What he wouldn't give to tip her over the edge.

He lifted his visor and Grace followed suit.

"How about a ride before I drop you at your place?"

She nodded, eyes sparkling. He revved the engine again. She bit her lip and her eyelids slid down. Holy crap. A visual slammed into his brain of Grace's sweet pussy pressed against the vibrating seat. Of course, she was naked.

Her hips shifted, her heat pressing against him. Her eyes opened, bright with arousal. Watching her was the biggest turn-on he'd ever experienced. Two more seconds of this and he'd be useless. He winked, slammed his visor shut and faced the inter-section.

The light changed and he rumbled forward, slow and easy, muscles tight. Damn, he needed to get a grip. So what if the most beautiful woman he'd ever seen was hot, bothered, and wrapped around him like a well-worn leather jacket. He was a grown man, not some horny teenager.

The vibration of the powerful engine beneath him increased as he accelerated. He could have sworn Grace whimpered as she pressed closer, rubbing against him like a cat. Unable to resist, he revved the motor again. Her head dropped against his back. Her sweet, drawn-out moan reached him over the low rumble of the bike. The painful erection wearing the imprint of his zipper throbbed in time with his pulse.

Had what he thought just happened, happened?


\*\*\*\*\*


Grace kept her eyes shut. Matt's heat soaked into her and the Harley vibrated beneath her. Her cheeks burned. She'd never been so mortified in her entire life.

In the middle of downtown Boise, in full view of cars and pedestrians, she'd gyrated against Matt like a cheap hooker and had an orgasm. How pathetic. So what if sitting on the bike was like riding a giant vibrator? She had more self-control than that. Except she obviously didn't.

She couldn't wrap her brain around such a complete loss of inhibition. If she hadn't felt the contractions shredding her sense of reality like nothing before, she wouldn't have believed it. How was she going to look him in the eye again? Matt would forever think of her as the woman who orgasmed on the back of his bike.

Fresh waves of humiliation washed over her and she swallowed a groan. She'd done too much of that already. The lack of certainty was another slap in the face. Did he know? It wasn't like she had laid back across the seat and screamed her pleasure to the cloudless sky overhead. A very aroused Matt between her legs, both of them naked—she bit her lip. Her body throbbed to life again.

Grace stared blindly at the dignified old homes along Warm Springs Avenue. Her day had spiraled out of control. A break-in at her condo and a solo orgasm on a Harley behind her boss. Her boring, ordinary life had become a soap opera.

Stark silence filtered into her senses, pulling her out of her memories. Matt had shut off the bike and was just sitting there. Not that she gave him any other option. Tight as she was holding on, the poor man would need a crowbar to pry her off him and the bike.

Heat suffused her cheeks. Yanking off her helmet, she clumsily scrambled off the bike and onto the pavement in front of her condo. Her knees buckled.

Heavily muscled arms snatched her up inches from the unforgiving pavement. Grace buried her hot face in the crook of Matt's neck.

"Think I'll go ahead and die of mortification now, thank you."

"No worries, sweetheart. It happens when you're not used to riding. My fault. I shouldn't have taken you so far."

His voice rumbled above her ear and vibrated through his chest. The arousal that had never quite gone away found new life. Held tight in his arms, her breasts nestled against him, his heat enveloping her, she fought a silent battle.

So it'd been a rough day. So her emotions where splattered like bugs on the grill of a semi. That was no reason to molest her boss. Even if he was sweet and considerate and sexy as hell.

"Grace?"

Finding intense fascination in the tight weave of fabric in his shirt, the smell of leather and man and rich cologne, she refused to look up. Matt jiggled her a little in his arms. She stared at the column of his throat, miserable with want and fear and who knew what else.

Did he have to be so freakin' gorgeous? The darkening shadow of beard stubble marking his strong jaw drew her gaze. She wanted to feel that stubble scraping against her bare skin. Grace stared at his lips and sucked her lower lip into her mouth. She had about a thousand places in need of his lips. Reluctantly, she met his eyes.

He quirked his brow. "You're awfully quiet. Everything okay?"

Her lips parted, but no response came to mind. She focused on his lips again, the dimple on his cheek teasing her. Her brain had gone fuzzy.

*Back up, Grace. I hardly know him.* Okay, so she'd worked for Matt for half a year and had an incredible orgasm on the back of his bike. Teensy details that meant nothing. Not in the grand scheme of things. She wasn't a hop in the sack with any Joe Blow kind of girl.

*Breathe in, breathe out. Shut down raging hormones; get a grip on out-of-control libido.* If this was what happened when she went too long between guys, maybe a battery-operated boyfriend wasn't such a bad idea. A girl could get into trouble operating at this level of neglect. It clouded her judgment.

She forced herself to smile. "I'm good. You can put me down."

"Are you sure? I don't mind holding you. As a matter of fact, I'd be only too happy to carry you up to your condo." His brown eyes twinkled.

"Up three flights of stairs, Matt? Get real." She wriggled.

He quirked a brow. "You're questioning my strength?"

His arms tightened around her and he started walking, his long strides eating up the distance to her building. Flattening her palm against his chest, she pushed and squirmed. His arms didn't budge.

"Matt," she hissed. "This isn't necessary. You're totally built, okay? A He-Man, an Adonis, a god among men. Just put me down."

He glanced at her and flashed a fully fledged, tooth-baring grin. Her heart skipped a beat and her muscles turned to runny pudding. No man had a right to be so gorgeous. Turning a girl into empty-headed mush should be illegal. No wonder Matt never smiled. He wouldn't get any peace, what with beating women off with a stick 24/7.

"Careful, beautiful. Your praise will go to my head." He was still smiling.

They stopped and he allowed her feet to drop. He didn't release her, instead holding her caged against his body, her feet dangling above the floor. Grace couldn't seem to find the presence of mind to drag her gaze from his.

One arm wrapped tight around her waist, he tangled his other hand in her hair. His gaze dropped to her lips and his head lowered.

His firm lips brushed across hers, feather-light, teasing. Not enough. Tilting her head, she lifted her chin a few notches and wrapped her arms around his neck. Complete surrender had never really been in doubt. She could be embarrassed by her behavior later. Right now, she had to taste him.

Matt's mouth settled more firmly. He nibbled at her lips and she parted them. So gentle, so erotic her breath staggered. He stroked her tongue, wrapped around and invited it to play.

Hesitation had never been part of her personality. Grace sucked on his tongue. When he retreated, she sucked his lower lip into her mouth and rubbed the underside with the tip of her tongue. Matt groaned and flattened her backside against a wall.

The slight shift brought their bodies into direct contact. His erection pressed against her. She wriggled, tightened her arms to raise up just a smidge. Oh, yes. Right there. She moaned into his mouth and fisted his hair in her hand.

A deep *WOOF* echoing up the stairs shattered the moment. Grace jerked back.

Matt grinned, rueful and wicked at the same time. Her stomach flip-flopped. His arms relaxed and she slid down to her feet.

He crossed his arms. "Not very nice of Apollo to interrupt."

Grace glanced around. They were in the passageway in front of her condo. She leaned against her front door. Matt hadn't been out of breath at any point while carrying her up the stairs. He really was a He-Man.

She opened her mouth then closed it. What was she supposed to say? Too much time spent studying and pursuing her career had left her a little too inexperienced on the ins and outs of relationships. Sex, yes. Actual dating, no.

"Thank you for an amazing evening, Grace." The naughty twinkle lit Matt's eyes again. A slow smile grew, bringing a single dimple into evidence.

"Dinner was wonderful." She wanted to bang her head on the door behind her. Could she be any more awkward? No, cancel that. She knew for a fact, she could.

He ran a finger down her cheek, along her jawline, tipping her face up.

"I'll see you Monday, sweetheart."

He pressed a soft kiss to her lips and stole her breath. Who knew such a big guy, one who was reserved and self-possessed at every moment, could be so achingly sweet?

Matt stepped back, then just stood there. Watching her. She relaxed into the door and met his gaze, arching her brows in silent question. His eyes sparkled and his lips twitched.

"Oh!"

Heat rushed into her cheeks and Grace spun around to unlock the door. Duh. He was being a gentleman and waiting for her to get safely inside before he left. Good grief. You'd think no one had ever kissed her before. Then again, they hadn't. Not like him.

Getting the door open took a minute too long as she fumbled with the dead bolts, the burning awareness of the patiently waiting man behind her making her hands tremble. She undid the last one and almost fell into her condo.

Turning, she forced a smile through her humiliation. "Good night."

"Sweet dreams." Matt's devastating eyes gleamed.

She closed the door and slid the locks home, then stood there panting like she'd just bolted up all three flights of stairs. Smooth, Grace. Real smooth.

# CHAPTER SEVEN

Sheriff John Sanford tapped his fingers on the steering wheel as he waited for the light to change. He hadn't done a whole lot of traveling in his life, but a natural sense of direction and a good map were all he needed. He just hoped he could figure out his final destination soon. A young woman's life depended on it.

The light changed and he stepped on the gas. Old brick buildings with century-old architecture lined the streets. The road turned into a small highway. Ten minutes later, he turned off onto a country road.

The urgency of the situation rode him hard. He ignored his impatience and focused on the here and now. The technique was one he'd learned early on in his law-enforcement career. Dealing with the ugliness of car accidents and violence required some sort of coping mechanism, and rushing in could get a man killed.

He pulled up in front of a big house, worn by the years but immaculate, despite the over-long grass. Instinct whispered up his spine. Big, spacious yards separated the houses. Big trees swayed in the light breeze, and bright sunshine made the day look deceptively warm.

Five minutes passed, then ten. Nothing stirred inside the house. No curtains shifted, no shadows passed in front of the windows, no sign of life whatsoever. A door slammed nearby.

Next door, a woman stepped outside. Flowered gloves, a wide-brimmed straw hat and a bag of gardening tools made her intent clear. Perfect.

She knelt beside a perfectly manicured flower bed as he climbed out of the Cherokee. She glanced over her shoulder when he closed the door, but the hat cast a shadow over her face and he couldn't read her expression. Keeping his posture relaxed and nonthreatening, he shoved his hands in his pockets and strolled over. A lawn mower grumbled a few yards down. The breeze carried a faint scent of freshly cut grass and spring bulbs in bloom.

"Excuse me, ma'am?"

The woman rose as he approached, a pair of well-kept gardening shears in one gloved hand. "Yes?"

Closer now, he could make out her face beneath the brim of her hat. Pointy chin, soft lips, small nose and dark, sober eyes gently lined with age. Her slight shoulders were ramrod straight.

"I was wondering if I could ask you a few questions about your neighbors there." He gestured behind him.

Her gaze flickered toward the house before settling on him again. Her smooth expression revealed little. Her eyes, on the other hand, were full of shadows.

"What's your interest?"

"I'm. . ." He hesitated, ran a hand through his hair. Well, no point in hiding it. "I'm the sheriff of a small town in Kentucky, ma'am. John Sanford's my name. There's a young woman I knew years ago, when she was just a little tyke, and I need to find her. She lived in that house for a while."

The woman's mouth firmed.

He bit back his impatience. "She's in danger."

She considered for a moment more, then nodded. "A lot of children have come and gone from that house. Laura Wells used to live there. She cared for foster children, quite a few over the years. I assume the girl you're looking for was in foster care?"

He nodded.

Her gaze shifted to the house behind him. "Laura died a few years ago. Her husband still lives there, but he was never involved with the children. Just kind of did his own thing. Stayed out of

69

the way. He worked a lot. I don't think he's uncaring, just reserved."

Sanford reached inside his jacket. The woman jerked and stepped back, flattening one of her pretty bulbs beneath the heel of her shoe. She didn't seem to notice. Her fingers tightened convulsively on the handle of her shears.

Slow and easy, he removed a photo. "Nothing to worry about. I'm just getting out a picture I'd like to show you."

He held it out. She stared at him, not even looking at the picture. Why was she so jumpy? Like she thought he was going to yank out a shotgun and start blasting.

He narrowed his eyes. "Has someone else been by recently, asking questions?"

She nodded.

"A man about my age?"

She nodded again.

"Did he hurt you?" His stomach knotted. She was such a little thing. "Was your husband around?"

"My husband died ten years ago, but no, the man didn't hurt me. He just. . . I don't know. I know he was trying to be charming, but his eyes were flat. He scared me."

"I can show you identification if you like. As I said, I'm a sheriff from down south and I have no intention of hurting you. I'm just trying to find this girl."

Her gaze dropped to the picture he still held out, and she stepped forward. A small frown brought her delicate brows together. Another step and she reached for the photo. "May I?"

"Yes, ma'am."

She took the photo in her fingertips. After studying it for a minute in silence, she glanced at him. "This picture is old and shows a grown woman. I thought you were looking for a young girl."

"I am. I don't have a current picture of Grace. I lost it. This was her momma. I understand they look alike and her momma is the same age in the photo that Grace is now."

She looked at the picture again. "The resemblance is amazing. She was younger when she lived there, of course, in high school, but I remember her. She was such a sweet thing, very reserved. I got the impression she didn't trust easily. She helped me weed during the summer. Four years she lived with the Wellses, before going off to college. Some big-name university, I believe. Purdue, that's it. She came back for holidays and such. I got the impression she and Laura developed a real bond."

"That's real helpful. Do you happen to know where she's living now?"

"No, I'm sorry." She shook her head, staring at the picture before returning it. "I haven't seen Grace since Laura died. Like I said, Darrell kept to himself around the children."

Sanford glanced back at the house. It squatted on the overgrown lawn, brooding and silent, despite the birds chirping and darting through nearby trees. His bad feeling deepened.

"Does Mr. Wells still live there?"

"Yes. I haven't seen him for a few days, but that's not unusual. Ever since Laura died, he's turned into a real hermit." She frowned, looking down the slight incline at the house. "Still, he's always real particular about his lawn. I swear he measures the blades of grass, and he never lets it get overgrown. I hope he hasn't fallen ill."

"Did the man who asked you about Grace talk to him?"

"I don't know. As soon as he left my yard, I hurried inside. There was something about him that wasn't right."

"Okay." He tucked the worn photo back inside his jacket. "Thank you for your help."

"I hope you find her, Sheriff. She was real sweet. Soft-spoken. She deserves a good life, and I hope she's found it."

A good life. Not shuffled from one foster home to another. Guilt had been a part of him for so long he didn't remember anything else. Every once in a while, though, it rose up and surprised him with its ability to suffocate a grown man. "Yes,

71

ma'am. Thank you. I'll just head on over and have a word with Mr. Wells."

He turned and started down the slope of well-manicured lawn. Not bothering with the sidewalk, he cut across to the porch of the house. Crossing the weathered boards to the front door, he rubbed the back of his neck. A lawman learned to listen to his instincts. His were going off like a fire alarm.

He rapped his knuckles on the door. Nothing. Spotting a doorbell, he reached over and leaned on it. Loud chimes played a Mozart symphony through the big house. Behind him, birds twittered and the drone of bees humming around spring flowers filled the air. In front of him, stark silence screamed.

Well, shit.

He tried the doorknob. The door swung open easily and a heavy stench smacked him in the face. Not good.

He drew his sidearm. The smell wasn't fresh, but you couldn't be too careful. With his free hand, he yanked out his cell phone and stepped inside, punching in 9-1-1. As soon as he finished relaying the information, he clicked the phone off, ignoring the operator yammering in his ear, slid it into his pocket and covered his nose with a handkerchief. There was no mistaking the ripe odor of death.

Cautiously, he checked each room before proceeding. A wide-open family room spanned the width at the back of the house. Furnished with the bare minimum, the smell hung like smog in the air. At first glance the room was empty. He walked in, wary.

The long windows on the far side overlooked a huge lawn pitching away from the house. Massive old trees loomed over the yard, providing shade and, no doubt, entertainment for young kids. He'd enjoyed climbing trees himself as a boy.

Sirens pierced the serenity. Good response time. He scanned the room and spotted a scrawny arm dangling over the side of a worn recliner in front of a large, wall-mounted television.

"Damn." He holstered his pistol and circled the chair. "You must be Darrell Wells."

The unusually warm spring weather hadn't done the body any favors. Flies buzzed around, crawling in and out of Darrell's orifices. No air conditioner hummed in the background and young maggots writhed on the blood-splattered, bloated gray skin. If he had to guess, Wells had been dead for around a week. The gaping bullet hole in the center of his forehead left no doubt as to cause of death.

The front door banged open, the local boys loudly announcing their presence. There went the rest of his day. He'd only planned an hour, two tops, at this stop. He just hoped they weren't too wet behind the ears.

He scrubbed a hand over his face, pulled his badge, and put his hands in the air in expectation of their arrival.

Bloody hell. He didn't have time for this. Every delay allowed a monster that much closer to an innocent girl—that much closer to living out his twisted version of truth, justice and the American way.

## CHAPTER EIGHT

Pleasantly squished between Matt's muscles and the wall, Grace ripped her mouth free and gasped for air. Her lust-hazed gaze focused on the numbers lighting up the elevator panel. Eight more floors to go. Swallowing, she shoved at Matt's shoulders. He didn't budge, busy nibbling on her highly sensitive thank-you-very-much earlobe. She moaned and dropped her head back.

"Matt."

"Hmmm?"

The vibration of his voice sent a whole new sensation racing to her happy parts. *Deep breathing. Think Tai Chi, Pilates, meditating.* She groaned. If only she actually *did* any of those things.

"We have to stop."

He raised his head. Heavy-lidded, desire-filled eyes met hers and he frowned. "It's your fault."

It took all her willpower to not snag handfuls of his hair and drag his mouth down to hers. His words registered and her eyes widened. Her fault? He'd practically leapt on her the moment the doors closed on the basement parking lot.

Matt backed up and swept his gaze over her from head to toe. "You've never worn shoes like that to work before."

They were fabulous shoes too. Strappy stilettos weren't appropriate work attire, in her opinion. It was hard enough to get respect. He didn't need to know she'd put them on with him in mind.

She blinked at him innocently. "Don't you like them?"

"If I liked them any more I wouldn't be able to form a coherent sentence." He braced his hands against the elevator wall and dropped his forehead to hers, so close her eyes almost crossed. "Why are we whispering?"

"Because. . ." *Because someone might hear.* She flushed. "Just because."

A charming grin curved his lips—his very, very fine lips—and her knees went weak.

He stepped back and she sagged against the elevator. Straightened his tie, smoothed his freshly mussed hair and tugged his cuffs down. All the while he never broke eye contact. He tucked in his shirt and she couldn't help taking note of the erection straining the front of his slacks.

In the interest of self-preservation, she closed her eyes and rapped the back of her head against the wall a few times. She didn't behave like this. Least of all with her boss. He was going to think she was a total slut. Easy Sleazy Grace Debry would be her nickname around town from now on.

His hand between her head and the wall prevented a third thud. Minty, toothpaste-fresh breath wafted across her face. "Grace, why are you banging your head?"

She peeked under her lids and yes, dry amusement lit his beautiful brown eyes. His hand cradled her head, stroking and soothing her abused scalp. Every fiber of her being wanted to lean into his touch and purr like a contented house cat.

"Grace?"

"You must think I'm a total s-l-u-t." She groaned and closed her eyes. When had she gotten such a big mouth? She used to be so fabulously reserved.

"You are not an s-l-u-t, sweetheart. You're a beautiful, intelligent, passionate woman." He edged closer, friendly erection saying hello against her hip. "You're responsiveness is an incredible turn-on, in case you've failed to notice." He leaned down, his mouth beside her ear. "Is there any particular reason we're spelling words?"

75

A reluctant grin tugged at her lips. "Well, it's not a very nice word."

"No, it's not." He shook his head, adopting a stern expression she recognized from numerous board meetings. "You shouldn't use it in reference to yourself. Ever."

She snapped her hand up in a mock salute. "Yes, sir."

He shook his head and spoke to the ceiling. "I've been harboring a smart-ass. A smart-ass who should know I'm serious." He met her gaze, the tenderness in his expression doing things to her she'd rather not think about. "Save those words for the bedroom, sweetheart. You can be my slut anytime, anywhere."

While she melted, he helpfully tucked her blouse back into her skirt, his long fingers brushing the lace band on her panties.

The elevator dinged and they jerked apart like teenagers caught necking. Matt hastily buttoned his suit jacket. The doors slid open on them standing several feet apart, serene business-like expressions on their faces. At least, she hoped so. Especially since several of her co-workers lounged around the reception desk, including Luke.

She stepped off the elevator and almost ran into Matt in her haste to escape. His hands on her waist kept her on her feet and set her nerve endings clamoring.

"Excuse me." Matt released her and smoothly stepped to the side. "Have a good morning, Miss Debry."

"Thank you, Mr. Duncan. You too."

The click of her heels followed her down the hall.

Luke caught up to her. "What was that about?"

*Let the inquisition begin.* "What?"

"You, Mr. Duncan, long elevator ride to the top of the building."

She frowned. "I ride in the elevator with people all the time."

"People, yes. Mr. Duncan, no. Besides, you're flushed. And your hair's down. And you're wearing those hot fuck-me shoes."

"You're critiquing my outfit?" They reached her office. She tossed her purse on the desk, faced Luke and crossed her arms.

"If I'm flushed, it's because Mr. Duncan was lecturing me about turning in that report late last week. Not that it's any of your business. What do my shoes or how I fix my hair have to do with anything?"

Luke lounged against the doorframe, grinning. "So you didn't get off so easy about handing it in late after all. Maybe I should start measuring your office to make sure my stuff will fit."

"What stuff? Everything you have belongs to the company." With him effectively diverted, she stowed her purse and sat in her chair. "Besides, you're not getting my office."

"You probably fluttered your lashes and distracted him with those big green eyes. He would have to be made of granite not to respond. Although, I could've sworn he *was* made of granite."

Damp panties reminded her of exactly how granite-like certain parts of Matt were. Even so, irritation flared. Where did he get off talking about Matt like that? She bit her tongue. Defending her boss would only get her in trouble.

Didn't mean she couldn't defend herself. "You're treading a fine line there, buster."

"Yeah, I know. Hey, I have tickets to a concert in a couple of weeks. Wanna be my date?"

A headache throbbed to life. "Luke, I'm not going to date you. You're sweet, but I value our friendship."

"So, you can be my friend date."

"You're fine with that? There isn't someone else you'd rather ask?"

He shrugged. "Nope. Besides, it's a Celtic Women concert. I know you love them."

"Ooh, I do. Yes. I'd love to go. Thank you."

"No problem. See you later."

He left and she spun her chair around to retrieve the Peterman Project files. The drawer was empty. She yanked open the one under it, then two more. All empty. She whirled back to her desk and her foot bumped something in the knee space.

77

Grace shoved back so hard her chair slammed into the filing cabinets. Under her desk, in neatly stacked piles, were her files. Air wheezed out of her lungs and black spots danced at the edge of her vision.

Snatching the phone up, she dialed and then put her head between her knees. Angels' wings, she hadn't hyperventilated since her nine-year-old foster brother hid under her bed and grabbed her ankle. That had been the first year she'd moved in to the foster home, a freshman in high school.

"Yes?" Matt's voice rumbled over the phone.

Some of the tightness in her lungs eased.

"Hello?"

"Matt?" she whispered.

"Grace? What's wrong?"

Just like that, his tone went from all-business to "who's ass am I kicking?". So willing and able to play hero to her damsel in distress. Sweet baby cherubs, he was dangerous.

"Someone's been in my office."

Silence.

"Hello? Matt, are you there?"

Nothing. Huh. So much for playing hero.

"Grace?"

She sat up so fast the room spun. Matt's rough, warm hands cradled her face. Taking a deep breath, she closed her eyes while the room reoriented itself. His thumbs smoothed over her cheeks. Warmth bloomed in her chest. Very dangerous, indeed.

Grace opened her eyes. He was down on one knee in front of her, concern darkening his eyes. Her heart jumped into her throat and choked her.

"You're pale as a sheet of paper, sweetheart."

*Breathe in, breathe out.* She could get through this. So not the time for silly romantic fantasies. Only, she'd never had a gorgeous, rugged hunk of a man drop to one knee before.

"What's wrong?"

Right. Business at hand. Finger trembling, she pointed under the desk.

Matt's gaze followed, and he frowned. "Are those your files?"

"Yes. I don't. . ."

He eased the phone from her clenched hand, punched in some numbers and barked a few orders. He replaced the phone then smoothed a hand down the back of her hair.

"Building security is on their way up." He glanced around. "I take it the files were removed from the drawers and stacked there?"

"Yes."

"Anything else?"

"I don't think so, no."

"Any notes?"

Her gaze flew to his and her stomach lurched. "You think this is related to what happened at my condo?"

"I think it would be foolish to dismiss the possibility."

Grace dropped her head to the desk with a moan, fighting a wave of nausea. "I was really, really hoping you wouldn't think the same thing."

His hand smoothed her hair again and some of the tension in her belly uncoiled. She lifted her head. Solid as a rock, his steady gaze reassured her. Oddly enough. She didn't like people taking over, bossing her around, not giving her the freedom to do things her way. She swallowed.

Uncharted territory made her nervous. Not knowing how things would progress, unable to guess at what would happen, her future twisting and turning until it disappeared in a kaleidoscope of confusion. Not how she liked things. She swallowed again against the acid rising in her throat and focused on Matt.

He paced to the door and back again. All that coiled energy— a restless lion in her office. Her gaze dropped to his butt when he walked away.

At least the view was nice.

# CHAPTER NINE

What was taking the security guys so long? Were they walking up the twenty stories instead of using the elevator?

Matt turned. A myriad emotions clouded Grace's face. He wanted to drive a fist through whoever the hell was scaring her. Shoving his hands in his pockets, he spun away. With a deep breath, he drew on a thin veneer of implacable resolve.

"Mr. Duncan?"

"Yeah, in here." He waved the two uniformed security guards into the office and shut the door against the curious faces peeking over the cubical walls. The office was cramped with so many people shut inside. Grace rose from her chair and edged toward the windows.

"Someone broke in. Over the weekend, I assume." Matt gestured toward the rear of the office. "He emptied Miss Debry's file cabinets and stacked the contents underneath her desk."

One of the men peered under the desk. His gaze shifted to Grace's legs and tension seeped through Matt. The jerk-off took his time standing up, staring at Grace the whole time.

"Is there a problem?" Grace stared the guy down, voice sweet as maple syrup.

"No, ma'am." The other guard glared at the younger one.

The younger guard managed to drag his gaze from Grace, glanced at the second guard and snapped to attention.

"If you two could step out of the office," the senior officer said, "we'll have a quick look around. I think it would be best if we called the police."

At least one of them had some sense. The other guy was still making calf eyes at Grace. She was busy ignoring him, deeply fascinated with the view from her window. Matt wanted to smack the guy upside the head.

"Sure. We'll be down the hall in my office. Miss Debry?"

Matt stepped back, deliberately herding the two guards into the corner of the office. Grace passed in front of him, flashing a look of gratitude on her way out. He closed the door behind him.

A crowd had gathered in the hall.

Luke stepped forward. "What's going on, Mr. Duncan?"

"Someone messed with Miss Debry's files. No need for any of you to worry. You can get back to work."

Giving orders came as naturally as chewing his food, and people always responded—even to the more subtle orders. They shuffled back to their desks, talking quietly to one another and glancing over their shoulders. Rumors would be flying within the hour. He ran his company with an iron fist and a twenty-foot wall of reserve, but that didn't mean he was oblivious to the under-currents.

Grace stood silent beside him. Awareness heightened his senses. He could stand in a crowd of five hundred, blind and deaf, and he'd still know the moment she was within reach. His pheromones liked her pheromones. Or something.

Hand on the small of her back, he steered her down the hall to his office. She went quietly, without even token resistance. Her unusual docility worried him.

He closed the door and faced her.

"What's wrong?"

"Some jerk is messing with my stuff and you're asking what's wrong?"

The battle spark in her beautiful green eyes surprised him. He couldn't help grinning. The woman was feisty and gorgeous. At least she wasn't hysterical. Dealing with an irrational woman wasn't exactly at the top of his to-do list.

Grace crossed her arms and glared. Hard to be intimidated by a five foot five curvy bit of woman.

"You find something amusing?" She arched her brow.

Her sweet tone didn't fool him. She was pissed and she needed an outlet for her anger. Apparently, he had a nice fat bull's eye painted on his chest. Which was fine. He didn't mind being her punching bag, surprisingly enough.

"I know it's stressful." He patted her arm. "I'm just glad you're not a blubbering mess."

Lovely arched eyebrows climbed skyward. "Wow."

"What?"

"Your sensitivity overwhelms me."

"Trust me. No guy in his right mind wants to deal with a hysterical female. No matter how high up the hotness scale she rates."

Grace blinked. "You think I'm hot?"

"Like you don't know." What was it with women? She was beautiful. Stunning, intelligent and sexy enough to freeze brain cells made her a triple threat.

Grace strolled over to stand in front of him. One white-tipped fingernail trailed down his chest to rest on his belt. His dick leapt to attention like a well-trained dog. Her fingertip burned a path back and forth across his abdomen, hardening everything in the vicinity.

"I think you're pretty hot too."

Unaware he'd even fisted them, he uncurled his hands and reached for her. Someone pounded on the door. Biting back a curse, he dropped his hands and memorized the desire glazing her green eyes. Lips full and pouty, eyelids drooping, cheeks flushed, she was a walking advertisement for sex. She made it damn hard to walk away.

"Mr. Duncan?"

He groaned. Grace spun away. The image of her nipples pressed against the delicate material of her blouse was imprinted on his brain. Front and center.

Striding across the room, he flung open the door. The two security guards on the other side stepped back. The man he assumed was a police officer did not.

"Come in, gentlemen." He shoved aside his impatience and waved them in.

"Uh, that's okay." The older guard remained rooted to the spot. "I think the police can take it from here."

"Fine." Matt shifted his gaze from the guard to the other man. "Officer?"

The police officer walked around the two guards and into the office. Matt shut the door without another glance at the petrified guards. He expected more gumption out of men in their position, even if he did sign their paychecks.

"Matt Duncan." He held out his hand to the police officer.

"Detective Spencer Harrison." Harrison shook his hand with a firm grip.

Detective. That explained the suit.

"Grace Debry." Matt gestured toward Grace.

She crossed the room to shake the officer's hand. "Pleasure to meet you, Detective Harrison."

"I understand your office was broken into."

"Not broken into exactly, as I don't lock the door. But, yes, it's my office."

Harrison glanced at him, obviously looking for confirmation.

He nodded. "After business hours, you have to enter a security code in the elevator panel to reach this floor."

Harrison made a notation on his pad. "Who has the code?"

"The majority of the employees. The exclusions would be temporary help and anyone who has worked here for less than ninety days. Unless they hold an executive position, in which case they're given the code immediately."

Detective Harrison glanced between them and scrubbed a hand over his jaw. "Doesn't look like they took anything, so it comes across as a prank. I'm not sure what you'd like me to do. You have a decent-sized company. That leaves an awful lot of people open as suspects."

Matt nodded. "I understand. Normally, I wouldn't have requested the police. But there have been incidents at Miss Debry's home."

"What incidents?"

Grace answered. "Someone has broken into my condo twice. The last was Saturday afternoon while I was out. I called the police."

"They filled out a report?"

Her eyes narrowed slightly. "Yes".

"Okay." Detective Harrison scribbled something in his notepad then stuck it in his pocket. "I'll pull it when I get back and add this to the report."

Frustration tightened Matt's gut. He understood there wasn't a whole lot the police could do, but he didn't have to like it. Plus, the timing bugged him.

"Thank you, Detective." After showing him out, he glanced at Grace. "You want some help putting the files back?"

"No." She sighed. "We've already got the whole office in a tizzy. Helping me sort through papers would set off a whirlwind of whispers."

"I don't care."

He didn't. He was too concerned about her reaction if she found another note stuck in the files somewhere. She shouldn't have to deal with this crap alone.

"Well, I do. I can manage just fine."

Slipping past him, she tugged open the door. She glanced over her shoulder. The picture she presented stalled his heart in his chest. Black curls cascading down her back, perfect butt, long slim legs, drawing the eye down to those sexy-as-hell shoes.

"Thank you for your help, Matt. Your swift response really. . ." Her lashes dropped to conceal her eyes. A small frown creased the skin between her brows. "Helped."

The door closed with a quiet click behind her. Standing there in the middle of his big office, he puzzled over her. Her admission had obviously cost her. Not surprising, considering a childhood spent in foster care. She'd probably learned to take care of herself and not depend on anyone at a painfully young age.

He couldn't honestly say he understood what her childhood had been like, the circumstances that would have driven her. Growing up the eldest boy in a typical suburban family, he hadn't had to cope with anything difficult. Nothing outside of the normal situations that arose in any family. His childhood consisted of two loving parents, a younger brother to pester him and sports, hunting, and horses to keep him busy.

Matt sat, swiveling to face the windows. Gray clouds hung low and heavy over the city. The balmy weekend had given way to weather more suitable to a wet spring. There wouldn't be any more rides on his Harley for a while.

The memory of Grace clinging to him on their ride after dinner and her low moan increased his heart rate. If she came like that, without being touched, how much more incredible would it be when he was inside her?

Damn. He had a meeting in fifteen minutes with a bunch of stiff-necked executives. They were considering using his firm to build a state-of-the-art factory near Salt Lake. An erection tenting his pants would not impress them.

# CHAPTER TEN

"I am so not dressed for this," Grace muttered.

She shifted again. Her job didn't usually entail crawling on the floor and a snug pencil skirt that did not lend itself to this sort of situation.

Her left foot had long since fallen asleep. Whoever did this hadn't bothered messing up the files. It shouldn't take her too long to restore order. They had a pretty odd sense of humor, but at least she wouldn't be wasting an entire day on her office floor.

Snagging another file, she shifted a little to improve blood flow. A flash of white caught her eye. She tilted her head. Taped to the underside of her desk was a square piece of paper.

"What now?"

She snatched the paper free and sat up. Unclenching her jaw and deliberately relaxing her tense muscles, she unfolded the lined paper.

*Nice office, slut.*
*You always did think you were better than me.*
*Too bad I'll be having the last laugh.*
*You're nothing but a trailer trash tramp.*

She sighed, closed her eyes and rested her head against the desk. The trailer trash thing again. Maybe one of the foster homes she was in early on had been a trailer. Memories from when she was little were fuzzy at best.

"Grace?"

Sweet dandelion blood. Pressing a hand to her racing heart, she peeked around the corner of her desk. Great. Luke.

"Yes?"

"Why are you sitting on the floor?" Frowning, he walked in and settled a hip on the side of her desk.

"How else do you suggest I deal with this mess?"

"Oh, the files? I don't know. I guess I didn't realize they were on the floor. Why would someone do that? I could see someone stealing them, though I don't know what they'd gain from a bunch of construction estimates and invoices. I mean, you'd think if they were going to break into someone's office it would be Mr. Duncan's."

"Yeah."

She tucked the note under the desk, where he couldn't see it. Recent events were too personal and disturbing to share with Luke.

"So, is anything missing?"

"I don't think so."

There was no reason to take anything if his sole purpose was to terrify her. A headache throbbed at the base of her skull.

"You wanna get lunch? A bunch of us are going out."

"It's noon already?" She groaned. "Time flies when you're having fun. No, thanks. I have yet to get any real work done."

"I'm sure Mr. Duncan will cut you some slack. You two looked pretty cozy."

Her head shot up and pain splintered up the back of her skull. She massaged her scalp and tried to come up with a reasonable response that didn't involve throwing things. Dealing with petty office drama on top of the break-ins was too much. She didn't know where this thing with Matt was headed. Burning her bridges for no reason wasn't appealing.

"I didn't realize a ride in an elevator constituted a relationship these days. If that's the case, I'm a real slut. I go both ways too, considering the women I've ridden up and down with."

"I didn't mean—"

A dry voice interrupted. "I don't think I like hearing one of my executives called a slut."

Luke's eyes widened. *"Oh, crap!"* clearly reflected in his expression. Stiff as a board, he turned to face Matt.

"That's not what I meant, sir. Grace was joking."

Matt nodded. "Good to know."

He didn't move. Luke shifted and crossed then uncrossed his arms. Clearing his throat, Luke glanced at her. "Well, I'll leave you to it then."

She bit back a smile. "Enjoy your lunch."

Matt stepped into the hall to let him past. Grace watched him watch Luke. She'd swear he was jealous. He had to be aware she and Luke were friends, and had been for almost as long as she'd worked there.

Luke had started a few weeks after her and they'd clicked immediately. As friends. She couldn't remember the last time a man had been jealous because of her. She kind of liked it. She felt desirable. "Making any progress?"

"Yes." She set down a file. "I've got about half put away."

Matt glanced up and down the hall, stepped inside and closed the door. His gaze a little too intense, too knowing, he crossed his arms and leaned back against the door.

Instantly defensive, she straightened her shoulders. "What?"

"Anything I should know about?"

Like a blazing bonfire, the little piece of paper refused to be ignored. Damn. Pretending she'd never seen it held a whole lot of appeal. With a sigh, she reached under the desk and grabbed the scrap of paper.

"Here." She thrust it at him.

His eyes darkened. "This is from the same person who left the last one."

"Yes."

"I don't like it."

"It's pretty creepy, but there's nothing threatening in all this. More pesky and annoying." She grimaced. "Just ask the police."

"I'd say this note is pretty threatening."

Grace sighed and rubbed the back of her neck, exhausted. "I really don't want to deal with this right now, okay? It's just some messed-up stuff and a few not-nice notes."

"Are you serious?"

She closed her eyes. "Shouldn't you be heading out to lunch?"

"Yes. Why don't you come with me?"

Was he insane? "I don't think that's a good idea."

"Why not?"

"Because everyone will think we're dating."

\*\*\*\*\*

Matt maintained a neutral expression despite the fury boiling through his veins at the bastard who was messing with Grace. The strain on her face and her uncharacteristic hesitance drove his frustration higher. He ached to protect her, to soothe her, but he'd settle for distracting her. The desire to date her, and potentially more, added a few nerves he didn't need to the mix.

"Is that a problem?"

Grace shrugged. "I don't know. Are we dating?"

"Considering the things I'd like to do to you, I'd say we're definitely dating." His voice emerged a husky drawl.

She cast her gaze to the side, one corner of her mouth turned down and a little frown pulling at her brow. Her vulnerability tugged at him.

A step closer and her scent teased him. He braced his hands on either side of the desk, fencing her in, and leaned close enough to make out the dark flecks in her eyes when she reluctantly met his gaze. Matt nuzzled the soft skin below her ear.

"I'm not easy and I'm not a one-night stand, Grace."

She chuckled and tipped her head to the side, giving him better access. "I thought that was my line."

Matt skated his lips lower, her unique blend of sweet spice singing through his veins. "I'm borrowing it. Things are about to get complicated, sweetheart."

"Complicated?"

He nibbled at the delicate spot where her neck met her shoulder. She sighed softly. "How?"

"I'm your boss." He followed the deep v of her blouse with his mouth, pulse thudding thickly. Desire was making it hard to remember why he'd set this course.

Her head dropped back. "Mm-hmmm."

"There could be implications from your co-workers. Can you handle that?"

Nudging aside Grace's silk blouse with his nose, he traced the edge of her lace demi bra with his tongue. So close. The scent of her was richer, stronger, more enticing there. Her soft, flushed skin enticed him deeper. He fisted his hands on top of the desk.

"Yes," she moaned softly.

Satisfaction curved his lips. Her desire played a siren's song, clouding his judgment. No way he was risking her reputation and dignity by fucking on her desk.

"Good. Because I have no intention of letting you go." Not until he'd sated his desire, at least. Time to end this before he lost the strained thread of his control. He lifted his head, straightened her blouse and dropped a quick kiss on her stunned, parted lips. "Come on. I'm starving."

He opened the door then stepped back, waiting. Her jaw snapped shut audibly. Eyes narrowed, Grace rose with feline grace. She smiled sweetly as she passed, her hand brushing across his throbbing erection on the way. He bit back a groan and followed, eyeing the seductive sway of her hips.

Glancing back over her shoulder, she fluttered her lashes. "Better button your jacket, honey-pie."

The vixen had come out to play. He dutifully buttoned his jacket to cover his obvious arousal.

"So, where are you taking me?" Grace smiled cheerfully at the heads peeping over the cubical walls. Eyes wide, they disappeared just as quickly.

Matt couldn't hide his grin or stop the bloom of pleasure in his chest. They were officially dating. His gaze dropped to the sassy sway of her ass, and he narrowed the distance between them.

"In the elevator," he growled in her ear. "On the floor. In a chair. Even the old-fashioned way, in a bed. I'm not picky."

She drew a sharp breath and her steps stuttered slightly as they stepped into the elevator. The doors sighed closed. Back ramrod-straight, Grace stared straight ahead. He deliberately invaded her personal bubble, forcing her to focus on him and not the asshole terrorizing her.

Matt skated his palm over the curve of her bottom and she swallowed audibly.

She spun to face him. "You're doing this to distract me."

Her brilliant mind attracted him as much, if not more, than her beauty.

He smiled slow and easy. "I certainly hope you find me distracting. I know my ability to function is severely impaired around you."

"No. I mean, yes." She narrowed her eyes. "I mean, you're doing this to distract me from the break-ins and notes."

Shrugging, he leaned back against the elevator panel and crossed his arms. "Trust me, making love to you is no burden."

"You weren't. We weren't. That was just. . ." she waved her hand, ". . . necking."

She had a gorgeous neck. Smooth and sweet. He'd like nothing better than to nibble for hours. Well, there were a few other things he'd like to do as well.

"Where would you like to go?"

She blinked. "What?"

"For lunch."

"Oh. I don't care."

They stepped off the elevator into the basement-level garage. Matt placed his hand on the small of her back, guiding her toward his black F350. He opened the passenger door as laughter reached them. A group of people from the office passed. One of them glanced their way and stopped. The frank assessment on Luke's face narrowed Matt's eyes. He stepped closer to Grace.

Luke crossed his arms. "You said you weren't going out to lunch today, Grace."

The rest of the group stopped. As they each spotted them standing together, the open door a flashing sign of the obvious, their chatter died. Grace shifted and he glanced down. Her arms were crossed and her chin high, staring them down. Pride filled him.

"I changed my mind."

"For a better offer, I see."

Luke's snide tone drew Matt's gaze and he contemplated the younger man. Interesting attitude. His dark eyes flashed to Matt then back to Grace.

"Good luck with that." Luke strode off.

The rest of the group was slower to follow. As the last one disappeared around the rear of the truck, Grace's shoulders sagged.

"Well," she glanced at him, lips trembling on a smile. "That could have gone better."

Causing her additional stress had not figured into his plan. Ticked off at himself, he rubbed her arm. "Don't worry about it, sweetheart."

"Easy for you to say." She scrambled into the truck. "You're the boss."

Matt leaned in and rested his hand on her thigh, rubbing his thumb back and forth. The height of the truck put them at eye level. "You can't let other people's attitude problems affect you or your decisions. I learned that lesson early on."

"I know." She sighed. "Trust me. I know. It doesn't always make it easier."

Her sadness pulled at him. He'd screwed up royally. Now she was upset over her co-workers behavior, something she didn't need on top of everything else. While rudimentary at best, he knew of only one way to totally relax her.

Cradling her head, he slid his hand higher up her smooth thigh and leaned in to brush his lips against hers. With a soft moan, Grace opened for him. He didn't hesitate to delve into the sweet depths of her mouth. Tangling her tongue with his, he slipped his hand beneath her skirt, moving aside the silky barrier of her panties. Using one fingertip, he teased her folds. So hot and wet.

She gasped into his mouth. He pushed his finger inside her and her intimate muscles clamped down—to keep him out or pull him deeper, he couldn't tell. Arousal wound around the base of his neck and pressed against his zipper, testing his self-control. Her arms wound around his neck. Tension held her body tight as she fought an orgasm. Not happening. Deepening the kiss, he pressed another finger inside her slick heat and rubbed her clit with his thumb.

Grace's muscles clenched tight around his fingers, she fisted handfuls of his hair and sobbed into his mouth. The world could have ended right then, with her convulsing around his fingers, and he wouldn't care.

He didn't release the pressure until the last muscle spasm passed. Slow and easy, he slid his fingers from her. She moaned. Holding her gaze, Matt brought his damp fingers to his mouth and licked them clean, never breaking eye contact. The taste of her nearly killed him. His cock throbbed painfully.

"Matt. . ."

He kissed her again, unwilling to allow regrets or recriminations to sour the moment. Letting her taste herself and his hunger. He wrapped his arms around her, battling back his desire to cradle her tenderly.

An effort Grace almost blew to hell and back when she wrapped her legs around his hips. Balanced on the edge of the leather seat, she kissed him deaf, dumb and blind. He squeezed her bottom and pulled her tight against him. The heat of her against his aching length was sweet torture. He dipped his head and gently sucked on her neck, careful not to mark her.

"Please. . ." she whimpered.

He sucked a little harder, struggling to rein in his desire in the face of hers. No way was he going to take her in the basement parking lot. He pried his fingers from her ass and rubbed her back. Softened the kiss. Eased their bodies apart several inches, every nerve ending screaming in denial.

Murmuring softly, he cradled her against him, gentling her. Denying himself in an effort to honor her and who she was, to herself and to him.

"Orgasms in public places aren't really part of my sexual repertoire," Grace murmured.

He glanced down. Her lashes were lowered and a blush stained her cheeks. Adorably flushed.

Matt grinned. "I'm glad to hear it."

Grace jerked her head back and met his gaze. Her flush spread. She licked her lips, and he clenched his jaw against a surge of desire that shot straight to his groin.

"Can't say it's a familiar experience for me, either." He stepped back and lifted her legs into the cab. "I liked it, though."

He winked and shut the door. At the rear of the truck, he gripped the tailgate and glared into the distance. Lust and fury tangled potently in his gut. Grace's eyes were free of fear and strain, but he remembered all too clearly how she looked in her office. He longed to get his hands on the asshole tormenting her.

Forcing his anger aside, he climbed into the driver's seat and headed for his favorite restaurant. Ten minutes later he pulled into a parking spot and shut off the ignition.

Grace looked at him. "Oh, you are good."

He grinned. "Thanks. Although, if you're just now realizing it, I need to up my game."

"I'm a little slow. Either that or you seriously scramble my brain waves."

Matt shook his head and reached across the console to wrap a tendril of her hair around his finger. "You are many things, sweetheart. Slow is not one of them."

Her cheeks colored, but she held his gaze. "Thank you, Matt. For distracting me."

Shrugging aside embarrassment, he jumped from the truck. Instead of letting her climb down, Matt grasped her around the waist and lifted her down. The feeling of her curves beneath his hands killed him all over again.

\*\*\*\*\*

Grace jogged down the Greenbelt, enjoying the chilly air and the moonlight dancing across the path with the sway of the trees. It had been too late to knock on Mrs. Freeman's door to take Apollo with her, so she'd dragged Lisette away from her painting instead. She glanced sideways and stifled a grin at her disgruntled expression.

A midnight run might not be the most brilliant idea, but she wasn't alone. Plus, exercise cleared her mind and released tension from her muscles. The atmosphere in the office had been strained when she got back from lunch. She hadn't seen Luke all afternoon.

There was no reason for everyone to get their panties in a knot over her dating Matt. He was a man. She was a woman. Both single. Both adults. Heck, there wasn't even a policy preventing inter-office dating.

The slap of another shoe on the blacktop reached her, and she glanced over her shoulder. Between the bright splashes of moonlight, shadows lay deep over the path and in the trees. She didn't see anybody. Their isolation settled between her shoulder blades like a target. This stretch of the Greenbelt was quiet, with no other late-night exercise enthusiasts to keep them company. Bare tree branches scraped together and the hair on her nape rose. She tried to shrug it off, shooting another glance at Lisie. There was safety in numbers, right?

"Um, did you hear something?"

"No." Lisie turned in a full circle without breaking stride, her long ponytail bouncing with each step, and shot her a look. "Did you?"

The taunting notes she had received loomed before Grace, and she unconsciously quickened her pace. Her bursts of breath misted in the cool night air, her normal well-regulated breathing gone. She squared her shoulders and forced a deep breath. There was nobody behind them. No one had ducked into the trees as soon as she'd glanced back. Just her overactive imagination at work.

Except, she hadn't been thinking about the notes or someone breaking into her condo, her car and her office. She'd been thinking about Luke's irrational anger and her co-workers' sidelong glances and whispered conversations. Her body had been busy remembering the feeling of Matt's long, skilled fingers inside her.

A branch snapped and she stumbled.

*Holy dog treats.*

"You heard that, right?"

Lisie's eyes were huge in the moonlight. "Yes."

"Shit." A map of this section of the pathway sprang to mind and her heart skipped a beat. The only way back was the way they'd come.

Grace glanced back again. No friendly jogger, no dog sniffing bushes. What had seemed so cheerful and refreshing was now threatening. Menace loomed thick in the air and she struggled to breathe.

"What should we do?" Lisie's soft voice wouldn't carry far, but Grace couldn't help another backward look.

"I'm not—" Her toe caught on uneven pavement and she flung her hands out to break her fall.

"Mon dieu!"

That hadn't been soft. Grace's knees slammed into the unforgiving surface, then her hands. She gasped at the pain.

"Drop and roll," she hissed at Lisie. Ignoring the sting, she flattened to the blacktop and rolled into the deep shadows between the path and river. She came to a stop alongside a tree trunk, rolled smoothly into a sitting position and shimmied behind the tree, thankful she'd chosen a black outfit.

Lisie followed seconds later, hitting a nearby tree with a little too much force. She sucked in a breath, glanced around, and crawled over to join her—blessedly silent in the underbrush.

Her heart pounded like a drumbeat and their combined breathing sounded overloud in the quiet night. Straining to hear, she pressed into the harsh bark. Seconds ticked by. Grace met Lisie's gaze and made a downward motion with her hand at the same time she slowly exhaled in an attempt to calm. Lisie nodded. Gradually, the hammering of her heart receded and her breathing pattern settled.

Sounds emerged. Tree branches rustled overhead. Wings beat the air and a whip-poor-will's quick chirrupy call made her jump. The bushes rustled. She stared hard into the darkness shrouding the path. A shadow shifted, separated from one then melded into another.

Oh, God. Holy mackerel, trout and salmon. Her heart tried to gallop off into the night without her, but she forced herself to remain still. Lisie grabbed her hand and they clung tightly to each other. They needed to slip away without alerting their stalker.

A sound caught her ear. A whirring. Like. . . Yes! A light appeared at the curve in the path, and she could just make out the shape of a cyclist headed their way. Oh, thank you, thank you, thank you.

Grace bit the inside of her cheek. She could clearly see the rider now. A big hulking guy, hunched low over the handlebars of his sleek bicycle. The breeze moaned through the trees, parting them for a split second to reveal a man across the path. He rose from a crouch, dressed in solid black with a large stick in his hand.

Her gaze flew back to the cyclist. What would he do? A stick to the spokes? Club the guy across the face? Her gaze darted between the two. She bit down harder on the inside of her cheek. The metallic taste of blood trickled across her tongue.

She made a quick decision, pried her hand free of Lisie's and darted out of hiding with a cry that would have done a screech owl proud.

The cyclist swore and swerved. Straight toward the man in black. The moon glinted off his eyes. He was staring straight at her. Ice slid down her spine. One step in her direction, then two, set him on a collision course with the big cyclist.

"Hey!" the guy shouted.

Too late. He slammed into the man in black and they crashed to the ground. A tangle of limbs and bicycle. Curses and grunts filled the air.

Grace spun and gestured wildly at Lisie. As soon as her feet hit the path, she grabbed her hand again and bolted. The paved path flew beneath her sneakers and the cold night air stung her cheeks. Not daring to look back, cringing against a hard tackle that didn't come, she stretched her legs and ran as if her life depended on it. Maybe it did.

She rounded a curve in the path, then another. Lisie was panting for air, but doggedly keeping up, despite her shorter legs. The dim lights of their condominium complex loomed light years in the distance.

Grace glanced over her shoulder, past Lisie's pale, frightened face, and caught a flash of something between the trees. Not daring to stare too long and risk tripping again, she spun back around. What she'd seen clarified her suspicion. He'd swiped the guy's bicycle and was chasing them.

A rush of fear-laced adrenaline lent her a burst of speed. She was practically dragging Lisie. So close. They breached the complex perimeter, but didn't slow. Their running feet on the stairs reverberated like thunder in the quiet night. At the first landing she dared a glance out into the shadows on the path. The bike's headlamp had disappeared.

Her throat closed. He could be anywhere. A quick look back showed an empty stairwell. Somehow that failed to reassure her.

On the last set of stairs, she released Lisie's hand and fumbled her key out of the zippered placket of her running shorts. The key slipped free of her clammy fingers and thumped to the hallway floor. Scanning the hall, she scooped it up and shoved it into her dead bolt. Lisie pressed close, patting hands at her back in a silent urge for speed.

A shadow moved in the stairwell. She sobbed in frustration and wrenched the door open.

Lisie scrambled in so close behind they nearly tripped over one another's feet, and Grace slammed the door so hard the pictures along the wall shifted. Shaking and light-headed, she slid the locks home then pressed her ear to the panel.

At first, she couldn't hear anything beyond the mad rush of blood through her veins and her own panting. Then a soft foot-step stole her ability to draw air.

"*Soc au lait!*" Lisie hissed. "What you doin'?"

Grace flapped her hand at her to be quiet. Another, the slide of a shoe against the floor outside her door. Her knees tried to give out, but she jerked upright and stared at the door. Evil oozed around the door frame. She stepped back. The floor creaked beneath her feet. A low, husky chuckle from the other side. The door seemed to vibrate in its frame. A shiver broke her trance and she snatched the phone off its base.

# CHAPTER ELEVEN

Matt groaned and rolled over to glare at the clock. 11:00 pm blinked back at him in highlighter yellow. Damn. He'd just drifted off. The phone rang again. He winced and snatched it off the nightstand.

"Yeah?" he rumbled, voice scratchy.

"Matt." The whisper of Grace's fear drifted through the phone. He sat bolt upright. "Grace?"

"He's here. Please." Something thudded and she whimpered. A soft, distant "mon dieu" reached his ear. "How fast can you get here?"

"You're at home?" Matt tossed back the covers, adrenaline flooding his veins.

"Yes."

"I'm on my way, sweetheart." Zipping up his pants, he fought to keep the tension out of his voice. "Are you alone?"

"Lisie is here."

The tiny Cajun looked like a stiff wind would blow her away, but it was something. "Hang up and call the police."

Silence greeted his order. Damn, this was not the time for her to pout over him being bossy. He jerked the phone away, yanked a T-shirt on, and brought it back to his ear.

"Baby. . ."

"I think he's gone."

Shoving his feet into loafers, he stuffed his wallet in his pocket, snagged his keys off the hall table and slammed the front door behind him. Thankfully, she'd called his cell.

"You can't be sure. Call the police." His powerful truck engine rumbled to life. Without giving the diesel time to warm up, he jerked the gearshift into drive and roared out of his driveway. "Grace?"

"I'm here." Her voice trembled, the unusual vulnerability killing him. "He's gone, I know it."

She was so damn stubborn. The tires squealed as he took a corner too fast. At this time of night, the streets were deserted and the lights were helpful enough to click to green at his approach.

"There's no way you can know." His gut clenched. He hated to scare her further, but. . . "He could be waiting outside for you to peek out or looking for another way in or jimmying your locks."

She whimpered. Damn. He was such an asshole. White-knuckling the steering wheel, he tore around another corner and into her parking lot. He stood on the brakes and the big truck shuddered to a stop, the anti-lock system objecting.

Without bothering to pull into a spot, he threw the diesel into park, jumped out and ran for Grace's building. No one crossed his path, and he didn't see anybody lurking in the shadows. At Grace's door, he gulped air and pounded on the door. Probably should've knocked more politely, considering the time of night and her terror, but the protectiveness roaring through him left no room for manners.

"Grace, it's me."

Stuffing his hands in his pockets, he listened for noise on the other side. Silence. His gut tightened and he glanced to either end of the hallway. The hair on the nape of his neck rose, but he didn't see anyone. Which didn't mean no one was there, watching from some circumspect hiding spot. The slide of Grace's locks brought him back around. She must walk like a cat. He hadn't heard a sound.

The door opened and Grace stood silhouetted by the hallway

light. The room behind her was dark. Her face was pale and her gaze wary as she glanced past him.

"There's no one out here, sweetheart." He dragged his thumb lightly over her cheek. "Let's get you inside, though, just in case."

Her lower lip trembled. She stepped back. He threw a final narrowed look up and down the hallway, fisting his hands against the violence running through him, wishing the perv would step into view, then closed and locked the door. Shutting the door blocked off the light and it took a minute for his eyes to adjust.

Grace stood directly in front of him, her eyes big and luminous in the pale oval of her face. A sparkly tear slid down her cheek. Might as well have been a punch to his gut.

"Aw, baby." Matt tugged her close, wrapping his arms around her. She trembled and burrowed closer. After the wild drive over, it was so damn good to hold her. To reassure himself that she was safe and sound. He edged toward the couch without releasing her. When he tried to pull back, she whimpered. So he sat with her wrapped around him like an octopus on steroids. There were worse things.

Lisette was a pale, tiny ball burrowed into the far corner of the couch, her face swallowed by enormous dark eyes. They exchanged a long, silent look.

He rubbed his chin against the top of Grace's head, soft strands of her hair catching in his stubble. "Tell me."

She curled up on his lap. Oh yeah, he could get used to this.

"Grace." He nudged her chin up with his knuckle. "What happened?"

She shivered and ducked her face into the crook of his neck. Her breath washed over his skin and goosebumps rose. Which, in turn, roused very friendly parts of his anatomy.

*Not the time, buddy.*

She mumbled something into his neck, which he understood exactly zero of.

"What?"

With obvious reluctance, Grace pulled back a little and rested her head on his shoulder. Which he was also okay with, as was junior. Especially when she wriggled her soft hip deeper into his crotch.

*Down, boy.*

She sighed. "I went jogging an hour ago."

Matt glanced at the glowing digital display on her DVD player. 11:15. He squeezed her and sighed. "Baby, I know you hate when I boss you, but seriously? Some guy breaks into your home, your car and your office, and you decide jogging in the dark is a good idea? Come on. You're smarter than that."

"Apparently not." Some of her typical sass colored her tone. Reassuring, that. "Since I did go running. In the dark. Like a total and utter moron. I had a too-stupid-to-live moment, okay? Like the blonde bimbo in slasher movies."

Matt chuckled and tangled his fingers in the silky curls tickling his forearm. He rubbed a strand between his thumb and fore-finger. "Hey, you were smart enough not to go alone."

She nodded and stretched her hand toward Lisie, who wriggled closer and grasped the proffered hand. "I'm not sure that really was smart. I put my friend in danger."

"No, sug. It wasn't your fault." Lisie's voice was soft and breathy with the remnants of fear, but firm. "I'm glad ya weren't alone."

"She's right, sweetheart." He met Lisie's gaze over Grace's head and nodded his approval. "So you were jogging. . ."

"We were fine for a while, enjoying the quiet night, the chill in the air—"

Lisie snorted. "Speak for ya'self. My thighs were screamin' objections and I'm pretty sure I swallowed a moth."

Their laughter was tinged slightly with hysteria. Matt rubbed Grace's back.

"Then. . . I don't know. I got creeped out. I kept hearing someone behind me, but I couldn't see anyone. I ran faster. Then I tripped, like a total klutz. I was so scared. We were so scared." She scooted closer and her breast pressed into his chest.

"F'sho." Lisie nodded.

This had to be the most horrifying, erotic story he'd ever endured. The rest poured out of her in rapid-fire staccato speech he strained to digest over the pounding of his pulse.

They sat in silence for a few minutes. Matt enjoyed the simple act of holding her, but there were issues to be addressed.

"As much as I love that you called me first, you shouldn't have. You have to get over this aversion to the police. It's their job, even if the guy is long gone. At the very least, they'll have a good look around and make sure he really is gone."

Lisette nodded emphatically. Grace sighed and relaxed a little, her body molding to his in a very distracting way. "I know. It's just. . ." A shudder shook her. "When I was twelve, a policeman picked me up to take me to a new foster home. Instead of going straight there, he pulled into a deserted parking lot. And he. . . um. . . did things."

"Oh, baby." Nausea and anger coiled tight in his gut, but he kept his touch gentle, stroking up and down her arms.

Lisette mumbled something that sounded like a mix of French swear words and Voodoo curses, and patted Grace's hand, which she had yet to release. He couldn't believe he was fighting an erection while sharing the couch with a strange woman. Threesomes weren't his thing, even if Lisette did have a unique sort of fae beauty about her.

Grace ducked her head beneath his chin, bringing the fragrance of her shampoo close. "I never told. He didn't, you know, penetrate me or anything. I haven't trusted the police since. Besides, the boys in the foster homes were always teasing and tormenting me, trying to scare me with bugs and snakes and frogs. I learned not to react and to hide my fear." She shrugged. "I guess some habits become so ingrained it's pretty difficult to fight upstream against them."

"I'm sorry, sweetheart. So very sorry."

"I imagine brothers would act the same way. I had plenty of

food, clean clothes and attended good schools. The adults were very kind and caring."

Matt bit his tongue. Kind and caring were a poor substitute for the love of parents. Besides, she was desperately trying to divert the topic from what had happened with the slime- bucket policeman. She showed poise and maturity in her acceptance of her childhood, and he admired the heck out of her for it. His brother had grown up in a loving, safe home and he hadn't turned out half as well. Just went to show people determined their life's path, no matter what their upbringing.

"F'sho," Lisette did more hand-patting. "My brothers still tease me somethin' fierce. Isn't no excuse for the police, though."

Matt firmed his lips to keep them shut.

Grace sat up and met his eyes. "I know what you're thinking, Matt. Don't even go there."

He settled his hand on the curve of her hip and raised a brow. "Really?"

Even in the poorly lit room, color flooded her cheeks.

"That's not. . ."

Lisette's light, lilting laugh flashed heat into his own face. For a second there, caught in the depths of Grace's eyes, he'd forgotten they had an audience.

Their audience hopped up from the couch. "Dat's my cue to head home. It's time to make dodo anyhow."

"I'll walk you home." He slid Grace's behind onto the cushion, immediately missing soft heat, and rose. Lisette opened her mouth, to no doubt object, and he arched his brow. One of her delicate eyebrows winged upward and sass sparked to life in her dark eyes.

She pursed her lips. "Dat's probably a good idea. Dawlin', I'll see you tomorrow. Holler if ya need me."

He was surprised by her easy acquiescence, if grateful. One stubborn woman was his quota. The women shared a quick, hard hug. Grace's lower lip trembled, but she schooled her expression before plopping back down on the couch. She was unnaturally subdued, and he may have been slightly rude as he hurried her friend across the hall and into her condo.

Lisette turned just inside the door and planted her hands on her hips. "You be good to her, ya hear? Life ain't been no bed o' roses for dat girl."

It was like being scolded by a dark-haired Tinkerbell. Matt fought to keep his lips from twitching. He doubted she'd respond well. "Yes, ma'am."

She scowled at him, but the twinkle in her eyes betrayed her amusement. "I know you wanna rush back ta Grace. Go on, git."

The door slammed in his face and he "got." Grace slumped against the couch, none of her normal spark to be seen. He frowned and scooped her back into his lap. Much better. The way she melted against him made his heart clutch.

"You doing okay?"

She shrugged.

"Hey." He tugged on a lock of her hair until she looked at him, then stroked his thumb back and forth across her earlobe. "Talk to me."

Her gaze dropped to his mouth.

He pushed aside the thoughts and feelings still shifting uncomfortable beneath his skin because of her earlier revelation and focused on the moment. On the pleasure of a lapful of soft sweet woman. Throw in the look she was giving him and a guaranteed conflagration of lust wasn't a stretch.

Working hard to keep in mind her recent fright, he pulled her closer, until they shared the breath between them. A shaft of moonlight spilled in, silhouetting the curve of her eyebrows, her straight nose, and the long lashes framing her green eyes. Then those lashes fluttered down and she closed the remaining distance.

He sank into her kiss like a thirsty man diving into cold, clear water. Her plump lips moved over his, parted for him, and he groaned. Burying his hand in her thick mass of hair and sliding the other one over the curve of her hip to her waist, under her shirt, he anchored her to him.

Grace wriggled until she straddled his lap. Full breasts pressed into him. Her nipples were heated points of desire arrowed right at his crotch. The heat of her core soaked through the denim of his jeans and she arched against him with eye-crossing enthusiasm. His brain short-circuited. Two seconds later she was flat on her back on the couch.

He cupped her breast, the thick fabric of her sports bra frustrating him. She moaned softly and sucked his lower lip into her mouth. Erection pulsating, he yanked her bra up and rocked against her pelvis. Palming her bare breast, the hard nub of her nipple pressed into the center of his hand. Had to be as close to heaven as a guy could get. She swiveled her hips. A hair's breadth away from humiliating himself, he levered up on his arms.

"Grace."

With a soft, feminine sound of need, she reached down and cupped him through his pants. His vision blurred. Damn. He locked his elbows, dropped his chin and endured her exploration.

So help him, if she discovered. . . and then she did. Grace rubbed her thumb over the exposed tip of his cock. Matt fisted handfuls of couch cushion, desperate for control. His hips jerked and a drop of pre-cum pearled at her touch. She leisurely spread the moisture around the sensitive tip. His lungs seized. An X-rated film played behind his eyelids, starring Grace. In the movie version, she wriggled down and replaced her wandering fingers with her mouth.

Swearing, he surged off the couch. Forearms braced against the far wall, he dropped his head and tried to steady his breathing and pounding heart. After all she'd been through tonight, this was not the time. Nor was it how he wanted their relationship to progress. Think about. . . Grandma Rose and Grandpa Edie doing it. He flinched. Damn, that was nasty. The intense pressure eased and he was able to draw a full breath.

Grace's hands smoothed up his back, right up the column of his spine. Desire slammed him down to the mat for the count. The muscles in his shoulders knotted.

"Matt? Did I do something wrong?"

Vulnerability coated her voice. He was an ass. "No, baby. You did everything right, believe me."

"Then why are you over here?"

Forcing his body back under control, he turned to face her. He ached to touch her, to hold her, but didn't trust himself. He crossed his arms. "This isn't the right time. I got carried away. I apologize. I didn't mean to. . . I'm sorry."

Clouds must have covered the moon, because the room went black as pitch. The scuff of her shoe and the lessening of her scent told him of her withdrawal as surely as if he'd seen it.

When she spoke again her voice had cooled. "I see. Well, I'm sure it's safe now. You can go. I'm sorry for getting you out of bed."

"I don't think so."

"Excuse me?"

He'd watched her every expression for so many months, he could easily picture her face right now. An inscrutable expression, cracked ever so slightly by a tightening around her lips and a tiny narrowing of her eyes. Her gaze would be nailing his ass to the wall. If he could see her. Unwilling to miss the hot spark of irritation in her green eyes after seeing her so pale and frightened, he flipped on the overhead light. Which didn't quite work out as planned, since Grace squeaked in protest and slapped a hand over her eyes. Hand still over her eyes, Grace turned in his direction. "What do you mean?"

Sounded like she was gritting her teeth.

Matt grinned, glad she couldn't see him. "I'm not leaving you alone tonight."

Her hands came down to fist on her hips and he was treated to a full-on glare. "Funny." Her tone was chilly enough to freeze tap water. "I don't recall inviting you to sleep over."

Hot enough to singe his eyebrows one minute, cold enough to shrivel his balls the next. Fascinated, he leaned against the wall. "I don't recall asking."

"No, you didn't. And since you're standing in my home, that seems to be a requirement you've overlooked."

"I didn't overlook anything and I'm not leaving. This guy has already gotten in once while you were sleeping and I doubt you've had the locks rekeyed."

She paled and dropped her gaze. No longer amused, he straightened from the wall. "Just tell me where an extra blanket is. I won't bother you, I promise."

"That's not. . . I wasn't. . ." Grace made a sharp gesture with her hand. "Look, Matt. I appreciate the old-fashioned chivalry and all, but I don't need a babysitter. Even if I did, which I don't, my couch isn't big enough for you. You'd be miserable."

After their make-out session he'd be miserable no matter where he slept. "I'll survive. Blanket?"

Frustration evident in every elegant curve, she shoved a hand into the curly mass of hair at her temple and glared. He glared back. She heaved a sigh and stomped into her bedroom. A few minutes later, she reemerged with a blanket and pillow in hand. She gestured toward the bedroom.

"You use the bed. I'll fit better on the couch."

With a snort, he shook his head. "Not gonna happen, sweetheart. So just march your little tush back in there." Deliberately, he loomed over her and leered. "I'd be happy to help you."

Instead of the annoyance he'd expected, her dark lashes dropped to half-mast and she fairly purred in invitation. His cock went rock hard between one heartbeat and the next, eager to accommodate. Giving his hormones a stern lecture on taking advantage of emotionally vulnerable women, he placed a hand at the small of her back and steered her toward her room.

"Goodnight, Grace."

In the doorway, she turned and swept him with a heated look.

A look that lingered on the erection straining his crotch. She pursed her lips. His cock twitched. A Mona Lisa smile curved her mouth, and she slipped into the room and closed the door. Which was what he wanted, damnit, even if the rest of him would happily sit up and beg to be taken to bed with her.

Matt flipped off the light and gingerly sat on the couch. Bending over to undo his laces wasn't an option, so he started to wedge them off with his feet. Then remembered his truck parked in the middle of the parking lot. Any number of people would be royally pissed in a few hours if he didn't move it.

"Grace?" He rose his voice to be heard through the door. "I'll be right back. I need to move my truck."

"There's a key beside the door, on the little table."

He snagged it on his way out. The cold night air went a long way toward easing his arousal, thankfully. Sleeping with a hard-on wasn't something he'd been looking forward to. Not like he could take care of it with Grace on the other side of the wall.

His interior truck light was on. He had hit the remote as he ran to Grace's apartment earlier. He remembered hearing the answering beep from the horn as the alarm set. What the hell?

A quick survey of his surroundings revealed nothing. He circled the truck. The doors were closed. Nothing was scratched or showed signs of tampering. Yet the light inside shone like a beacon.

Matt tried the door. Locked. A press of his finger to the remote released it and he opened the door. The instant dinging to remind him the interior light was on sounded overloud in the quiet night, and he glanced around again. If someone had sabotaged his truck, they had probably stuck around to giggle over the discovery of their handiwork. He checked the doors, under and around the seats, then climbed behind the wheel and started the truck.

A white piece of paper, jagged around the edges, lay on his dashboard. He craned his neck to read it.

*Nice truck, asshole.*
*She belongs to me.*
*Stay away from her and keep your hands off*
*or I'll start taking things that belong to you.*

White-knuckling the steering wheel in an attempt to control his temper, he read the note several times, committing it to memory, then pulled out his cell phone. Grace might have justifiable compunctions about calling the police, but he didn't. If this dick-wad wanted to jerk him around, he'd better come armed for bear.

## CHAPTER TWELVE

Grace paced her living room. A glimpse at her clock tightened her belly another notch. Matt had been gone an hour. One whole hour to move his truck. If not for her earlier experience, she'd have left thirty minutes ago to find out what the heck was going on.

Especially when the eerily silent flash of blue and red lights entered the parking lot. A look through her windows had revealed nothing. A giant oak tree blocked her view of most of the parking area, a fact she'd appreciated until tonight. Nibbling on her nails, she made another sweep of the room. Nothing would be left of the manicure on her left hand soon.

The lock rattled and she ran to the door, pressing her eye to the security peephole. Relief weakened her knees, but anger burned on its heels. Mumbling beneath her breath, she wrenched the door open and glared at Matt. If fury had power, he would be nothing more than a pile of ash on the floor.

"Uh. . . hello." He eyed her. "Guess I should have let you know what was going on. I hoped you were asleep."

She smiled sweetly. "Yes, you should have. And no, I'm obviously not asleep. After my experience tonight, knowing you were out there alone, sleep was the very last thing on my mind."

"I'm sorry." He edged past her, cautious as a lion tamer minus his whip inside the lion cage. "Could we continue this discussion inside? I'd hate to disturb any of your neighbors."

"My. How considerate of you." If her smile stretched a little thin, was that her fault?

Shutting the door, he surveyed the brightly lit condo before returning his attention to her. She greeted his delinquent gaze with raised brows and saccharine sweetness.

"Your friend left a little note in my truck. I called the police. I wasn't in any danger. I'm sorry you were worried."

Her anger drained away. "What did it say?"

"Just some crap about staying away from you." He shrugged as if it were nothing. "I gave it to the police."

Her shoulders slumped and she glanced at the clock. 1:00am. "I have to. . . *we* have to work in the morning, so I need to get whatever sleep I can at this point." She nibbled her lip, glancing at him hesitantly. "Thank you for coming, Matt. Do you need anything?"

"I'm good. And again, sorry for worrying you."

"It's okay. Good night."

"Night."

In her room, Grace climbed into bed. The down pillow welcomed her and soft sheets encased her. She should have slid easily into sleep's embrace, yet she lay staring at the wall.

He'd left a note for Matt. Inside his truck. Matt was now in danger because of her. Hell would freeze over before she let some psycho freak dictate her love life. She might kick him to the curb because his bossiness pushed her too far, but not because of some random loser stalker freak.

Grace flipped the ham and mushroom omelet half a second before it blackened. Hopefully Matt liked well-done eggs. The sound of the shower running in the other room had her distracted to the point of oblivion. Instead of watching the cooking food, she kept picturing Matt naked, water sluicing over rock-hard abs, muscles bunching and flexing as he shampooed and soaped. She groaned aloud. At this rate, she'd have to change her panties before she left for work.

The water shut off and a new image sprang to mind. Water droplets beaded on taut skin, the soft towel rubbing across all those yummy parts she wanted to rub up against like a cat. Too late to save her panties, she at least attempted to rescue the omelet. She snatched a plate out of the cupboard and slid the omelet from skillet to dish. A door opened and she flew into a whirlwind of motion. Filled mugs of coffee, dumped chopped fruit next to the omelets, and snagged forks. She winced as the plates landed on the breakfast bar with a graceless clatter.

Matt sauntered out of her bedroom. She swallowed hard and grabbed the bottle of flavored creamer out of the fridge. The cool air felt good on her flushed skin. She paused, pretending to search for something.

Anything to stop herself from tackling him and ripping off his clothes. Liquid arousal gathered between her legs. She slammed the door closed with more force than necessary, disgusted. A restless night spent tossing and turning to the tune of erotic dreams didn't excuse her hyper-active libido.

Straightening her shoulders, she sent her hormones airmail to Perdition and faced Matt. He lounged against the bar with negligent grace, watching her with the eyes of a hungry predator. Hard to be cool, calm, and collected when faced with that first thing in the morning.

Grace forced a smile. "Good morning." She set the creamer on the counter, remaining safely on her side of the half wall. "Sleep well?"

"Fine, thanks. How about you?"

"Like a log," she lied without qualm.

"Good. Breakfast smells delicious, but you really didn't have to go to the trouble."

"Please." Her cheeks were starting to ache from her determined smile. "It was the least I could do after you endured a night on my couch playing knight-errant."

Matt's dimple winked at her and the panty dampening resumed.

"Knight-errant, hmm? I didn't realize you were a romantic."

114

"I'm not." There went his smile. Pity. "Sit down and eat your food."

"Yes, ma'am."

He obediently sat on a bar stool and picked up his fork, then glanced from the other plate of food to her. "Aren't you going to eat?"

Grace eyed the food. Reluctant as she was to be in close proximity to him, she couldn't very well slide the plate back across the counter. That would be far too revealing. "Of course."

Rounding the counter, she sat on the bar stool next to Matt. Oh. My. Word. Her olfactory senses went into overdrive, her vaginal muscles clenched and her nipples pebbled. How on earth did a man smelling of her soap turn her on to the point of pain? She was a freak of nature.

Swallowing with some difficulty, she snatched the creamer and dumped some into her coffee cup. "I hope you like ham and mushrooms in your omelet. It was all I had."

"My favorite. It's good. Thank you."

"You're welcome." She shoved a bite of omelet into her mouth and barely managed to choke it down. A swallow of coffee helped unclog her throat. "So. What's on your schedule today?"

"I'll be at the Eagle Road jobsite all morning. I have meetings with contractors. Back at the office around one or so, after lunch with Brian McKenzie."

Ugh. Brian McKenzie was the superintendent on the jobs and had been for the last five years. He'd been a busy, busy boy during those years, working his way through every woman in the office— single and otherwise. Smooth to the point of oily, he did nothing for her.

"And you?"

She hid an eye roll behind her large coffee mug, before remembering they were doing the polite chitchat thing and pretending they hadn't made out like teenagers last night. Maybe he was having better luck with that.

Peeking over the rim of her cup, she met the blazing intensity of his dark eyes and her face heated. Then again, maybe not. If he kept the *'Let's screw like wild animals'* look on his face much longer, she'd be forced to oblige.

"Grace?"

Like the coward she was, she ducked back behind her coffee cup. "Uhm-hmm?"

"Are you feeling better today?"

"Better than what?"

"Better than last night."

"Well, yeah." She grinned. "The light of day demolishes all sorts of things that go bump in the night, don't ya know." The brown of his eyes deepened. Her skin prickled with heat. She resisted the urge to fan herself. "Why?"

"Because if you're back to yourself, there's no reason why we can't finish what we started last night."

Grace's eyes widened. To her dismay, she couldn't even summon a response.

"Not right now, of course."

No? But she was embarrassingly ready.

Matt leaned closer and rubbed his thumb over her lower lip. "We have to go to work and I intend to take my time. Then, just in case we don't get it right the first time, I plan on doing it again."

Again? Her tongue darted out to moisten her lip and encountered Matt's thumb instead. Holding his stare, she sucked his thumb into her mouth and wrapped her tongue around it. A flush darkened his cheekbones and his gaze dropped to her mouth.

"As many times as it takes," he murmured.

Oh, wow. She really would have to change her panties. Matt hooked a finger in the waistband of her skirt and tugged her close. He popped his finger free and took her mouth in a consuming, fiery kiss. Body humming and ready to go—to bed—she moaned. Instead of hauling her off to the bedroom, he pulled away. Not later, *now*.

116

"Sweetheart," he groaned when she latched onto his shirt. "I have to run home and change before my meeting."

Pouting and not real proud of it, she released him.

"Fine." Her lower lip wanted to stick out, so she sucked it into her mouth instead.

Matt rubbed a thumb over her cheek and leaned his forehead against hers. "I promise, tonight you'll have my full, undivided attention. Not only that, today is Friday. I'm yours for the weekend."

He did know how to soothe ruffled feathers. The whole weekend. A girl could get carried away with so many days of decadent indulgence spread before her. She grabbed her purse, mentally writing a very special shopping list.

They walked out to the parking lot together. Another brain-cell-searing kiss rendered her lips tingly before she climbed into her car. Along with other body parts she tried hard not to think about.

At the office, her high heels ricocheted inside the concrete-lined basement-parking garage. The cold crept inside her jacket and she shivered. For the first time, the place creeped her out, and she regretted parking so far from the elevator.

Was a second set of footsteps following her? Her stride increased. Tension crept up her spine. Grace ran a hand through her hair and ever-so-casually glanced over her shoulder. The usually well-lit garage space seemed shadowy and dark, but she didn't see anyone.

She picked up her pace until she was jogging, grateful when she spotted the elevator. So close. She was being silly, but she didn't care. Oh, freak. The echo no longer matched her footsteps. She glanced back again. A tall guy with sandy hair was a few parking spots back and rapidly closing the distance.

Her heart jumped into her throat. The elevator doors opened. Laughter spilled out, along with three men and a woman.

Grace slowed to a more normal walk, swallowed hard and

turned. The man had disappeared. Exchanging smiles with the group, she slipped onto the elevator in their wake and repeatedly pressed the door-close button until they finally obliged. She sagged against the brass railing and pressed trembling fingers to her mouth.

He could've been anyone, going to one of the many businesses in the high-rise. But there was the whole disappearing thing. Maybe he had dropped something and bent to pick it up. Or any number of things, really.

The elevator arrived at her floor. She stepped off and nearly ran into Luke.

He steadied her with his hands on her upper arms and winked. "Hey, Grace. Final day in the long haul. You're here bright and early."

"Ten minutes isn't exactly early."

"I figure anything above and beyond is early." He grinned. "Too early. You know me."

"Yeah."

Luke fell into step beside her as she headed for her office. "So, what are your plans for the weekend?"

No force on earth could have stopped her smile.

Luke stopped walking.

She turned. "What?"

"That's my question. I have *never* seen that particular smile on your face."

She cleared her throat and glanced away. Fiddled with her purse strap. Shrugged. "You know. Just. . . looking forward to the time off."

Luke's eyebrows shot up. "Ri-i-i-ight. Uh-huh. And I'm Lex Luther."

Grinning, she held out her hand. "Hello, Lex. I'm Grace Debry."

He grasped her hand and tugged her forward until they stood uncomfortably close. "Funny, Grace. What's going on?"

"Luke." She yanked her hand free. "Respect the bubble, bud." She spun on the ball of her foot and started walking.

"Come on. I'm curious."

Finally reaching the relative safety of her office, she plopped into her chair and crossed her arms. Her belly roiled with acid. Maybe coffee had been a bad idea. "Grace. I'm sorry, okay?" Luke knelt beside her, maintaining a careful distance. He gestured to the empty air between them. "See? I'm a fast learner. Personal bubble respected. Forgive me?"

"If I have to." She rolled her eyes. Like she could stay mad when he pulled those puppy-dog eyes and brown-nosed so beautifully.

"So. What are you doing this weekend?"

"Oh my word." She rolled her eyes. "I'm looking forward to relaxing, like I said. I have big plans to pamper myself." Leaning forward, she whispered, "I may even give myself a pedicure. Exciting, isn't it?"

A cocked brow relayed his skepticism loud and clear. Too bad. What she had planned was none of his business. Not now, not ever. It wasn't like she went around poking her nose into his personal business, demanding to know how he spent his time away from work. Like she wanted to know. Ick.

"Fine. Don't tell me." Pulling a very believable pout, Luke rose to his full height and scowled at her. "Keep your precious secrets."

"Thank you, dahling, I will." A big, toothy grin and fluttery lashes accompanied her statement. Luke's lips twitched.

"What-ev." Luke walked out.

Grace shook her head. So typical of him.

By late afternoon, she was nearly crawling out of her skin. She was certain the clock was broken. Exasperated, she stood. Maybe a loop around the floor would settle her. Two more hours until she could leave—she'd go insane at this rate.

Her phone rang before she made her escape. She cocked a hip on the desk and answered.

"Grace?" a soft female voice enquired. "Grace Debry?"

"This is she."

"The same Grace Debry who used to live with the Wells in Indiana?"

Straightening, Grace frowned. "Who is this?"

"You probably don't remember me, dear. This is Mrs. Growsky from next door. You used to come over and help with my flower beds."

"Of course I remember! How are you? Is everything okay? How did you find me? Oh, Mr. Wells has my information. How are you?"

She had fond memories of Mrs. Growsky. Hot summer days and warm fragrant dirt between her fingers. She had relaxed and shared thoughts she never would have dared otherwise. Mrs. Growsky had been a wonderful confidante and encouraging mentor during her high-school years. "Oh, I'm fine. How are you?"

"Great. My job here is great, I love my place and I have wonderful neighbors." She had wanted to keep in touch, but knew better. When Laura died, she'd severed ties.

Mrs. Growsky calling out of the blue tightened her stomach.

"I'm sure you're wondering why I'm calling. To tell you the truth, I debated long and hard about this. I've had your new phone number and address for ages, you know. I knew you were uncomfortable with me asking to stay in contact, but I wanted to know you were doing okay after you left."

Grace furiously blinked back tears. Of course, Matt chose that moment to walk through her door. One look at her face and he shut the door behind him, frowning. He reached for the phone. Unable to speak over the emotion clogging her throat, she shook her head. He sat on the edge of a chair. All this time, Laura's neighbor had watched over her.

Mrs. Growsky sighed. "Some strange things have been going on. Since they seem to involve you, I had to warn you."

Warm fuzzies banished to Neverland, Grace's nerves tightened again. "Warn me?"

"Yes, dear. I'm sorry to alarm you, but. . . Well. . ."

"Please. Just tell me."

"Darrell Wells was murdered last week."

"What?" Her gaze flew to Matt. He was by her side in an instant. He tried to take the phone from her, but she jerked free and very carefully lowered herself into her chair.

"Well, he was actually murdered about a week earlier, but no one discovered the poor man until that nice sheriff came along." She hmm'd softly. "Where did he say he was from?"

"Why would anyone want to hurt Mr. Wells? He kept to himself to such an extent he was practically a hermit. Without Laura around, he probably became exactly that. What happened?"

"I don't know, dear. Several people have been asking about you, though."

She dropped her head to the desk, vaguely aware of Matt rubbing her back and murmuring. . . something. Oh, he still wanted the phone.

"What?" Her brain felt fuzzy.

"A man came by two weeks ago. Last I saw, he was headed to the Wells' house."

"Looking for me?" she repeated faintly.

"Yes. Then, a little over a week later, that nice sheriff stopped by. He asked about you too. He showed me a picture of your mother. My goodness, you're her spitting image. I knew right away he was talking about you."

Goosebumps chased one another across her skin. "He had a picture of my mother?"

She'd never seen a picture of her mother. The foster-system workers had explained there'd been nothing with her when she was brought to them. Yet some stranger had a photo. Of her mother. She couldn't seem to wrap her mind around that.

"She was beautiful. What a shame she died so young. You really are her mirror image, dear. I could have been looking at a photo of you. Of course, I knew it wasn't you because the photo was old and worn. The clothing styles weren't right either. And her hair, my goodness. No, I can't imagine you doing that to your beautiful hair. All those glorious curls, and your mother chopped them so short." She tsked. "A crime, that's what it is. You're still wearing yours long, aren't you?"

"Yes."

Mrs. Growsky had always rambled. Not that she was going to complain when she was rambling about a mother Grace had never laid eyes on. At least, not that she could recall. Obviously, she'd seen her as an infant. Now she was rambling. In her thoughts. Which seemed worse, somehow. She shook off some of the numbness.

"Do the police have any leads on Mr. Wells' murder?"

"I couldn't say. They wouldn't talk about that with me. They interviewed me about the man who'd been by a few weeks ago. I cooperated, I assure you. Told them everything I could remember about him and what we talked about."

"I'm sure you were very helpful. Would you mind telling me?"

"Of course, dear. I rather thought you'd like to know, seeing as how he asked about you. I even wrote down all the details. Let's see. Where did I put it?" Paper rustled. "He was a tall man, taller than my Lawrence was, making him over six feet, I would guess. Shaggy dark-blonde hair, which I know for a fact he colors. He was in his fifties. No man his age would still have blonde hair." Her little sniff of disapproval brought an unwitting smile. "Blue eyes and a strong nose. Had an athletic build too. One of those men who played some sport when he was younger and kept active as he aged. My Lawrence was like that, you know."

Grace was peripherally aware of Matt staring at her. She wrapped the phone cord around her finger. "I do remember you telling me that. What else do you remember? What did he want to know?"

"Well, I can tell you, I didn't like him. Despite his movie-star good looks, something was off, if you know what I mean. I'd say

122

he has a mean streak. So I played dumb. Said I remembered seeing a black-haired, green-eyed little girl staying with my neighbors for a while, but you hadn't been around in a long time. He wanted to know where you are now. Far as I knew, you hadn't stayed in touch after you left. Told him about Laura dying too and how Darrell hadn't been involved with you children. I assured him Darrell wouldn't know anything about any of you, but he insisted on talking to him anyway." She sighed. "I do wish I'd done something. I knew nothing good could come of it. I feel so bad about Darrell dying all alone like that."

"It is not your fault. I doubt you could have done anything for Mr. Wells, but you've been very helpful to me. And the police too, I'm sure. Thank you so much for calling. I'm sorry I didn't stay in touch with you. I just. . . I didn't. . ." She bit the tender underside of her thumb. Nobody cared about her issues.

"Oh, you don't have to explain, dear. Growing up in foster care is difficult. You don't expect things to last, especially relationships. I'm always here if you need an ear, though. You remember that."

"I will. And I promise. . ." Grace hesitated. Promises weren't her forte. She avoided them like the plague. Still, Mrs. Growsky deserved that much. She forced the words past the constriction in her throat. "I promise to stay in touch. As a matter of fact, why don't you give me your address and phone number. I've moved a few times and I'm afraid I don't remember it."

She flicked a glance at the man hovering protectively when she finally hung up. Approval softened the hard lines of Matt's face. Why that mattered, she didn't know. Or didn't want to know. Same difference.

"Well?"

Frowning, she stared out the window. "Over two weeks ago, a man showed up at my old foster parents' home in Indiana looking for me. A week later, Mr. Wells was found murdered in his home by some sheriff from I-don't-know-where." She rolled the pen between her fingers. "Seems rather coincidental. Some guy shows up there looking for me, then somebody starts harassing me here. Plus. . ." Biting her lip, she dropped her gaze to the desk.

Matt turned her back to face him with a finger beneath her chin. "Plus what?"

"A man followed me through the parking garage this morning."

His eyes narrowed.

"I mean, I think he followed me. I could be wrong. I saw some guy walking behind me and kinda freaked. Some people came along and he disappeared." She shrugged. "It was probably nothing, except. . . the description Mrs. Growsky gave me was markedly similar."

"Damnit, Grace. Why didn't you tell me this earlier?"

"I told you. I wasn't sure. Besides, what could you have done after the fact? And don't talk to me like that." Crossing her arms, she sat back and glared.

He glared right back. "I can't help you if you don't tell me everything. Everything. I could have had the security guards check out the garage. I could have, and I *will*, arrange an escort to and from the building from now on."

She lunged to her feet, banging her chair into the cabinet. "Like hell you will."

"This is not the time to prove how independent you are." Matt's eyes glittered dangerously. "This is not about independence or your ability to take care of yourself. It's about staying safe and staying alive."

By the time he finished his impassioned little speech, she was pinned between Matt and the filing cabinet, her crossed arms brushing against his chest. Blood hammering in her ears, she debated her options. Because, damn him, he made sense. The desire to assert her independence burned the back of her throat. To show him he wasn't the boss of her. Not in her personal life anyway.

"Fine," she mumbled.

"What?" He inclined his head.

Her gaze dropped to his mouth.

"I didn't hear you."

"I said fine. The stupid security guards can escort me to and from my stupid car like I'm some stupid kid." That was rather a lot of stupids.

Matt's brow climbed and his lips twitched. Of course, he would have to notice.

"Now that we've settled that, I vote we kiss and make up." His voice dropped to a lovely low timbre and naughty thoughts sparked.

She averted her face. "I don't think so."

"Why not?"

Hot breath tickled her ear. Hotter lips nibbled. He nipped her earlobe and she surrendered. Even tilted her head a few degrees to allow him better access.

"I'm mad at you." Yeah, anger explained her racing pulse and shortness of breath.

"Hmm. . ." He sucked gently on an especially sensitive, previously undiscovered, erogenous zone below her ear. "What can I do to get in your good graces again?"

His hand burrowed into her hair and tugged her head back while he paved a burning path down her neck, then reversed direction. When he reached her chin she forgot how to breathe. Really didn't seem necessary at the moment anyway. Then, drat the man, he stared straight into her surely glazed eyes.

"I care about you, sweetheart. Nothing is more important to me than your safety and well-being."

Oh, man. How could a girl resist? It wasn't fair. And he still wasn't kissing her. What the heck? Did he need absolution first? "Fine. You're forgiven."

Brown eyes flared with satisfaction, which ticked her off. Then she didn't care, because he was kissing her as if his continued existence depended on it. She wound her arms around his neck and hung on for dear life.

Something somewhere pinged. She yanked her mouth free and gasped for air. Matt's hair was adorably mussed.

"Aren't we starting the weekend a little early?"

"I don't care." He claimed her mouth again. "I say we. . . call it good. . . and. . . take off. . . now," he said in between kisses.

"You are the boss."

## CHAPTER THIRTEEN

Matt opened his truck's passenger door. One shapely leg emerged, then the other, the skirt hitching high on Grace's thighs as she stepped onto the running board. Man, he loved her legs. Instead of letting her step down, he wrapped his hands around her waist and lifted her down. He'd have her naked and under him in fifteen minutes.

Then she lifted swirling pools of green desire and his erection gained another painful inch. She draped her arm around his neck and her body against his.

"Matt?"

He swallowed pooling saliva. "Yeah?"

"If you don't get me up to my condo in the next thirty seconds, we're going to have sex against the side of your truck." She brushed her smooth cheek back and forth against his, her voice gone husky.

The rush of breath across his skin made his chest expand; the words sent another arrow of desire to his groin.

"I'm wearing almost non-existent panties and it's making me feel very, very naughty."

On a groan of pure agony, he slammed the door closed, grasped her hand and headed down the sidewalk in a ground-eating stride. The truck alarm beeped as an afterthought. Grace trotted to keep up, her soft laughter following him up the stairs. Much as he longed to take them two at a time, she'd never be able to do the same. Gaining her place alone held little appeal.

He waited impatiently while she unlocked the door. He nudged her inside, shut the door with his foot and grabbed her. Her belly was against the door a second later, and she flattened both palms against the paneling. The pose nearly unmanned him. One hand protecting her cheek from the door, he nibbled her neck and palmed her delectable ass.

She gasped and he wanted to taste that too. So he did, licking his way into her mouth. Her moan tasted of sin. Hot, wet, mind-numbing sin.

Before he grew too distracted to think, he flipped the dead bolts. The building could be on fire; he wouldn't care so long as no one disturbed them. Grace did some sort of shimmy against his cock, and he swore. Cupping the side of her face, stroking his tongue in and out of her mouth, he jerked her blouse free of the waistband. Soft-as-cashmere skin met his fingers.

Grace's bra clasped in the front, proving there was indeed a Mistress Fate. And she liked him. Feverish with wanting her, he cupped both of her breasts in his hands, pinching her nipples gently and thrusting against her ass. She freed her mouth with a gasp mingled on the same breath as a moan.

He had to. . . he needed to. . . Shit. He was behaving like a caveman again. Five seconds away from taking her against the door and, for the life of him, he couldn't release her breasts. Matt dropped his head back and sucked in air like a dying man, kneading soft handfuls of heaven. Not helping.

Grace deserved better. Rose petals and flickering candles. Silk sheets, soft music, and a slow seduction. His damn heart clutched at the thought of how beautiful she would look in candlelight. Like forever. But at this point, if he could manage to drag them both to a soft surface, he'd call it a win. He would do the other stuff later. After he'd been inside her for about a week. She squirmed against him.

Make that a month.

"Grace, the bed."

Pushing off the door, forcing him back, she turned and made for the bedroom. Making excellent use of the otherwise wasted time, if he did say so himself, he managed to unbutton his shirt one-handed. Grace tossed her shirt and bra across the bedroom. Her skirt followed, leaving her in red heels and a scrap of black lace held in place by several thin straps across her hips.

He reached for her, intent on removing the last vestige of barrier between him and the promise land. Her playful slap on his hand stopped him short.

"Patience," she murmured.

She reached up to slide his shirt off his shoulders and her hardened nipples brushed against his bare chest. They both moaned. His shirt fell and she repeated the motion then shifted side to side, erotic torment at its finest. Grace's eyes slid closed. Flushed with pleasure, lost in sensation, she was the most beautiful creature he'd ever seen. He fisted his hands at his sides to keep from throwing her to the bed.

A low growl rumbled in his throat without his permission, but he'd been pushed as far as he could go. He would be ashamed of his animalistic behavior tomorrow.

Backing off a little with another of those smiles he was coming to love, she reached for his belt. He covered her hand with his. "Sweetheart?"

Warm green eyes met his. "Hmm?"

"Let me finish this. Go lie on the bed. Please."

The corners of her lips tipped up farther. "Still bossy, but you're learning."

She turned and walked to the big bed.

Tickling the crevice between the beautiful pale globes of her bottom, little sparkling balls at the end of a black satin bow bounced with each step. He swallowed his tongue. He should find out where she purchased her lingerie and buy stock.

He almost hit the floor when he forgot he was still wearing his shoes. Swallowing a curse, he yanked them off and his pants

129

followed. Matt paused at the mattress to admire the view Grace presented draped across the cream comforter. So beautiful. So much more than all of his fantasies. Still wearing those panties.

Twitching with the urge to smooth his hands over her silky skin, he forced himself to hold still. Turnabout was fair play. He was only peripherally aware of her gaze skimming down his body, fixated as he was on the rapid rise and fall of her breasts. His erection surged in response. She fisted the comforter and her tongue flicked out to moisten her lower lip.

Her hands went on a leisurely journey over the top of her thighs, across her smooth stomach, to cup her breasts like a pagan offering. Glittering emerald eyes met his.

"Grace," he groaned.

"Come here."

Stopping just short of lunging, he nudged her legs apart to make a home for himself between them. The valley between tempted him to pause and linger, but he resisted, not stopping until they were eye to eye.

"I feel like I've waited my whole life for this. For you. This moment."

"So stop waiting already," she whispered.

Brushing his lips back and forth across hers, he found he could breathe freely again. As if with her permission to devour, he'd regained control. With unending patience, he applied himself to the task of driving her out of her mind. Starting at the top and working his way down, he nibbled, licked, and kissed every inch of her lithe body. He lingered over her breasts, loving the breathy moans he elicited each time he drew her nipples deep into his mouth. Kissed along the valley to her belly button, nibbled along her hips. Discovered sensitive spots at the inside of her thighs and her ankles. Then made his way back up to settle between her thighs.

"Matt."

She wriggled beneath him. He anchored her with a forearm

over her belly and spread her knees wide with his other hand. The damp, sheer barrier of her panties offered little protection. The sight and scent of her arousal nearly drove him beyond the ability to form words.

"Let me."

She stilled.

Her thigh muscles quivered, as if she was fighting against the desire to close her legs. That desire to please him, to strain her comfort zone for him, touched him and wrapped tentacles around his heart. He wanted to give her the world, but for right now, he'd settle for giving her an orgasm.

Running his tongue along the damp bit of silk, he tasted her. Addictive. Not nearly satisfied, he nudged aside the little triangle of cloth. He explored and tasted every hidden secret until she writhed and her cries filled the room. He nudged his tongue inside her then licked his way further north. She strained against him, muscles tightening. He pushed a finger inside and sucked her clit into his mouth.

Grace cried out and clamped her legs around his head. Her body arched and her fingers tangled in his hair, pushing him away and pulling him closer at the same time. He pinched her clitoris and sent her flying again.

Waiting, aching and throbbing with desire, until every muscle in her body had gone limp, Matt pushed his thumb inside her. She contracted around him and made a little hum of pleasure. Resting his forehead against her pelvis, pulse thundering in his head, he massaged and teased her back up. When she moved with him, meeting each thrust of his finger, he rose.

Crawling up her body, very much enjoying the view of her flushed and panting beneath him, he rummaged around for the condom packet he'd tossed on the bed earlier. She'd twisted the comforter and dislodged pillows.

He'd done that to her. Smugness battled desperation. Where was the damn condom?

"Matt," she moaned, pulling on him.

Fumbling, shaking, he searched harder. Slender hands caressed his chest, moved lower and wrapped around his erection. He froze. Grace guided the head between her legs, tugging until he rested against the hot, wet opening he so desperately wanted to sink into. Against his will, his hips surged forward and the head slipped inside. That little hum of pleasure came again and she grasped his butt, nails digging into him, trying to pull him deeper.

"Matt. . ."

"The condom." He groaned, arms shaking. "It must have fallen off the bed."

"I don't care." She whimpered, wriggling.

He shook harder. If she'd just hold still for two seconds, he'd find the strength to move, pull out and find the freakin' condom. Obviously not in a cooperative mood, she moved again. Nibbled on his chest while curling her hips up and taking him deeper. On a muffled groan, he lost what little control he'd been hanging on to and buried himself to the hilt inside her pulsating, wet heat.

Another little wriggle and he slid deeper. Grace wrapped her legs and arms around him, holding him to her. He cradled her to him, awed by how precious she felt.

"Grace, I'm not wearing any protection. I want to take care of you."

Pulling away a little, she blinked, so beautiful it physically hurt to look at her. Made him ache in places that had nothing to do with his dick and everything to do with his heart.

She played with his earlobe. "Are you safe?"

"Safe?" He tried not to think about his dick, buried in all that perfect wet heat. Safe. . . Oh. Duh. "Yeah. I haven't been with anyone in a while, and I've been tested since then."

An adorable grimace came and went. "Well, I definitely am. I haven't had a boyfriend since high school." That would explain the incredibly tight muscles making his head explode. "I'm not

132

a one-night-stand kind of girl. Plus," the sex kitten look she cast him made him twitch inside of her, "I'm on the pill. So we're fine. If. . . you're fine."

Sex kitten turned uncertain, shy librarian. Both mind-numbingly erotic.

Oh, he was more than fine. He pulled back, almost all the way out. Resignation flashed across her face, then he thrust back in. Resignation became bliss. Sliding a hand down, he grasped the round globe of her bottom and tilted her hips. Thrust again. Her beautiful green eyes went hazy and unfocused. The pretty porcelain-doll skin of her cheeks turned pink.

So beautiful. The tempo built with a will of its own, sweeping him away in a symphony of desire tangled inexorably with love. Reality crashed into him, the ripple effect moving outward and blinding him to everything but the woman moaning beneath him. Harder and faster, he pounded into her, the four-poster bed groaning in protest.

In the back of his mind, he recognized he was out of control and tried to rein it in, but it was too late. Climax gathered at the base of his spine. Grace tightened around him. Her arms wound around his neck, pulling his head down. He breathed in the scent of aroused woman. Long legs hooked around his hips, insisting he move faster and he obeyed. Tight inner muscles fisted him, demanding he give her release.

Cradling her head in his hand, he sucked on the sweet skin beneath her ear. His other palm tilted her hips higher, allowing him to surge deeper. Once, twice, climax drew undeniably closer. He slammed home and she shattered in his arms. Her thin scream raised goosebumps, and he caught the sound of her pleasure in his mouth.

Matt pumped into her, her climax milking him. Orgasm swept up his spine. Buried as far as he could go, he was afraid that more than his seed spilled into her lush body. His heart followed.

Still holding him tight, the aftermath of her orgasm rippling over him, the selflessness with which she accepted him shook him to the core. He ripped his mouth free of hers and pressed his forehead to her neck.

Brain function returned in small increments. He needed to get off her. Dragging himself free of her wet heat brought a groan. She was still so damn tight. Taking her with him, he rolled over. Limbs boneless in spent pleasure, she lay across his chest.

Oh yeah, he could get used to this.

"Matt?"

"Yeah?"

"That was incredible."

Matt's chest swelled, along with other parts of his anatomy. "I was a virgin until just now."

Grace burst into laughter, rolling off him onto her back in helpless giggles. He lifted onto an elbow and enjoyed the way her breasts jiggled. Unable to resist, he leaned down and caught a nipple in his mouth.

She gasped his name, arched upward, and the giggles stopped.

"As I recall, I made some promises this morning." Enjoying the way her body curled into him, he moved to the other breast.

"I don't think I can."

He sucked harder and her head fell back on a moan thick with ripening desire.

"Then again. . ."

Since she could still talk, he clearly needed to up his game.

\*\*\*\*\*

Sheriff John Sanford glared from the crinkled map spread across his hood to the stretch of road disappearing into a jagged canyon. How the hell had he gotten this far off track? He slammed a fist down, denting his SUV. Not a second to lose and he'd gotten lost. How his wife would have laughed.

Fresh grief slammed into him. Thirty-five years together, and only a month since she'd been gone. The first stroke had taken her entire left side. The next. . . damn. He pinched the bridge of his nose. The way her eyes had pleaded with him still shook him. As if begging him to put her out of her misery. Like she was trapped inside her body and desperate for a way out.

In some ways, the final stroke had come as a relief. Even if he sometimes thought the pain of living without her would kill him. He couldn't bring himself to care if he lived or died. His cell phone rang and he fumbled for it, welcoming the distraction.

"Hello?"

"Hello, Son. Are you finished with this foolishness yet?"

Deep breath in; deep breath out. He would not yell at his mother. "No, I'm not. I feel responsible." His voice rose on the last decibel. He paused and took another deep breath. "I've explained this already."

"It doesn't make sense, John. Why did you go to so much trouble to hide this girl? From what?"

His molars ground at the whine in her too-high voice. "I ignored all the signs. Hell, her momma came into the station with a black eye and begged me for help. You know what I did? I called her husband and told him what she'd said. I grew up with Deke. Played ball with him in high school, protected his ass when he became quarterback. Maybe that's the whole problem. I got in the habit of covering for him and it extended into my job."

"Don't use that kind of language with me, young man. I still don't see why you hid her, or why you're so determined to find her now."

"Because I'm the sheriff and have been for years. It's my job to protect people. I failed miserably with her momma and she's dead. All these years I've watched her daughter, making sure she was safe and happy. And then you. . ."

He bit his tongue so hard he tasted the sharp metallic tang of

135

blood. He'd always been respectful of his mother. Then his wife had died and he'd seen another side of her. A side he hadn't liked. Not only that, she'd seriously endangered one of the few people left he genuinely cared about.

A cloud of dust appeared on the horizon, headed his way. Thank you, God. The information that had sent him on this particular wild-goose chase was obviously false. No way the man he knew would hide this far from civilization. The guy liked his creature comforts.

"Mom, I've gotta go. Take care of Roxy, okay?"

"As if I'd let your dog starve, John."

"I know. Bye."

A battered old pickup bounced down the rough road, jerked to and fro by the deep ruts. The hair on the back of his neck rose, and he straightened. Squinted against the sun.

The truck passed out of the trees and the sun shone through the open driver's window. Of all the dumb luck. Sanford unholstered his service revolver and stepped into the road, pointing through the windshield.

"Stop!" he bellowed.

Deke grinned. It was all the warning he got before Deke stepped on the gas and the truck roared toward him. His eyes flew wide and he made a desperate leap for the tall grass bordering the road. The hot grill of the truck slammed into the lower portion of his airborne body, throwing him to the hard dirt with such force the breath was knocked clean out of him.

He stared at the sky overhead, so clear and blue he had to shut his eyes against the unbroken brilliance. The grind of brakes came, then the rumble of the old motor died and a door slammed. Well, shit. To come all this way and die in the dirt of the Idaho foothills seemed wrong. He thought of his sweet wife, swallowed thickly, and let his head loll to the side. Heavy footsteps vibrated the ground. Sanford held his breath and prayed harder than he had in years.

"Well, well, well. Long way from home, Sheriff."

A foot nudged him, but he stayed lax and unresponsive. A knee thudded into the dirt next to his ribcage. The sunlight darkened, blotted out by Deke's big form kneeling beside him. Please, God, don't let him be smart enough to feel for a pulse.

"Hell, Sanford. Who'd have thought it would end this way?"

A heavy hand came down to rest on the middle of his chest, making him very thankful he was holding his breath. Deke had never been the brightest bulb in the pack. He had to be turning blue, which would make it look more convincing.

"Just to be sure," Deke muttered.

Fireworks exploded behind Sanford's closed eyelids and velvety darkness rose to envelope him.

Sanford groaned and opened his eyes. Wide-open skies sprinkled liberally with stars greeted him. A huge moon hung heavy in the sky, dipping toward the mountains lining the horizon. Struggling into a sitting position, he leaned to the side and heaved up everything he'd eaten in the last two weeks. When his stomach quit trying to turn wrong side out, he gingerly felt along his scalp.

A lump the size of a lemon met his exploring fingers, and his vision tunneled, sparks lighting off in his peripheral.

"Damn."

Deke never had been fond of firearms, thank God. Staggering to his feet, he looked around. Squat pine trees, sagebrush and thigh-high grass. Not another soul in sight.

Cursing a blue streak, he walked to where he'd left his Cherokee on the side of the road and stared at the empty plot of grass. Twin rows of bent grass in the bright moonlight led him deeper into the sagebrush. Fifteen minutes later, he found his Jeep behind a small group of tangled pine trees. The keys dangled in the ignition. Deke had probably hoped some kids would take off with it.

He gingerly slid behind the wheel, then waited until the horizon resettled. Odds were he had a concussion and shouldn't be driving, but sticking around meant risking discovery by the wrong person. Based on the size of the bump on his head and his empty holster, Deke was now armed—if he hadn't been before.

Rubbing his sore ribs, he started the SUV. Thankfully, the truck had only gotten a glancing blow when it struck him. Not enough to do any real damage, but it'd probably be a good idea to get checked out at a hospital. He was no spring chick.

Hours later, Sheriff Sanford walked out the emergency room exit and eased into his Cherokee. Sunrise tinted the sky various shades of pink. The road was deserted.

From a hidden spot beneath the passenger seat, he removed a file folder. "GRACE DEBRY" was written on the tab. The few pages did little to improve his mood. Hospital staff had tried to talk him into checking in, wanting to watch him for twenty-four hours. He'd squashed that idea quicker than a roach skittering across the kitchen floor. Time was of the essence. Somewhere in this city, Deke roamed free and Grace lived on borrowed time.

With the help of the Indiana police department, he'd found information about Grace in old local papers. A black and white from the sports section showed her frozen forever in time crossing the finish line in a track event she'd won her senior year of high school. Another black and white, this time of Grace as the class valedictorian at her graduation. There was a notation at the bottom saying she would attend Purdue University. That still made him grin. The tiny girl he'd cradled in his arms twenty-five years ago in Kentucky, grown up and attending a big university like that.

The passenger door opened and a big man climbed in, baseball hat pulled low. "Alright. I'm here. Now what's so damned important you got me out of bed this early?"

Sanford grinned. "Damn, it's been a long time."

The flash of his smile revealed a gleaming gold tooth. Sanford almost laughed. Only Gunner would do something so cheesy.

"We gonna sit here and gossip like old women, or you gonna tell me what you need?"

Sanford handed over the slim folder. "This is all I have. I want you to watch her. Don't let on, though. You'll freak her out."

Gunner flipped through the papers, pausing to read a few. Finally, he shook his head. "At least now, your county is known for having some of the toughest domestic abuse laws and sentences in the country. You did something, even if it was too late for the rest of the family." Gunner glanced at him. "You said you hid her real good. What's happened?"

"My mother"

"Huh?"

Sanford started the Cherokee. "Let's take a drive while we talk. We can get some coffee and I'll show you where Grace lives."

\*\*\*\*\*

Matt woke to orange-hued sunlight across his body. Pretty funky. The beautifully curved female draped across him, on the other hand, had a lovely pale-pink hue to her skin. He could spend hours exploring her. His morning erection throbbed. As he debated his options, she shifted the rest of the way onto him and nestled her face into his neck. His heart turned to pudding and his cock to granite.

Which pretty much decided the matter. He grasped her hips and positioned her. Pressing upward and pulling her down, he slid home. Thick pleasure flooded his veins. Her slick pussy holding him tight, with nothing to separate them, had to be the best thing in the entire freakin' universe.

One of her arousing little noises vibrated across his skin, then her lips opened and pressed to his chest. He thrust.

"Mmm. . . Good morning." She nibbled along his collarbone.

A hard thrust. "Morning." Then another. Hands pressed to his chest, she lifted up. Taking in her sleep-tousled hair and sparkling eyes, the uniquely Grace-motivated emotion expanded inside

139

him. His erection throbbed. Grace tossed her hair back and rode him faster.

Man, he loved a woman who went for sex in the morning.

He loved her.

Fuck.

His balls tightened and he reached between their bodies. Slick moisture coated her pussy. He smeared it around and rubbed her hard little clit. Moaning, she increased her pace. Thrusting up to meet each downward drive, he teetered on the brink. He gritted his teeth. He wanted her to come with him. Back in control, he pinched her clit firmly between his fingers. With a sharp cry, she convulsed around him. He thrust hard a few more times and let his climax sweep through him.

Pulling her down, he wrapped his arms around her, savoring the intimacy. Savoring the intimacy? What the hell? Since when did he get all sentimental? Next he'd write flowery poetry. Didn't stop him from holding her, though.

His heart ached at the beauty of the woman in his arms. Not physical beauty, though she had that in spades. Her spirit, strength of character, aptitude at work, and even her sass made her far more beautiful than temporal physicality. Even so, he wasn't about to blurt out his feelings. His momma hadn't raised a fool. It was way too early, Grace was incredibly skittish, and he didn't really understand what love involved. The business side of his nature wanted to know the parameters of what such a relationship included.

Grace sure as heck hadn't mentioned anything remotely love-like. Hadn't even cried out anything emotional in the throes of passion.

That realization chilled him to the bone. He tightened his arms around her. She made a soft noise of contentment, nestling more securely atop him. Asleep again, but he had worn her out. They hadn't slept much through the night.

Much as he hated to disturb her, nature called. He slid out from beneath her. Afterward, another call demanded his attention—the muffled ring of his cell phone. He dug through the clothes scattered around Grace's bedroom. Nothing.

The phone chimed a voicemail receipt and he walked into the living room. His jacket lay on the floor beside the front door. He pulled his phone from the interior pocket and swiped his thumb across the screen. His parents' number. His gut clenched and he tapped the CALL button.

"Hey, Robert. What's up?"

His step-dad cleared his throat. "Your mother's having a rough time. The doctor wants to operate first thing Monday. He's worried about the size of the tumor. If it's tangled in any neighboring organs. . ."

The silence stretched, filled with the stench and tension of a recent battlefield. Matt didn't know what to say. Robert wasn't a real touchy-feely kinda guy. Neither was he.

"Anyway, she'd like to have you and Jeff over for dinner tonight."

"Yeah. Sure. I'll be there." He gazed toward the bedroom, where his heart lay sound asleep. "I know it's not a great time, but I'd like to bring someone."

"Actually, I think that'd be a great distraction for your mother. Get her mind off things. I assume you're talking about a woman?"

"Yes."

"She'll be pleased."

"Good. I'll see you later then. Six?"

"Yep. Have a good day."

"You too, Robert."

Clicking off the phone, Matt stuck it back in his coat pocket. Nerves he'd rather not admit to spiked at the thought of asking Grace to meet his family. Despite their phenomenal sex marathon, their relationship had the solidity of Jell-O prior to refrigeration. Which he would know, since making Jell-O was the extent of his cooking skills.

## CHAPTER FOURTEEN

Grace pulled her robe on and wandered out of her room. Based on the clothes still scattered across her floor, Matt hadn't left. Since her bed lacked a muscular, sexually gifted man, it begged the question: where was he?

A glance across her breakfast bar revealed the answer and then some. Grinning, she leaned against the bar.

"Now there's a sight I don't mind waking up for."

Matt turned, improving the view. Not that there was anything wrong with his lovely, well-muscled butt. His defined chest was sprinkled with just the right amount of hair and a narrow trail of hair arrowed to a very, very nice. . . she lost her train of thought as his cock sprang to life with unmistakable eagerness.

Good grief. He was like an X-rated version of the energizer bunny.

He set down the package of coffee he'd been scooping grounds out of and advanced. Butterflies took flight. Ridiculous after spending an entire night with him. She backed up.

"Now, Matt." Holding up a hand, she almost toppled over an end table. She caught her balance and the table.

"Grace."

"Matt."

He lunged, taking her with him onto the couch. In a feat of impressive, and arousing, athleticism, he twisted as they dropped so she landed on top of him. His deft fingers rid her of the robe in a blink. He pulled her down and kissed her senseless.

Matt grasped her bottom in one hand, adjusted her position and slid inside her. She gasped into his mouth, wincing a little as tender muscles adjusted to accommodate him. To his credit, he froze, fully buried inside her, pulled back and frowned.

"I'm sorry, sweetheart. Did I hurt you? Not enough foreplay?"

To her utter horror, his bluntness heated her cheeks. Guess she wasn't as worldly as she liked to think. Trying to hide her embarrassment, she sat up. His cock sank deeper, which brought another wince along with a moan. Incredible.

"Foreplay isn't really the issue." She closed her eyes, trying hard to be as upfront as him. "I'm just not. . . That is. . ."

Okay, so she wasn't even a little bit sophisticated.

"Ah." His knowing tone forced her eyes open. He cupped her cheek, his expression so tender her heart ached. "That's right. You said it'd been quite a while for you. You must be sore. I'm sorry, baby."

He twitched insistently inside her, his body demanding even when he wasn't willing to be. So deep, he pressed against a rather— she wriggled experimentally and fresh pleasure pulsed—sensitive spot inside. Focused on the sensation, she closed her eyes and curled her fingers in his chest hair.

"You don't have to. . ."

She circled her hips and whatever he'd been about to say died on a groan. Feminine power glowed, alongside another surge of pleasure. If she only moved in certain ways, maybe she wouldn't notice her tenderness.

Rocking back and forth, keeping him buried inside and adding the occasional hip swivel, need built until she was aware of little else. She dropped her head back. The soft caress of her long hair down her back brushed across her bottom. His coarse hair and firm muscles bunched beneath her fingers. She quivered. Bloody daisies, the feel of him beneath her and inside her—liquid fire between her thighs.

His fingers bit into her hips, holding but not inhibiting her movements. She whimpered. Burning from the inside out, she licked her lips and opened her eyes. Matt watched her, eyes narrowed, skin tight with passion. The muscles in his arms clenched. Grace rocked faster, so close.

As if he sensed her desperation, how close she was, and knew exactly what she needed, he released one hip and pressed his fingertip against her clit. She jerked, but he maintained contact and pressed harder, holding her gaze.

"Grace, I can't hold out. . ."

She circled her hips. His hand on her hip clenched, the one between her thighs dragged across her clit, and his cock spilled inside her. His orgasm triggered hers, wave after wave of pleasure crashing through her while her muscles milked and rippled along his deeply buried erection.

Time stuttered to a stop. So intimately joined, the cresting pleasure carrying them both, they melded into one for an awe-inspiring space in time. She winced at the fanciful, romantic thought.

*Silly girl, it's only sex. It's always only sex.*

Amazing, soul-melting, temporary sex.

Her bones melted and her spine collapsed. He pulled her down against his chest. The harsh sound of his breathing and the pounding of his heart were loud in her ear. Time took up its incessant cadence, to her relief.

She wanted to laugh at her foolishness, but the lingering after-effects wouldn't allow it. Besides, she didn't want to upset Matt. He might think she was laughing at him, which would be beyond ridiculous. He had serious skills.

"You didn't have to. My ego, and my dick, could have dealt with the blow to their psyches. I don't want to hurt you."

"Uhm." She nestled her head to a more comfortable spot. "I'm fine. I promise."

His hand coasted down her back and curved over her bottom.

Little tingles trailed in its wake. The spark of sexual attraction between them was like the shock from an electrical outlet. Sex hadn't diminished it one iota.

Grace shifted to get up. He was still semi-erect inside her, but she was famished. She arched her eyebrows. His warm brown eyes sparkled beneath half-closed lids.

"What can I say?" He shrugged. "I'm ambitious."

With a snort of laughter, she rolled off and scooped her robe from the floor.

"That's the understatement of the year." She pulled on her robe, heading for the kitchen.

Pulling open the fridge, she contemplated the contents. Rather sparse. She hadn't made it to the grocery store yesterday. In fact, they hadn't even had supper last night. Matt must be starving. Her stomach growled agreement.

"How about," Matt gently pushed the door shut and wrapped an arm around her waist from behind, "we take a quick shower and head out for breakfast? Or more like brunch."

"*We* take a shower? As in, together?"

He swept aside her hair. "Mmm-hmm." He nibbled her neck. She tilted her head to give him better access. The hand on her stomach slipped inside her robe and she shivered. "I'm all about water conservation."

"Very green of you." His hand headed south.

"Matt." She choked on a laugh and grabbed his errant hand. "I really can't. I won't be able to move."

"That's a problem?" His teeth sank into her earlobe, not hard enough to hurt, and she discovered that therein lay a direct line to her clit. She melted.

Matt scooped her into his arms.

She squeaked. "Matt. I'm too heavy. Put me down. I'm perfectly capable of walking."

He snorted. "Don't insult me, woman."

"Woman?"

"Besides, I'm helping you conserve those lovely tender areas we want well-rested. I have plans for them."

"Oh, so we're conserving those now too? My, my. You're a regular nature boy, aren't you?"

"Nature-loving *man*, yes."

He set her gently on the bathroom floor and started the shower. She held up the bathroom counter like a delicate Victorian maiden while Matt grabbed towels out of her cabinet, checked the water temperature, adjusted the spray to a pulsating massage, and tugged away her robe.

How was she supposed to go back to normal life after being so thoroughly pampered? Something akin to panic fluttered along her skin, but she shrugged it off with the robe. Her motto was enjoy it while it lasted.

Well, her motto now, anyway.

He nudged her into the shower and crowded in after. She used to think her shower was roomy. Herding her under the spray, he lifted handfuls of her hair and smoothed it back from her face until it was soaked. Then he pumped entirely too much shampoo into his hand. She wanted to laugh, but his expression was so serious and tender as he rubbed the shampoo into her hair. Her burst of humor dissipated into the steam.

Once every square inch of her hair was clean, he pulled the shower head loose and rinsed so carefully, not a single drop of water trickled down her face. He repeated the process with conditioner. Relaxed beyond belief, Grace wrapped her arms around his waist and rested her head against his chest. He rinsed the conditioner from her hair with the same meticulous care.

Lathered with her scented soap, his big hands slicked down her back, over and under her bottom. He knelt and ran his hands down the back of her legs. One foot, then the other, his soapy hands massaged her arches and between her toes.

Yet another spot with a direct line to her clit. Her lovely relaxation fled. He rinsed her feet and worked his way up the front of her legs. His thumbs massaged the inside of her thighs, applying gentle pressure until she parted them. His fingers rubbed and circled every millimeter of her pelvis. Tension wound through her. She dropped her head back onto the warm shower tiles.

Gentle fingers rubbed her nether lips, sliding farther back, teasing her with the temptation of a touch that never came, then up over her belly and around her breasts. He soaped her and rolled her nipples between his fingers. Grace moaned. He rinsed her with the handheld shower head. Lower and lower, until the water pulsed over the tender skin between her thighs. The heat soothed even as it wound her tighter.

"Matt," she moaned.

"Shhhh."

Without applying pressure, he skimmed his fingers over her throbbing clit and circled her entrance. Around and around, again and again, until she shattered. Her legs buckled. He caught her, cradling her in his lap on the floor of the shower. His hand up and down her spine soothed her. Settled her.

She reached between their wet bodies and wrapped her fingers around the erection throbbing insistently against her belly. He gently disengaged her fingers.

"But. . ."

He kissed her. "I'd rather wait until later. I want to be inside you."

Grace glanced down at the perfectly lovely erection eyeing her back. Seemed a shame to waste. "I don't mind. Really."

"I appreciate that." His broad hands curved around her bottom and he helped her to her feet. "I'd still prefer to wait."

Muscles the approximation of boiled pasta, she leaned back against the shower wall. She wasn't used to this sort of abuse. Marathon sex had never figured into her daily schedule. He soaped and washed his hair, treating her to a lovely play of muscles in his arms and chest. She sighed appreciatively.

Then he turned, proving he was an equal-opportunity kind

of guy. Which she appreciated. So much, in fact, that she couldn't resist running her hands over his truly fabulous butt. Said butt went taut beneath her fingers. Willpower dissolving into mush, she stepped closer, skimming her hands around to his front, resting against him. Eyes closed, she made excellent use of the soap sliding down his body and massaged his cock.

Not that it needed any help into full arousal. Matt's groan vibrated through him and into her. Tightening her hold, she pulled up, swirled her fingers around the head, then back down. His hand covered hers, stilling her but not removing her hand. For several seconds, they stood in a frozen erotic tableau. His fingers tightened, both of their hands squeezing him, before he pulled her hands away.

"Not playing fair." He shut off the spray and turned. Color rode high in his cheeks and his eyes were the color of dark chocolate. She glanced down. Junior twitched in approval.

He spun her to face the glass door and smacked her butt. "Out."

"How rude." She lifted her chin and stepped out. "I mean, really. I was only trying to lend a helping hand." The towel she threw hit him square in the chest and her laughter bubbled free.

Matt's sparkling eyes narrowed and he advanced. His bobbing erection considerably diminished the threatening approach. She giggled, snatched a towel off the counter and bolted.

Grinning, she put a chair between them and turned. He stood gloriously nude in her living room. Matt could have posed for Michelangelo's *David*. Her gaze drifted lower. Except for his manhood. Poor David looked like he'd been dipped in an ice bath. Either that or Mother Nature really disliked him.

A drop of water trailed down his thigh, joining another headed south. Water dripped onto her expensive, designer, World Jeffet rug. The nerve.

He stepped one way, she danced the other. Another giggle welled.

"Hold still, wench. I intend to teach you a lesson."

"Oh, really?" Giggling like an escaped lunatic, she darted left when he went right. "Since you'd have to catch me, and that doesn't seem a very real possibility, I'm not worried."

"Why isn't it a possibility?"

Grace did her best to look solemn. "Well, you are sooo much older." His eyes narrowed, "And heavier." Muscles flexed in his arms. "And really. . . horribly. . . grossly. . ." He took a step forward. ". . . out of shape."

"Oh, it's on."

He dodged around the chair. The incessant giggling made it hard to run, but she lit for her bedroom and slammed the door. His palm slapped against the door panel and kept it from closing. She scrambled to the other side of her bed.

He glowered. "Old? Grossly out of shape?"

Her sides hurt from laughing. Another burst of giggles weakened her knees. Tears of laughter clouded her vision. He scaled her bed, grabbed the front of her towel, and dragged her onto the bed beneath him. She couldn't stop laughing.

Matt leaned over her, intimidation melting into a smile. Not that she'd bought his scowl. His warm brown eyes made a mockery of the most menacing expression. Hard arm around her waist, he pulled her snugly into his side.

Her giggles subsided and contentment crept in. Too warm, happy and sated to contemplate moving—even for breakfast—she tangled her legs with his.

Matt broke the comfortable silence. "My mom and step-dad invited my brother and I for dinner tonight. I told them I'd be bringing you."

Dinner with the family? She stiffened. Not just no, but hell no. She didn't do families. Especially families of men she was dating. Meeting the family implied things. To all parties. It went against her creed.

"I'm sorry, but I'm busy tonight."

She slipped from beneath him, snagging her robe where it lay draped over her nightstand, tugged it on and went into her bathroom. Brushing her teeth suddenly seemed terribly important. Dental hygiene shouldn't be overlooked.

Matt followed. "I was under the impression we were spending the weekend together."

Spitting the toothpaste into the sink, she rinsed her mouth and tried to marshal her thoughts. She cared for him. Throwing away their right-now relationship because she knew it wouldn't last long-term was silly.

Her belly cramped and a wave of panic hit, but she fought it off. This was ridiculous. No way did she care for him that much, for pity's sake. This had to be delicately handled. No matter what, she didn't want to lose him. Not before she had to.

Bracing her hands on the sink, she met his gaze. "Look, Matt. I'm not a meet-the-parents kind of girl. Maybe I've seen *Meet the Fockers* too many times." Not so much as a twitch. Okay. That joke fell flat. Kinda like his eyes had gone flat. Uh, yeah. Not good. "You confided in me about your mom being sick, and that was really sweet and I appreciate it. The thing is, my last foster mom died of cancer."

Some of the stiffness left his body, but he didn't exactly relax. "That's all it is? Bad memories? It's not because you don't see our relationship going anywhere and would rather spare me the pain of my whole family knowing?"

Wow. That came out of left field. He couldn't read minds, so what brought it on? Ah. Lightbulb moment. She cocked her head. "Is this past experience rearing its ugly head?"

He shrugged. Stuffing her guilt, she flattened her palm against his bare chest. "Between your mom's illness and the newness of. . ." She gestured between them. ". . . this, I'm just not ready. *Capisce?*"

His lopsided grin tugged unfairly at her heartstrings.

He pulled her close. "Yeah. Sorry for getting defensive."

Remorse popped up to sit uncomfortably in her tummy. Winding her arms around his neck, she pretended to ponder his words. "Huh. I could have sworn that was offensive. Then again, I'm not real up to par on my football terminology."

Matt groaned. "Nobody mixes football and golf terms. There are laws, woman."

Grace nudged her hips forward. "There should be laws about this. Did you eat a whole crate of oysters before you came over?"

"You're complaining? You women are never satisfied."

"You women?" Arching her brows, she pulled away. "You act like there's a whole harem tucked away in my closet."

She went into her bedroom to find something with a little more coverage. Feeling his gaze on her, she glanced over her shoulder. He stood with a shoulder resting against the door frame, arms crossed, emphasizing really nice pecs.

"Get some clothes on, stud muffin. Then I'll let you feed me. Surprisingly enough, I've worked up an impressive appetite. I might eat an entire side of beef."

Dimple winking, he straightened. "I'd better make sure my wallet can handle the abuse."

"As if."

Hours later, Matt left for his family dinner and Grace sat on her balcony, staring over the river. As she'd grown into adulthood, one thing had remained firmly planted in her heart and mind. Relationships weren't for forever. People came for a day, or a semester, and then went. Some stuck it out for a whole year. Until high school, each new school year had brought a new foster family.

A few hazy memories of being pried from the arms of foster mothers lingered. In her heart, those foster mothers had clung to her too. Her head shook in disgust every time her heart tried to run the show. Wisdom came with experience. Wasn't that the point of life lessons? Especially when repeated with such fierce rigidity.

At the beginning of freshman year of high school, she was dropped on Laura's doorstep.

She nursed her glass of moscato, sighing at the memory. Her barriers had crumbled sometime during sophomore year. The four-year stay was likely to blame. Not that it was Laura's fault their relationship had ended. Laura hadn't wanted to die. Still, it reaffirmed what Grace had already known. Some people were meant to walk through life alone. She was one of them.

Which led her back to Matt. The thought of no longer having him in her life brought a deep-seated ache. Right in the region of her heart, damn it all. When would she learn? After all these years, the walls around her too-fragile, too-soft, too-emotional center should be miles high. Unbreachable. Matt had bulldozed right on through. His stupid, crooked smile and blasted dimple were to blame.

Oh, who was she kidding? The entire Matt Duncan package rendered her helpless as a newborn kitten. She glared at the dumb trees. Sweet dandelion blood-ridden baby cherubs from heaven. Grace tossed back the rest of her wine and stomped into her condo. Of all the stupid, idiotic, moronic times to stop swearing, this had to be at the top.

The phone rang. She wanted to toss it off the balcony.

"Hello?"

"Hello, dear." Mrs. Freeman's voice crackled paper-thin across the phone line. "I saw your gentleman friend leave."

"Oh, yeah. That was Matt."

"Your boss? Never mind, dear. I don't mean to be nosy. I'm calling about Apollo. He's been pacing the apartment, and I wondered if you might be able to spare some time to take him out for a walk."

"I'd love to. I'll be down in five."

Setting the phone back on its base, she dashed into her bedroom to throw on her jogging clothes. An outing with Apollo was exactly what the doctor called for. A final tug on her runners and she was out the door, bounding down the stairs with an enthusiasm the Great Dane would be hard pressed to rival.

Which was her first mistake, she realized ten minutes later, running for all she was worth. Clearly the big, lovable hound had been cooped up for far too long. At this rate, they'd find her at dawn, dead of a heart attack, stroke, and suffocated from her inability to gasp air fast enough. Another giant lope from too-long doggy legs yanked her arm into screaming agony. Add a dislocated shoulder to the list.

"Son of a. . . Great Dane mother. Apollo. Give me a break, buddy."

The dog looked back as if to say, "*What's the problem? You're young.*" His droopy lips flipped up in a grin as he ran.

She narrowed her eyes. Oh, that was it. One bossy male in her life was more than enough. Angling toward the grass, because even in her irritation she cared about the big slavering mutt's joints, she threw on the brakes and hauled on his leash. For a split second of eye-widening terror, she thought Apollo was just going to keep running with her arm still attached to the leash, while she remained behind. Then he arced around in a circle and panted to a stop.

In a brief moment of exhausted delusion, she swore he was laughing. She shook off the image and collapsed onto the grass. Apollo dropped down beside her and rested his drool-foamed jaw on her belly.

"Oh, gross."

For a woman who'd spent all night, and a good portion of the morning, becoming reacquainted with certain parts of her anatomy, a mad dash down the Greenbelt was more than she'd bargained for. Much, much more. Her breathing returned to normal, her heart rate calmed, and finally the rest of her body caught onto the lack of movement.

Vaguely aware of curious looks tossed her way by passing joggers, bikers, and other exercise enthusiasts, she preserved her dignity by staring up at the wide expanse of blue sky.

Until a shadow blocked her view. A gravel-laden voice accompanied the shadow. "You okay, lady?"

Squinting up, and then up some more, she made out a huge man in a jogging suit. Light gleamed off his bald head. Apollo raised his head at the man's approach but hadn't stood or assumed a protective stance.

Muscles screamed as she pushed to her feet. "Yeah, yeah," she muttered.

"Sorry?" The Hulk frowned.

Gaining her feet, she forced a smile sharp enough to cut glass. "I'm fine, thanks. This beast was just trying to kill me. No biggie."

"Oh, yeah?" Black eyes cut to Apollo.

Grace rested a protective hand on the dog's back. He'd risen and must have picked up on her tension, because he bristled beneath her hand.

"By running like he was competing for the Triple Crown."

"Oh."

Those steely eyes came back to her. She fought the urge to take a step back. Purely on description, she doubted this guy was her stalker. Still, the world was full of wackos.

"Well, as long as you're fine."

"Yes. Thank you."

With a nod, he started walking. In the opposite direction of her condo. Suddenly exhausted, any interest in further exercise evaporated.

"Come on, boy. Hope you had fun, because that's all you're gonna get this time around."

She was shocked to see how far they'd come. Amazing the distance covered with a long-legged dog plowing ahead. Mrs. Freeman seemed surprised to see her so soon but accepted Apollo's return with her usual calm poise. Grace staggered upstairs, focused on collapsing on her bed.

At the top of the stairs, the hair on the nape of her neck lifted.

Her front door stood ajar. No way had she left it open. Maybe Matt had returned. But why would he leave the door open?

He wouldn't.

One foot found a lower step, then another and another. Eye level with the hall floor, a shadow passed the opening. She turned and ran.

Not sure where she was headed, since her purse and car keys were upstairs in her condo, she tore around a corner and hurtled straight into a rock-hard masculine chest. A scream stuck in her throat.

## CHAPTER FIFTEEN

Sheriff Sanford drummed his fingers on the steering wheel. What the hell was taking so long? Speak of the Devil. . .

Gunner barreled out of the pawn shop and dove into the Cherokee like he'd just ripped off the joint.

"Go, go, go!"

Sanford threw the Cherokee into drive and peeled out of the parking lot. Hanging out with Gunner had gotten him into heaps of trouble during his teen years. Some things never changed. Glancing in the rear-view mirror, he winced at the black skid marks he'd left. A man ran out of the store, a nasty-looking shotgun in hand. Sanford glared at Gunner.

Patience hanging by a thread, he faced the street. "What did you do?"

His passenger tried an innocent expression. Shiny bald head, thick neck, black eyes, and rough-looking face—innocent wasn't a good look for him. "All I did was ask a nice young man a few very polite questions about anybody trying to pawn a police-issue handgun recently."

"That was not a young man tearing out of the building and shouldering a twelve-gauge."

"Probably the young man's father."

Sanford's fingers tightened around the wheel. This was as bad as dragging answers out of Billy when he'd hauled him in for holding up the 7-11. "Why would the young man's father have a desire to fill your hairy backside with holes?"

The dad would have to get in line.

"Could have something to do with me hauling the scrawny kid's pimply face across the counter and threatening to pound it against the glass until he lost the snotty attitude." Gunner snapped the seat belt into place and sat back with the air of a man highly satisfied with a job well done.

Sanford spent a solid thirty seconds visualizing smashing Gunner's head into the dashboard. No sane man would voluntarily go up against the beast seated next to him, which meant his sanity had taken a hike. Not exactly news. "I don't suppose you managed to get anything useful out of the. . . interview?"

"Ya know, once I smacked his head into the counter, the information poured out. Along with some blood, but you probably don't want to hear about that. Or the broken nose."

Gunner popped a few knuckles while Sanford mentally itemized the reasons he couldn't pull over and kick Gunner's ass. Number one: He wasn't positive he could take him. Number two: Gunner had been unruly since birth, and would no doubt die that way. How he'd lived to be so old was a mystery.

"Anyway, someone matching our guy's description was in yesterday, right at closing time. The kid's dad sent him packing."

"Too bad. I'd like to have my gun back."

An evil grin accompanied more knuckle-cracking. "We'll get it back."

Sanford winced. "How are things with Grace? You haven't seen Deke?"

"Nah. I did talk to her once. Some horse of a dog was giving her trouble. I made like I was just another jogger on the path."

"Hell, Gunner. I said not to make contact."

"What, you want me to keep Deke from mauling her but a dog can have at it?"

Sanford gritted his teeth, then counted to fifty. "No. I don't want anyone mauling her."

"There is another guy. Pretty sure he's doing more than mauling." Gunner smirked.

He glanced sharply at him. "What do you mean?"

"Unless I miss my guess, which I never do, they're doing the horizontal polka. I did some checking and he's her boss. Dirty pool, man." He shook his head. "Dirty pool."

"He's not some old geezer, is he?"

"Like us?" His big, booming laugh reminded Sanford of the time the two of them snuck around the back of Principal Gordon's house and saw him banging the secretary. Thankfully, Gunner had waited to laugh until they were out in the barn guzzling the whiskey he'd swiped from his dad. Even then, he'd had a laugh to wake the dead.

"Nah." Gunner shook his head. "The guy's in his mid-thirties, but everyone knows the boss-man has no business screwing an employee. If she were my daughter, I'd take the SOB for a walk and teach him a thing or two about respecting women."

"You think he's just using her?" Sanford's gut tightened. Bad enough they had to deal with Deke squirming out of the wood-work. "He have a rep for sleeping with his female employees or something?"

Gunner rubbed his bald head. "Far as I can see, the guy's love life has been pretty nonexistent until Grace. Had an ex-fiancée a few years back who apparently slept with his entire family." He shrugged. "Maybe this thing with Miss Debry is on the up-and-up. Can't say as I'd blame the guy. If I were a few years younger. . ."

Sanford snorted. "Yeah, knock off twenty years, get an attitude transplant and major plastic surgery. You might stand a chance."

"I resent that." Gunner fluttered stubby lashes and placed a hand on his chest. "I could've been married five times over if I'd wanted an old ball and chain to drag around."

Sanford's halfway good mood evaporated. Focusing on the road, he steered the Jeep toward downtown Boise. Since that's where Grace lived and worked, Deke couldn't be far. According

158

to Detective Harrison, Deke had sullied every aspect of Grace's life. Pity they had no proof. They couldn't arrest him on Sandford's intuition.

"You doing okay, John?"

Sanford shot him a glance. Gunner never called him by his first name. "What do you mean?"

"Your wife dying and all. Gotta be rough, after being married so long."

Tension shot up his back and a headache exploded in his temples. All the effort he'd put into redirecting his attention was destroyed. "I'm trying not to think about it. Why don't you go back to watching her home? I'll head on over to where she works and keep an eye on things there. Deke's bound to show up sooner or later."

"Question."

"Shoot."

"Why haven't you gone to Grace and told her the whole story?"

All of his nerve endings tightened, until his face felt made of glass. A light tap in just the right place and he'd shatter. Sanford swallowed. "Fact is, I'm ashamed. I don't want to face that girl and tell her the role I played. I don't see the point. My going to her won't make any difference. Won't catch Deke or help keep her safe."

"You're too hard on yourself, man. After all these years and everything you've done to keep her safe, you need to cut yourself some slack. Ease up."

"Maybe, but the guilt is fresh as ever."

*****

Matt braced himself half a second before Grace slammed into him. He wrapped his arms around her trembling body and stared at the blind terror in her eyes. Her fingernails dug into his arms, then her expression blanked, her eyes rolled back into her head, and she crumpled like a stringless marionette.

"What the hell?" Heart slamming into his ribs, he lifted her in his arms. Her head rolled back, exposing the slim column of her throat. His heart skipped a beat. "Grace?"

No response. The flutter of her pulse beneath the pale skin under her jaw reassured him. Somewhat. He needed to get her home and call for help.

He took the stairs two, three at a time. Her door stood open. He frowned. Vividly aware of Grace's vulnerability as she hung limp in his arms, he approached the door.

"Damnit." He glanced up and down the hall. Nothing. Nowhere he could stash a helpless, unconscious woman while he dealt with a possible intruder. He thought about thumping on Lisette's door, but immediately discarded the idea. Too noisy, and Grace wouldn't appreciate it if he exposed her best friend to danger.

Somewhere in the distance a dog barked. Apollo. Her neighbor. Mrs. Freeman. An old woman, she'd be on the first floor.

Back down the stairs he went, careful not to jostle Grace. His pulse skittered and leapt. He glanced at the handful of doors. Process of elimination. He headed for the closest one and banged on the door with his foot.

A low, throaty growl greeted his pounding. What were the odds? He waited with rapidly waning patience as the door clicked and rattled, clicked and rattled, and finally opened. A petite, white-haired, wrinkled lady peered up at him. Apollo loomed behind her.

"Mrs. Freeman?"

"Yes?" Her faded blue eyes swept over him and landed on Grace's pale face. She straightened. "Is that Grace? What happened? Never mind." She shuffled aside. "Bring her in, young man. You must be Grace's boss, Mr. Duncan."

The eyes might be faded, her eyesight strained, but there was nothing wrong with her mind. Sharp as a tack. "I don't mean to be rude, but could I leave her with you? She fainted, but I don't think anything serious is wrong. I need to check something upstairs, and it's not. . ." He hesitated. No need to scare her. "Can I leave her here for a few minutes?"

"Of course. Set the poor dear on the couch."

Matt passed a walker as he crossed the room. He gently arranged Grace on the couch. A sigh passed her lips to whisper across his face, and he couldn't resist a quick kiss. "I'll be right back," he murmured, even though she couldn't hear him.

Rising, he turned. Mrs. Freeman was directly behind him. For an old woman, she moved with the silent feet of a cat.

Her eyes sparkled. "You take Apollo with you. He'll help."

He and the dog eyed one another. "Uh. . ."

Paper-soft fingers gathered one of his hands between them. "You take him. I know you two haven't bonded yet, but that's a male thing. You're still circling, sniffing one another, figuring out what role you'll each play in her life." She patted him. "Take him."

What could he say but, "Okay."

Mrs. Freeman turned to Apollo. The massive beast nuzzled her side, gentle as a bunny rabbit. The two met almost eye to eye. Matt had to strain to hear her words, and he did, shamelessly.

"You take care of this young man, Apollo. I know you're worried about your Grace, but he's a good man. They're two halves of the same whole. Help him."

The dog stared at her, slavish devotion clear in his eyes. When he turned those eyes on Matt, he swore intelligence shone in them. Running a hand through his hair, he tried to shrug off the ridiculous fancy. Damn. What a day.

"I'll be back as soon as I can, Mrs. Freeman. If she wakes. . ." He rubbed his neck.

"I'll tell her you'll be right back." Her small smile held all the knowledge of her eighty-odd years. Yeah, Grace was safe.

Hound at his heels, he headed out the door, then waited for the snick of the dead bolt before jogging lightly up the steps.

Grace's door creaked. A breeze had kicked up. He paused close to the wall and listened. Silence.

Glancing down at the dog, he wanted to impart a few words of wisdom. Which made him feel stupid on several levels. Who talked to a dog, let alone gave one advice? Watching the old woman had rattled a few brain cells loose.

Staying to the side, he pushed the door open. Nothing stirred. The breeze swept through, tugging on the door and seeming to give it life. Creepy as hell.

He stepped across the threshold, flattened against the opposite wall, and flicked on the light. Apollo leaned against his legs, hackles raised and unmoving. Damn dog weighed a ton. It took a concerted effort to peel away from the wall.

Matt made his way methodically through the apartment. He searched the closets, under the bed, inside the pantry, and out on the balcony. Nothing. Not only that, but nothing appeared to be disturbed. His hair stood on end. He and the dog made a pair. Not a freakin' thing, yet they were both wired and on edge.

He stared around the living room and rubbed his neck. The breeze whipped past him and something fluttered on the couch. Smack dab in the middle sat an old doll with a piece of paper pinned to her ratty dress.

"Shit."

Apollo nudged his head under his hand. Absently petting him, Matt bent down to read the note. He recognized the handwriting on the torn paper.

*Recognize this?*
*I told you, you can't hide from what you are.*
*Nothin' but trailer trash.*
*I'm coming to take you home where you belong, slut.*

Now, why would a man who seemed to harbor such a strong dislike for a woman say he was going to take her home? Unless he meant home as in eternal resting place, and that would happen over Matt's dead and decaying body.

Apollo whined.

"You're right."

Pulling out his cell phone, Matt dialed 9-1-1. His thumb hovering over send, he stared at the dog. Great. Now he was talking to the damn animal. Shaking his head, he hit send. The police were getting to be regular fixtures.

After hanging up with the dispatcher, he paced the condo. Everything appeared undisturbed, down to the damp towels hanging on the towel rack from their morning shower. Back in the living room, he screeched to a halt.

Grace stood in front of the couch, staring at the doll.

A litany of profanity rolled through his head.

Her pretty porcelain complexion turned gray. She swayed and Matt was by her side in an instant, wrapping an arm around her waist and pulling her to him. She fit against him, her lithe body soft and molded to his. His chest expanded. Everything about her was so right it hurt.

He smoothed her hair back. The curls sprang right back into place, refusing all attempts to be tamed—like the woman herself. Her vibrant green eyes didn't waver from the tattered doll. Seeing her like this tore him up. Something dark and ugly welled, but he swallowed it back down. He needed to save it for the sick fuck tormenting her.

A knock sounded and Grace flinched, stiffening. Matt turned. The same police detective they'd dealt with last time stood in the doorway.

"Not the best idea." The detective gestured toward the open door.

"Yeah, I know."

Grace stirred in his arms and at last turned her back on the doll. "Hello, Detective. I'm sorry to cause you more work."

Her voice was soft and extremely polite. Distant. Matt frowned. His arm tightened.

163

The detective's gaze visibly softened.

"No need to apologize, Miss Debry. None of this is your fault. All part of the job." He moved farther into the room. "So what've we got this time?"

Grace pulled away and Matt clenched his hands to resist pulling her back. She was reasserting her independence. He could respect that. Didn't like it, but he respected it.

"I went out this evening, took a neighbor's dog for a quick jog. When I returned, thirty or forty minutes later, my door was open. I left and. . ."

She trailed off. His beautiful girl was reluctant to reveal weakness. Fainting would definitely fall under that category to her. Unsure when he'd begun to think of her as his, he shifted uncomfortably and filled in the breach for her.

"I encouraged her to stay at a neighbor's for a few minutes while I investigated. I figured it would be safer. Nobody was up here, and nothing was disturbed or taken, from what I've seen. Grace should look around to be sure." He glanced at her. She was staring at the damn doll again. "I spotted the doll on the couch and called you guys."

"Next time, call us first. This guy may be armed and violent. You have no idea what you could be facing. I don't want anybody to get hurt. Let us do our job, Mr. Duncan."

Matt had to admit he had a point. On top of which, he felt like a total ass. The detective remembered his name, but he couldn't pull up anything more than "detective." The guy knelt in front of the doll.

"Do you recognize this?" The detective looked at Grace. And damned if admiration didn't fill his expression.

Grace was too busy staring to notice. She stretched a hand toward the doll then hesitated and glanced at the detective. "May I?"

He shrugged. "Sure. We have your prints on file from the earlier break-ins, so we can eliminate them easily enough."

She picked up the doll. With an almost vacant expression, she fingered the age-yellowed dress and matted black hair. And it hit him—Grace and the doll shared a disturbing likeness.

Grace tipped the doll back and plastic eyelids closed over green eyes. Tipped her upright and the lids bounced open again. Freaky as hell. Kids actually played with stuff like that?

"I don't know. There's something, but I spent time in so many foster homes."

"That's okay, Miss Debry. If you'll just set her down, I'll bag and tag her."

Eyes widening, Grace did as she was told. "What will you do with her?"

"Collect a few samples. Determine her age, find out what we can about her origins. Look for fingerprints." He tipped his head toward her. "Other than yours, of course."

"You won't harm her, will you?"

Matt massaged the back of his neck. They could chop the thing up and use it for firewood as far as he was concerned. What he couldn't understand was why Grace didn't share his feelings.

"We can try to take unobtrusive samples."

"I'd appreciate it." Her big eyes were full of vulnerability and glued to the detective.

Matt fought the urge to growl. *Down, caveman.*

"I. . . I think I'd like her back."

"If you're sure."

The detective looked from Grace to the doll. For once, he and the detective were on the same page. If he never set eyes on that thing again, Matt would die a happy man. Grace nodded and the detective left.

"What's the deal with the doll, Grace?"

"I don't know. I can't explain. It's just. . . I look at her, touch her, and it's like some distant memory is trying to break through." She shook her head. "That sounds totally bizarre, I know."

Matt relaxed a little. That sounded more like the Grace he

165

knew. "Maybe not all that bizarre. The doll probably reminds you of one you played with as a child, or one that another kid you knew had."

"Yeah. I guess."

"Come here, sweetheart." He tugged her into his arms. "You scared me, fainting like that."

The way she leaned in and wrapped her slender arms around him, stole another piece of his heart. He breathed her in. Soft, feminine perfume, a fruity shampoo and underneath it all— Grace. His arousal was instant, painful, and totally inappropriate.

"Sorry," she mumbled into his shirt. "I don't know what happened. I've never fainted."

Someone cleared their throat. The detective hesitated in the open doorway, looking irritated and impatient. Matt's arms involuntarily tightened around Grace. His, every cell in his body proclaimed.

"This'll just take a second." A pair of plastic gloves over his hands, Detective Harrison picked up the doll and deposited her inside a large, clear plastic bag. "We'll take good care of her, Miss Debry."

"Thank you. And thank you for personally coming again, Detective Harrison."

"No problem." The detective faced Grace. "Call me directly if you have any further problems."

She paled. "You think I will?"

"Unfortunately. This guy has made it pretty clear that he's not giving up until he gets what he wants." The detective headed for the door. "I'll have a cruiser do a drive-by as often as possible. I would strongly recommend having new locks installed and keeping every set of keys on you at all times."

"I'll do that. Thank you."

Matt gritted his teeth. He'd told her to get new locks a week ago. Apparently, she hadn't listened. The detective closed the door behind him. Matt didn't hesitate to cross the room and flip the locks. Then he pulled out his phone and opened an internet search.

"What are you doing?" Grace stood in the middle of the room, arms crossed, lines around her lips and on her forehead, tension radiating from every line of her gorgeous body. The sick freak had succeeded in making her uncomfortable in her own home, and that pissed Matt off no end.

"Finding a locksmith. I want these locks changed now."

Grace blinked. "Excuse me?"

"You heard me. I'll pay for it."

Dark pink bloomed across her cheeks and fire sparked in her gaze. "Last time I checked, my name is on the lease. My condo, my locks, my bills. None of which is your responsibility."

"You are my responsibility."

He hadn't thought it possible, but she stiffened further. An icy mask blanked her expression. Maybe he should have thought that one out first. Ticking her off hadn't been part of the plan.

"I'm your responsibility? At what point did that occur? When I became your employee? When you took me out to dinner? Or when we screwed like wild bunnies?"

Her words cut deeper than he'd thought possible, slamming his defenses into place. He unclenched his jaw. "I may have phrased that poorly, but you're overreacting."

Her arms crossed, giving her full breasts a boost they didn't need. "I am no one's responsibility. Now or ever."

"Funny, I thought we were in a relationship."

"Funny, I don't recall you mentioning taking over my life."

"I am not taking over anything."

"Please. Given half a chance, you'd run me as ruthlessly as you do your business."

He narrowed his gaze. "What is that supposed to mean?"

"I thought it was obvious. Inciting terror in your employees and making unreasonable demands of them is a full-time hobby for you. You run that place with an iron fist. Obviously it's a

167

compulsive thing for you, since you're trying to do the same thing with our 'relationship.'"

The emphasis on "relationship" seemed like a bad thing, but he was beyond caring. "It's my business. I built it from the ground up, and I'll run it any way I damn well I please. Leave it to a woman to bring something entirely unrelated into an argument."

"You need to leave."

Some of the anger drained out of him. Damn, he was making a mess. He shoved his fingers through his hair. "Baby, I'm sorry. I'm not trying to take over anything here. You call the locksmith. I just want to make sure you're safe."

She smiled, the edges sharp enough to slice a block of cold cheddar cheese. "That's so sweet of you to recognize my capability. You still need to leave. I'm exhausted and desperately in need of some quality alone-time."

"Grace." He reached for her. "This got way out of hand. I didn't mean to—"

She held up a hand and he froze. "I don't really care what you meant. Maybe I will in the morning, but right now. . ."

His stomach sank.

"Just leave, Matt."

Frustration left a bitter tang in his mouth. "I'm not leaving until these locks are changed and I know you're safe."

Eyes narrowing, her smile slipped a few degrees. "I don't recall giving you a choice. If you really are refusing to leave, I suppose I could give Detective Harrison a call." She held up her hand, the detective's business card between her fingers. "Somehow, I think he would be only too happy to throw you out."

So she had noticed. He dropped his phone into his pocket with deliberate motions and enunciated carefully.

"Fine. Just please call someone about the locks."

"I'm not stupid," she snapped.

Neck tight, he headed for the door. Damnit, he didn't want to leave. Even without all the crap going on, he wanted to be right here, with her. He'd always been a fuck-up when it came to relationships, but he'd hoped to get it right this time. Hell, he'd hung his heart on it.

"Just go." The weariness in her voice forced him out the door.

Matt thumped his head against the wall across from her door. He wanted to rage, but the tattered remains of his self-control were just enough to stop him. Instead, he turned and stared at Grace's door. His ex-fiancée would be laughing her ass off to see him now, cold satisfaction in her smile.

"*Mon dieu*, what 'ave you done?"

He wearily rolled his head to the side. Lisette stood in the hallway, the golden light from her condo illuminating an oversized T-shirt, neon-green leggings, and crossed arms, all of which was smeared liberally with rainbow-bright paint.

She shook her head. "You'd best come in for a drink, beau."

"I can't."

Her slender eyebrows winged north and she studied him, obviously unimpressed by his growl. As quietly as she'd arrived, she spun on her heel and disappeared back into her home.

Matt sighed. What the fuck kind of man snarled at a little bit of a girl? He slid down the wall to sit on his ass and stare morosely at the door Grace had firmly closed in his face. God, he was pathetic.

Those eyeball-searing leggings blocked his view, then turned and sat cross-legged beside him. She waved a squat glass beneath his nose. His eyes watered and he jerked his head back, bashing his skull on the wall.

"What the hell is that, paint thinner?"

Lisette muttered something that didn't sound complimentary, then held out the glass again. "Is excellent gin that I brought up from N'Awlins, beau. Drink it."

He reluctantly took the glass.

"You're welcome." More muttering.

"Thank you." He took a cautious sip. The liquid seared a path

169

down his throat and he coughed up a fireball. "Gin my ass!"

Lisette snorted, took the glass from him and tossed back the contents. "My family has been making gin for generations. This is a particularly fine batch."

He noted the lack of flames licking along her words with narrow-eyed suspicion.

She rolled her eyes and tilted her head toward Grace's door. "What'd you do?"

God, he'd rather drink more of that pipe cleaner she called liquor. He scrubbed a hand over his face. "I may have been a little. . . bossy."

"Lawd above." Laughter tinkled out of her for a solid two minutes. Finally, she wiped her eyes and twisted to face him, her expression sobering. "Fellas aren't all that bright when it comes to romancing, so I'll let you in on a little secret. Women don't like being bossed around and treated like they don't have two brain cells to rub together in their pretty li'l heads."

Matt frowned. "But I didn't—"

A paint-smudged hand smacked up a half inch from his nose. "You sittin' out here in the cold, ain't ya?"

He crossed his arms.

"Grace is whip-smart, but she's also terrified of anything that looks too much like a relationship. Even friendship is hard for her. Ya have to walk softly, not plow through with all the finesse of a gator in a tea party. You bossin' her feels too much like. . ." she flicked her fingers, ". . . like permanence. Like you demanding a place in her life, when she don't wanna give ya one, and sure as heck don't believe you'll stay."

A man appeared in the stairwell carrying a heavy tool box and sporting a snazzy work outfit emblazoned with the company's insignia. Pushing to his feet, Matt extended his hand to Lisette. She snagged it, rose gracefully to her feet, and surprised him with a quick, fierce hug before disappearing back into her condo as quickly as she'd appeared.

Matt nodded to the workman as he passed, then jogged down the stairs. Lisette's parting whisper rolled through his mind.

"Stick like taffy, no matter what. She needs you, even if she doesn't know it yet."

At least Grace had called a locksmith. Hopefully, with some, or a lot, of groveling, he could fix the disaster he'd made of things. If not. . . He shook his head. No, he couldn't even contemplate that. It'd kill him.

## CHAPTER SIXTEEN

Grace shut the door behind the locksmith and slid the shiny new keys into her pocket. On her person at all times, Detective Harrison had said. Taking an extra step of precaution, she'd even had the guy install a sturdier lock on her balcony door. He'd sworn on his "sweet dead granny's" grave she held the only keys to her new locks.

With a groan of sheer exhaustion, she collapsed onto her bed. Except it didn't feel like her bed. She religiously made her bed every morning. This bed was a disaster and didn't smell right. It smelled like musky sex and Matt. She pulled a pillow over her face. And inhaled Matt. Just her luck.

She scrambled off the bed, shucked her clothes, and tossed them in the hamper. Then she stripped the bed and tossed the sheets and pillowcases in the hamper. She remade the bed, arranging the fresh sheets and blankets with exacting precision. OCD impulses satisfied, she crawled beneath the covers and buried her face in a pillow—that still smelled like Matt.

"Mother loving stinkin' pansy petals."

She flung the pillow across the room. It made a dull thud against the wall. She yanked another pillow across the bed and smacked it into shape. Tugging the blankets over her shoulders, she rolled onto her stomach. Then onto her side, cursing a green streak and insulting every flower she could think of.

Matt's scent permeated the fibers of every single bit of bedding she owned. He hadn't even slept on this pillow and she could smell him. The covers pulled up around her nose smelled of him. How the flip was she supposed to sleep? A girl couldn't even throw a guy out without being haunted by him.

Flopping onto her back, she stared at the ceiling. She could admit. . . grudgingly. . . to herself at least, that she could see Matt's point. He had suggested—as if he knew how to "suggest" anything—she get the locks changed a while ago. She hadn't. Plus, she had kinda glazed over after seeing the doll on her couch. His truly spectacular job of totally pissing her off had jerked her out of that bizarre state.

Maybe the doll was laced with some weird inhaled narcotic.

Regardless, she'd probably come down pretty hard on Matt. Snuggled into her very big and very empty bed alone had little appeal. She glanced at the alarm clock on her nightstand. 11:42 pm. Sighing, she glared at her bedside phone. What kind of desperate woman called a man in the middle of the night to come over?

Her fingers twitched. Well, she wasn't calling to demand sex. They didn't even need to have sex. Her pebble-hard nipples and the insistent throb between her thighs said otherwise, but she ignored them.

She reached for the phone. If he didn't answer in two rings, she'd hang up. One. . .

"Hello?"

"Matt. I didn't expect. . . I mean, did I wake you?"

"No. I couldn't sleep." The sound of his husky baritone made her arousal worse. "Is something wrong?"

"No. I, um, had the locksmith come out. I even had a new lock installed on the balcony door."

"That's good."

Twining the blanket round and round her finger, she stared at the play of shadows across the wall. How did a woman go about asking a man to come over in the middle of the night, anyway?

Matt cleared his throat. "I'm really sorry about the way I acted tonight. I know how you feel about me bossing you around. I just. . ."

"I appreciate your concern. I. . . uh. . . I haven't had a relationship in a long time. This is new and weird and I reacted badly. I'm sorry."

"Wow. I didn't think women said they were sorry."

She frowned. "Is that some wisecrack or are you actually serious?"

"I would not be cracking wise right now. Scout's honor."

"Then you're serious, which is somehow even more disturbing. So, what was her name?"

Silence. "Uh, Grace?"

"Yeah?"

"It's nearly midnight. Did you really call just to chat?"

Well, crap. She sighed and mumbled, "I sorta called 'cause I missed you and wondered if you'd come over."

"Come again?"

"Seriously? You're gonna make me repeat it?"

"Yeah, you'd better. I'm pretty sure I just fantasized you saying you missed me and wanted me to come over. Now."

Giggling, she rolled onto her back. "Probably because I did."

Click. Eyes going wide, she sat up and stared at the phone. Had he just hung up on her?

"Hello? Matt?"

Her lower lip jutted out and she slammed the phone into its cradle. Great.

Burying her nose in the Eau de Matt pillow, she shut her eyes and counted sheep. Then cows. Out of desperation, she switched to Great Danes. At the eighty-ninth Great Dane, someone pounded on her front door and she bolted upright.

"Grace?"

He'd come. Grinning like a fool, she clambered out of bed and flew across the condo. Throwing open the door, she didn't get a chance to say a word before he swept her into his arms and kissed her. What a kiss! She wrapped her arms around his neck and her legs around his waist and kissed him back with abandon.

The door slammed shut. Matt fumbled for the locks without breaking their kiss and carried her to her room, bumping into things a handful of times before hitting the side of the bed. His warm calloused hands roamed her body. Only then did she realize she'd answered the door in her birthday suit. His hands coasted around to cup her bottom and she forgot to care.

He set her on the bed, to her mewling objections. She had needs. Needs that needed addressing. Now. When he started yanking off clothes, she quieted. Watching a man strip was incredibly erotic. Especially when his erection sprang free.

Grace slid off the bed and dropped to her knees as he wrestled with his clothes, swearing under his breath. She leaned forward and wrapped her hand around the base of his cock, licked her lips and guided him into her mouth. He stilled as she sucked him deep. Pulling back, she sucked the head and swirled her tongue like he was a Tootsie Pop.

His hands fisted in her hair, but he didn't try to take over. He just held on. A move she rewarded by taking him all the way to the back of her throat and swallowing. His thigh muscles turned to steel beneath her hand and his shaft pulsed. Easing back, she increased the suction of her mouth and ran her tongue across the tip.

"Grace, I can't. . ."

She swallowed him again and he broke off with a deep, guttural groan. Cupping his sack in her other palm, she rolled it gently between her fingers and swallowed. Hands gentle, he cupped her cheeks and withdrew from her mouth. She released him with an audible, reluctant "pop." The taste of his sex lingered.

He bent down, stepped in the middle of the shirt he'd been struggling to remove and yanked. With a loud rip of fabric, he was free.

He didn't linger over the wreckage of his oxford. He lifted her off her knees and tossed her on the bed. His enthusiasm set off giggles. He followed her down and thrust deep in one smooth motion, cutting her off mid-giggle.

Raw sensation spun out. She arched and hung on for dear life. He found a sharp, hard, pounding stroke. The tempo shot her straight to the edge and held her there.

Matt wrapped one arm beneath her shoulders and cradled the back of her head in his hand, kissing her in a blatant echo of his hips. His other hand ran down her side, over and under her hip. Cupping her bottom, he angled her hips up and thrust deeper. Orgasm washed over and through her, and he followed, his muscles tensing and groaning his release into her mouth.

In the aftermath, she clung to him, savoring his weight. His lips trailed down her jaw to her neck.

"I missed you," he murmured against her skin.

Too breathless to laugh, she smiled. "You weren't gone long."

"Felt like an eternity."

He rose onto his elbows. The deep-brown depths of his eyes were sober. Terrifyingly serious. No. She didn't want serious. He moved inside her and her thoughts fractured.

"You're insatiable."

"Only with you." He held her gaze. "I could make love to you for a hundred years and it wouldn't be enough."

His words rang with sincerity and she recognized her own feelings in them. Panic flowed beneath the surface of her desire. Another deep thrust buried the alarm deeper, but she knew it would be there. Waiting.

Grace blew hair out of her eyes and resumed scrubbing. The en suite bathroom sparkled. The floor was the only thing left. Taking a scrub brush to it had seemed a touch over the top, but she'd shrugged and gone for it. Once she was finished with the bathroom. . .

A spot caught her eye and she attacked with relish. Anything but think about the hunk'a-hunk'a-burnin'-love sleeping in her bed—and the declaration in his eyes. He hadn't run out of steam until almost two a.m., it was now six and she'd been up for an hour. At least her bathroom was lemony fresh. She was pretty sure her stove needed a thorough cleaning too. It would be getting one regardless.

*"I missed you."*

*"It felt like an eternity."*

She scrubbed harder, backing toward the door as she went. The bedroom carpet forced her to stop and drop the brush into the mop bucket. Rocking back on her heels, she draped her forearms on her knees and stared at the shiny bathroom.

Long-term didn't work for her, no matter how much she wished otherwise. No matter how much her feelings had deepened. Not a good sign. Then again, calling him in the middle of the night hadn't been a great sign either. What had she been thinking?

*Sex. It was just sex.*

If only she could believe that, but the big galoot had won over much more than her body.

"Ruby-red roses," she moaned.

"What was that about roses?" a husky masculine voice asked from behind her.

She turned. He lay on his side, head propped on his hand, sheet draped low over lean hips and looking yummy with bed head.

She couldn't help smiling. "Nothing."

"What are you doing over there?" His brow rose. "And you're dressed. The rubber gloves are kind of kinky, but I'm willing to give anything a go once."

Peeling them off and draping them over the side of the bucket, she laughed. "Hungry?"

"Yes."

The low rumble in his voice warned her half a second too late. Warm, delicious-smelling male arms tugged her backward into

177

the bed. Another half second and his hand was beneath her shirt. Liquid desire pooled between her thighs.

"Matt, I can't."

"Why not?" His mouth skimmed her throat.

Despite her denial, she angled her head to accommodate him. "I won't be able to walk tomorrow."

"Walking is overrated."

"I can't just. . ." She moaned.

Blunt fingers pinched her nipple and rolled it, while he found her favorite spot along her neck.

"You're not playing fair."

"Did I say I would?"

"Seriously, I. . ."

The hand tormenting her nipple traveled south, slipped inside the loose waistband of her sweats and spread her liquid arousal in ever-widening circles. Her eyes might have crossed when his fingertips glided over her clitoris. Breathing ceased when he inserted two fingers. Panting, she tried to think. She could have sworn she had declared a ceasefire with her body, written up a truce of accord and agreed single life really shouldn't be underestimated.

Instead, her body betrayed her by arching into the naked man tormenting her and incited a mutiny. The nerve. This whole sleeping-with-the-enemy thing had gotten totally out of control.

Pretty sure she couldn't move a single muscle if her life depended upon it, Grace sprawled on her back and stared at the ceiling. Her chandelier was dirty and cobwebby looking. Maybe she should have tackled the fixture instead of her bathroom. Taken it down and dismantled it for a thorough cleaning.

Sounded like a lot of work. Her eyelids drooped.

The bed shifted as Matt climbed out. She was a limp noodle and he was full of boundless energy. Must've sucked all her energy out with sex. Rolling over, she curled into a ball and let her eyes close.

A firm whack on her backside brought her upright and glaring.

Matt grinned. "Come on, sleepyhead. You mentioned feeding me."

"That was before." She lay back down.

The grin grew. She ignored the dimple and closed her eyes. Covered a huge yawn with her hand. Warm hands wrapped around her ankles and dragged her across the bed.

"Matt," she moaned.

He freed her ankles, grabbed her wrists and hauled her up until she was sitting. A few really choice names came to mind. Then his chest pillowed her head and she relaxed. Never mind. This worked.

He wrapped his arms around her and dropped a kiss on the top of her head. "I can carry you out to the car, but I don't know any restaurants offering nude dining."

The humor in his voice tickled the edges of her temper, but she was too tired. He was abnormal. No one should be in such a good mood first thing in the morning. Sleep sang a siren song and she settled deeper into him.

"Go without me," she mumbled.

"Not gonna happen, sweetheart. Come on. On your feet."

He tugged her off the edge of the bed. Her feet hit the floor and her knees buckled. If he hadn't been holding onto her, she would have landed flat on her face.

"I thought you were joking about not being able to walk."

"Um, no." She yawned.

Matt scooped her into his arms. At this point, she was willing to sleep anywhere, so she curled into him. The welcome darkness of sleep fogged the edges of reality.

Water hit her skin and she jolted upright, heart pounding in her throat. Matt held her in his arms, but he'd stepped into the shower stall with her. She glared daggers. If there was any justice to be found, he'd collapse on the floor in agony. He grinned.

179

She crossed her arms and contented herself with pouting.

He bent his head and sucked her nipple into his mouth. Fine. She was awake already.

"You can put me down."

"I like holding you." He switched to the other nipple.

"Matt. If we're going to be in the shower we should at least wash."

"Me first." He let her slide down his body. His freak of nature erection almost slipped right inside her, but she angled her hips away.

"No, me." She snatched the bath pouf and liberally dribbled on her scented bath soap. Stepping behind him, she enthusiastically scrubbed his backside. By the time she hit his ankles, his skin glowed pink. Not the slightest bit remorseful, she circled around and glared at his bobbing erection.

"Bloody begonias."

The man had far too much energy. She started on his feet and worked up. A cursory once-over with the sponge was all his testicles got. If the rest of him was rushed, well, shoot her.

His eyes twinkled when she glanced up. She glowered.

If he thought they were having sex again, he was nuts. Loony. Out of his gourd. She pitied the poor woman who would have to service his needs for the rest of her natural life.

The thought of him with another woman hit her with the subtlety of a sledgehammer on a flower blossom and she flinched. Then tried to brush it off. So she liked the guy. The tightness in her chest made a lie of that statement. Okay, she cared about him. A lot. She wasn't the kind of girl who ran around sleeping with every Tom, Dick and Harry, after all.

She slapped the pouf into Matt's hand and presented her back. He gently smoothed the soapy pouf from her shoulder down the back of her leg to her ankle. Then from the other ankle all the way up to the other shoulder. He repeated the action on her front.

He dropped the pouf and ran his fingers along her nooks and crannies until she was squeaky clean. He rinsed her with the same gentle efficiency, then wrapped his arms around her and pulled her back flush against his front. Arousal hummed, but she was too rattled to deal with it. His ever-present erection nudged into the small of her back and she tensed.

"Easy," he whispered in her ear. "The status of my dick isn't your responsibility. You're beautiful, so lush and feminine. I can't help getting aroused pretty much every time I look at you. Doesn't mean you have to take care of it."

She relaxed, although it was hard, er, difficult, to ignore the thickness pressed against her. "What would you like for breakfast?"

"I didn't spend the weekend with you so you could cook for me." He shut off the water, nudged her out of the shower and handed her a towel. "I know a place that serves amazing French toast. If that's okay with you?"

"Sure." Bending over, she wrapped her hair in the towel. His fingers brushed down her spine and across her bare bottom, then he was gone.

Emerging some fifteen minutes later, she found him stretched across her bed, perusing the Sunday paper and looking more delectable than any man had a right to.

She smiled. "I see you're making yourself right at home. What are you going to do about your shirt?" Torn from the night before, it revealed more than she cared to share with the rest of the world. She was selfish like that.

"I have a spare in the truck."

Her eyebrow rose. "This happens often, does it?"

"Not until you." He grinned. "I always keep a spare in case I need to change after visiting a dirty job site."

Resisting the urge to stick out her tongue at him, she gave him her back instead and grabbed matching panties and a bra out of her dresser and shimmied into them. Not all that at ease with a man watching her dress, she fought a blush and walked into her closet. She came out fully dressed, down to her shoes.

"Ready?"

Matt was staring at the wall.

"Matt?"

"Hmm?"

*What the heck?* "Breakfast? Are you ready to go?"

He blinked. "You expect normal brain function when you cover your gorgeous butt with sheer black panties then put a matching bra over the most incredible breasts known to man? I've been carefully storing those forty-five seconds to fuel my fantasies. The brief glimpse of your pussy right before the material covered it, the flash of nipple as you slipped your arm into the strap. . ." He shook his head. "You've ruined me."

Would the floor just open up and swallow her already? Her face felt hot enough to light a campfire and she was pretty sure she would never voluntarily dress in front of a man again.

He stood and wrapped his arms around her. Grace buried her burning face in his shoulder.

"I don't know why you're embarrassed, sweetheart. You should flaunt a body as incredible as yours. On second thought, scratch that. Go ahead and be shy. As a matter of fact, you should dress like a librarian. A really old librarian. With mothballs."

Laughing, she pushed away. "Alright already. You've had your fun. Now feed me before I get grumpy."

"Yes, ma'am. When we're done, we get to come back here, right?"

"No. When we're done, you can show me where you live."

Matt grinned. "You're on."

Locking the door behind them, she blanched. Talking tarantulas, what the flip was she doing? Next she'd be offering him a key to her condo, which was beyond stupid. He wouldn't stay. No one ever did. She glanced at Matt from beneath her lashes, heart clenching at the thought of leaving him, of never feeling his hands on her or his warm voice in her ear.

*I am so in over my head.*

They walked down the stairs, her hand tucked firmly within his.

*Oh, what a tangled web we-of-little-brain weave.*

# CHAPTER SEVENTEEN

Matt let Grace inside and stepped back to watch her take in his home. He'd sensed a shift in her after they left her place that had solidified over breakfast. Much like his breakfast—a load of bricks in his gut.

Tossing a smile over her shoulder that didn't reach her eyes, she wandered into his kitchen. "This is a great place."

He used to think so, but now he realized it lacked something. Trailing behind her like a love-struck teenager, he pictured her in each room. Sipping coffee at his breakfast table in the kitchen, wrapped in his robe. Curled up at the foot of the couch in the rear family room, reading a book. Stretched out beside him in bed sleeping.

He needed to get a grip before he dropped down on one knee and proposed. From her body language the past hour and a half, a flat "*No*" would be his answer. Clearly, he needed to work on romancing her more than bedding her.

In the family room, Grace settled into a chair and studied the room. A natural river-rock fireplace stretched to the ceiling, while the open wood-beamed architecture opened up the ceiling. Metal work tables emphasized the warmth of his leather furniture on the wide-planked floors. At the moment, he couldn't care less about his décor, too preoccupied with why she'd chosen a chair instead of the couch.

Gritting his teeth, he sat in another chair. This was what he hated about relationships. The self doubt. The questions you didn't dare lay out in the open. God forbid anyone refuse to play the game. Polite, putting your best foot forward. Sincerity and honesty not only weren't expected, they were unwelcome. Right now, he wasn't feeling especially polite.

"Would you like something to drink?"

Giving him a strange look, she shook her head. "No, thank you. Are you feeling okay?"

"Fantastic." He sat back and raised his ankle to rest on his knee.

"Um, good. I like the fireplace."

"It's wood-burning." Like she cared if it burned logs or cow chips.

"Must be nice during the winter."

"Yep."

They'd perfected inane conversation.

"I never asked you how dinner went last night with your family. I'm sorry. How's your mom doing?"

"Dinner was good." His mother had deflated a bit when he arrived alone, but she'd recovered. "Mom is okay. Not looking forward to the surgery on Monday."

Grace's head bent, her hair falling forward to cover her face. Frustration sang through his veins. "I'm sorry."

Simple and to the point, yet it touched him. Besides, what more could a person say? Empty platitudes wouldn't help. Nothing would help. Polite, inane conversation wasn't so bad after all. He thought for a second.

"Did you play any sports in school?"

She tucked some curls behind her ear, baring the side of her face. "Track. What about you?"

"I loved baseball. Teenage rebellion included quitting the team, though. Part of me always wondered if I could have gone big. Pretty pathetic, I guess."

Green eyes focused on him and she smiled. A soft, sweet, Mona Lisa smile that left everything to the imagination and tied his gut in knots it'd take years to unravel.

"I suppose we all have those things in our life. The what-ifs we wonder about as we grow older."

He grinned. "Yeah, 'cause you're so old. What could you possibly have to regret?"

Just like that, the soft expression disappeared. Too damn late, he remembered her childhood. Man, he was the king of sticking his foot in his mouth.

"I didn't mean. . . I forgot." He winced.

With fluid grace, she rose from the chair and strolled to the window overlooking his backyard. "Nice pool. I've heard summers are hot around here, which will be nice after the long winter."

And there went any progress. "Grace, I know I've got a special talent for saying the wrong thing with women, and I'm sorry. What is going on with you today? You've been acting weird ever since we left your place this morning."

"Weird?" She didn't turn around.

"Yes, weird. Your sense of humor has fled and you're barely talking to me."

"Nothing is wrong with my sense of humor." When she did turn, he flinched. Her beautiful green eyes were cold enough to freeze the balls off a brass monkey. "I didn't realize your ego was so fragile that we had to speak every moment we were together. I apologize."

Fuck. What a disaster. He scrubbed a hand over his face then rubbed his neck, trying to ease some of the tension.

She edged toward the door. "I need to get home. We're not far. I'll walk. I need the exercise and time alone."

He opened his mouth to argue but snapped it shut. She needed time alone. Wasn't that code for she wanted away from his sorry ass as fast as humanly possible?

Giving him a wide birth, she made a beeline for the front door. Every swear word he knew pounded through his brain. He even made up a few for the occasion. They were pretty good. Maybe he should submit them to Websters for consideration.

186

*Fuck me.* He followed her down the hall. "You don't have to walk, sweetheart. I'm happy to drive you."

Grace laughed, but the sound lacked humor. "Please. I exercise every day. This'll be nothing. I'll enjoy it. Don't worry about it." She opened the door then faced him. "Thank you for breakfast. I'll see you tomorrow."

Thank you for breakfast? He'd fallen so far that after a weekend of incredible, mind-altering sex, she was thanking him for feeding her. He'd just go stand in front of a train now.

The door closed. His own freaking front door shut in his face. The urge to smash his fist into it grew until his fingers curled and he stuffed his hands into his pockets.

Tires squealed. A feminine scream raised all his body hair. Matt yanked the door open.

An old pickup sat cockeyed in the middle of the street, the engine running and the driver's side door hanging open. Looking up and down the street, his gut twisted. No sign of Grace. No sign of anybody. Shit.

"Grace!"

He jogged down the street and looked up and down both streets at the intersection. Nothing. Turning, he ran back to his house. As he approached, he glanced at the gate into his backyard. It was hanging open.

As quietly as possible, he edged past the gate. A bird exploded out of the bush beside him and he jerked back. Damn. He crept down the brick path alongside the house and paused at the side of the rear patio.

A flash of color disappeared around the far side of the house. Grace wasn't wearing plaid. Smiling grimly, he ran across the yard. There wasn't a gate on that side. Few people could vault a six-foot cedar privacy fence.

He cleared the corner in time to see a pair of ratty denim-clad legs and tennis shoes disappear over the top of the fence. Well, damn. He sprinted to the fence. A motor revved and he levered himself onto the fence. The idling truck peeled out.

Matt dropped back to the ground and doubled back. The people who'd owned the house before him had done a fantastic job landscaping. A wilderness of trees, bushes and boulders spread out, a little waterfall merrily splashing over rocks. Even though the trees hadn't leafed out yet, the mixture of plants created depth and fullness. There were a lot of hiding places. The guy might have found her. Hurt her.

No. He couldn't think like that.

"Grace?"

The breeze whispered through the trees. A car honked in the distance. Someone was grilling their Sunday lunch. He walked along the edge of the bushes, peering through the thick branches. The scent of rich soil filled his nose.

If he weren't such a thick-skulled dumb ass, this wouldn't have happened.

Some sort of evergreen shrub butted up against the fence. He didn't see how anybody could fit back there, but he checked anyway. There she sat, curled in a tight ball, her face pressed into her knees and her arms wrapped over the top of her head. Her position reminded him of the tornado drills he'd done in elementary school. Especially when she shivered and edged farther into the bush. The thing looked about as soft as a cactus.

Matt crouched down and rested his forearms on his knees. He wanted his arms around her so bad he ached, but her position screamed, *"Don't touch me."*

"Grace, sweetheart, it's Matt."

A shudder wracked her slender frame and she drew into a tighter ball. His heart clenched. Damn, she was killing him.

"Baby, come on out of there. The guy's gone. He drove off. You're safe."

She didn't move. Didn't utter a sound.

Screw it. Dropping to his knees in the damp mulch, he leaned forward, skimmed his hands down her arms to her elbows and tried to tug her forward.

A whimper rose from the neighborhood of her knees. "Please," she whispered. "Please, don't hurt me."

Shit. Just cut his heart out.

Hell if he knew how to fix this situation.

He edged around the bush where the landscaping opened a bit and sat down near her hip. The damp ground soaked his butt, but she had to be in a similar predicament. He stroked his thumb back and forth across her delicate wrist. Scratches streaked bright pink across the exposed skin of her forearms. After spending the weekend worshiping her incredible skin, he resented the hell out of anything marring its perfection. He tossed about for something to say. Anything. A distraction.

"I'm really sorry about what I said inside. Sometimes my mouth runs ahead of my brain. Not that I'm making excuses. I know life hasn't been a bed of roses for you. Well, I mean, I don't know, but I can try to imagine what it was like, going from one foster home to another. Never having any real stability in your life. The faces of the people who are supposed to love you and care for you changing constantly. I don't think I can imagine, honestly. It amazes me, humbles me, really, to see how you grew into this incredible woman." He shook his head. "Truly unbelievable, beautiful, strong, independent woman. You inspire respect in every single person who spends more than two minutes with you."

The muscles in her hand seemed to ease a bit, relaxing. He dared a little more and gently took her hand in his.

"Sure, I've achieved success in my business. I'm proud of what I've built. Personally, though, I'm pretty much a disaster. You picked up on that yesterday, so I'm sure it'll come as no surprise to hear I was engaged before."

She shifted a little and her head came up. Her eyes glistened with unshed tears. He damn near felt like weeping himself.

189

"It was the longest engagement on record. Leslie kept telling me she wanted to graduate from college before we got married. A few months before she graduated, I walked in on her practicing her reverse cowgirl position with some other guy. My father, to be specific."

"I'm sorry."

He shifted uncomfortably. Where had that story come from? He shared it with no one, and telling the woman he loved what a stupid moron he'd been in the past wasn't the brightest idea.

Grace crawled into his lap. This woman slayed him like nothing else. He didn't wait for an invitation to wrap his arms around her and hold on tight. Her head nestled beneath his chin, the scent of her shampoo and the evergreen bush mingling. The worry coiled in his gut eased.

"You always seem so capable." She fiddled with the buttons on his shirt. "Like you can handle everything and anything. I can't imagine you in that kind of situation. Did she break your heart?"

Matt wanted to deny it but hesitated. He took a moment to think, then grinned a little. "Ya know, I don't think so. It was almost a relief. The betrayal hurt, but what my dad did was worse. A few months later, I found out she'd been screwing my brother too. My parents divorced a few months later."

She smoothed her hand down his chest. "I'm sorry. You deserve so much more."

Feeling like a total loser, he shrugged. "I don't know about that."

She sat up, almost taking out his chin in the process. Her beautiful green eyes narrowed. "Listen up, Matthew Duncan. You are a highly intelligent, successful, sweet, wonderful man. Beneath the harsh exterior you present to the world is a heart of gold. You deserve a woman who will love you with all of her heart and soul. Who will think of you as her best friend, confidante, lover, soul mate, and the best thing that ever happened to her."

To his mortification, his cheeks got hot. A grown man of thirty-five did not blush. Not even when the woman he loved and adored complimented him in the most incredible way.

Okay, so he was blushing.

He ran his fingers along the petal-soft skin of her cheek, gently wove them in her hair, cupped the back of her head and kissed her with all of the love he couldn't contain. This woman tangled him up. Made him realize Leslie had done him an enormous favor.

He eased back and met her gaze. "Now, tell me what happened."

"Thank you for. . ." She lowered her gaze, long black lashes sweeping down to hide her eyes. ". . . for sitting on the wet ground with me. I was so scared. Out of my mind petrified, really."

"Anytime, sweetheart." He watched her carefully, hoping she didn't retreat again.

"I had just reached the sidewalk in front of your house when a truck flipped a U-turn, cutting off another car, and screeched to a stop in front of me. It startled me. Scared me. I glanced up and the driver was staring at me. His eyes. . . God, Matt. No one has ever looked at me like that before. Desire and hatred so hot it burned. So I ran. I knew he was coming after me. I knew I had to hide, because if he found me. . ." Grace shuddered and met his gaze. "Could we go inside? Could you just hold me for a while?"

Matt's heart clenched. "Whatever you want, baby."

He stood, scooped her into his arms and strode into the house. The way she nestled against him. . . If she hadn't already owned his heart, she would have stolen it in that moment.

# CHAPTER EIGHTEEN

Grace rolled over and glared at the blaring alarm clock. Going to work did not appeal, especially since she'd left Matt's house so late. Yawning, she buried her head under the pillow. Maybe she could play hooky. She was on intimate footing with the boss.

The noise got louder. If she was going to sleep in, which she wasn't, she should at least turn off the stupid alarm. She slapped the OFF button and slid out of bed, stumbling into the bathroom.

Thirty minutes later, she stood staring out her balcony doors and sipped the nectar of gods. Or coffee, as some people preferred to call it. The night had brought a heavy frost to coat everything in shimmering white.

A few joggers braved the path below. One glanced up, she could have sworn looking directly at her balcony, as he passed. She frowned. The guy seemed familiar. Puzzled, she headed into the kitchen to rinse out her cup.

Watching the black dregs of coffee swirl down the drain, it hit her. The man who'd offered her help on the Greenbelt on Saturday. No surprise there. A lot of people regularly jogged the Belt. Pretty creepy that he'd appeared to be looking at her place. She made a mental note to mention him to the police next time.

Ugh. She didn't want a next time.

Caffeine buzzing through her system, boosting her energy if not her mood, Grace jogged down the stairs to her car. She appreciated the fact that it still sat, undisturbed, in her parking space. She scooted in behind the wheel, buckled her seat belt and inserted her key into the ignition. A white square on her dashboard caught her gaze. Gooseflesh rose.

"Crap." She scanned her surroundings before reaching for the torn sheet of paper.

*I knew it'd only be a matter of time before you found another Sugar Daddy, skank.*
*Did he fuck you good and hard yesterday, slut?*
*I'm gonna have to work real hard to remind you you're nothing but a trailer trash tramp.*
*After I'm done with you,*
*I'm gonna slice his dick off for sticking it in you.*
*Next time you won't get away so easy, bitch.*

*Well.* She set the paper on the passenger seat with trembling fingers. *He's becoming downright wordy.* Nausea swept over her and the view through the windshield wavered.

Really, she'd been fine with the short and not-so-sweet notes. She rested her forehead against the steering wheel, breathed deeply through her nose, and pretended she was somewhere else. Like the Caribbean. Seated on the white beaches of Barbados, listening to waves against the shore and the wind in the palm trees overhead.

Knuckles rapped against her window and she jerked upright, her heart in her throat. Matt frowned down at her. "Open the door."

Pressing a hand to her racing heart, she climbed out of the car. "What are you doing here?"

"I told you I'd come by and pick you up this morning when you insisted on returning home last night. . . alone. Don't you remember?"

The wind blew a strand of hair across her cheek and he tucked the curls behind her ear. His touch went all the way down to her. . . Clearing her throat, she leaned back against her car.

"Guess my memory is going in my old age."

Matt quirked an eyebrow. "Yeah. Those gray hairs must be sucking the brain cells right out of your head." His gaze moved to the interior of her car. "Why were you just sitting there?"

"I was envisioning myself on a beach in Barbados."

"Really? You've been?"

"No, but I watch the travel channel. I've looked into going a few times, but it never seemed like much fun. Going alone, I mean." She stared at her toes peeking out from her open-toed heels. A pedicure might be in order. Bright pink, maybe. Or coral pink, like the inside of a seashell.

She sighed. Persistent as he was, he'd find out sooner or later. "I got another note."

Swearing, Matt tugged her into his arms, rubbing her back, cradling her against him. Yeah, that partially answered her question. He mumbled something into her hair and she lifted her head. Her heart ached just looking at him. Holy cherubs, he was gorgeous. Big and manly, staring down at her with warmth and concern, willing to protect her from all the ugliness in the world. Only, who was going to protect her heart from him?

Right there, standing in the parking lot in front of her condo with the chilly morning breeze ruffling her hair, a scary note lying on her seat and her nose full of his cologne, she admitted it. To herself, anyway. Matt had used a wrecking ball on her protective walls and dug his way right into her heart. She slid her arms around his waist and fisted the back of his shirt. A tremor swept through her, and he pulled her more firmly against him, no doubt thinking it was a shiver of fear. All she could do now was hold on for dear life and wait. Wait to find out how badly she would be torn up when he left.

Grace wanted to scream and shake her fists, but it was pointless. *"Tis better to have loved and lost, than never to have loved at all."* Ha. Tennyson didn't know diddly-squat. What a crock of ground-up dandelion petals.

194

"What did it say?"

Huh? Everyone knew what Tennyson. . . Oh. Right.

She shuddered. "It's on the passenger seat."

Matt rounded the car and opened the passenger door. He tilted his head, lips flat-lining as he read the note. A muscle leaping in his jaw, he straightened and slammed the door shut.

"Well, I suppose we'd better call Detective Harrison."

"Yeah." Grace glanced at her watch. "We'll be late."

He pulled out his cell phone and started dialing. Well, he was the boss. What difference did it make if they were late for work? She wrapped her arms around her waist. Work provided a welcome distraction from the psycho haunting her life, so there was that.

"I *am* the boss."

She stared. Weird. It was like he'd read her mind.

"What?"

She parted her lips to answer, but he held up a finger and started talking into the phone.

What a spectacularly miserable day. Grace collapsed on the couch and glared at her television. All day, her co-workers had given her a wide berth. She'd been glared at and gossiped about, repeat narrow-eyed glances thrown in her direction. It had been difficult to resist punching them. Or sticking her tongue out.

They were totally overreacting.

So what if she'd walked in half an hour late with the boss? It wasn't like he'd bent her backward over the nearest desk, stuck his tongue down her throat and his hand up her skirt. She shifted and crossed her legs. Matt was turning her into some horny freak of nature if that turned her on. Which it did.

Pushing to her feet, she stomped into the kitchen and flung open the refrigerator. Flipping thorny rose bushes. She never had gone grocery shopping, and lasagna with a side of mold wasn't appealing. Heaving a sigh, she grabbed the bottle of soft red wine and slammed the door shut. Wine was made from grapes, there-fore it was a fruit and totally counted as real food.

Besides, she'd worked there for months. If she'd slept her way into the position, wouldn't that little tidbit have emerged sooner? Did people think they were having sex in the restroom and supply closet all this time? Although, the supply closet had a comfy stack of toilet paper. She shook her head.

*Wow. Obsessed much, Grace?*

Okay, so they'd had amazing sex. Complete with mind-blowing orgasms. Multiple ones. Didn't explain the preoccupation she'd developed in the past seventy-two hours. It could be Matt and not just the sex.

Her doorbell rang and she hurried across the condo, eager for a distraction. Detective Harrison stood on the other side of her peephole. Hope surged. Maybe they'd caught the guy. She opened the door.

"Detective Harrison. Hi."

"May I come in for a few minutes?"

"Uh, sure. Yeah." She gestured him inside, shifting her shoulders in an attempt to ease the tension. "Can I get you anything to drink?" Grace held up her wineglass. "Some wine, maybe?"

Chuckling, he sat on her couch. "No thanks. I'm on the clock."

"Right. They probably frown on that."

"Yeah, just a little."

Silence settled like a thick wet blanket. The detective stared at her until she wanted to check for stains on her blouse or large hairy warts on her nose.

"Oh." He flushed. "Uh, the reason I'm here. You're probably wondering."

"Yes."

"The guy you've noticed on the Greenbelt, have you seen him again?"

"No, but I just got home."

He pulled a slim portfolio from his jacket. "Good. I brought some pictures along, if you wouldn't mind looking through them. I thought your home would be more comfortable than the station."

That was sweet. "Thank you."

He handed over the album and she flipped through the pictures, staring at each face for a few seconds. The quiet of the room seeped into her. She sipped her wine.

The pictures were creepy. Not men she wanted to meet on a well-lit day in the middle of Boise Towne Square, let alone the Greenbelt. Around the middle of the book, she stopped. "This guy. I'm positive he's the one."

She stretched across the coffee table to hand Detective Harrison the album while pointing to the photo. His lips thinned.

"This is a private detective. He's quite well-known around the station. Name's Gunner. We've never had a problem with him."

Her shoulders sagged. Didn't seem like such a good lead after all.

Rising from the couch, he tucked the picture into his jacket pocket. "I'll get in touch with him and find out what's going on. I promise I'll call as soon as I know something, Miss Debry."

She started to insist he call her Grace then met his blue eyes— just as his gaze rose from her chest. Maybe not. "Thank you. I appreciate it."

*Buh-bye now. Have a nice day. Don't let the door smack you on the ass on the way out.*

Something must've shown in her expression. Detective Harrison flushed and bolted out the door.

"Hey, Grace, we still on for the concert in a few days?"

Luke rested his shoulder against her doorjamb. "I know it'd be wild and crazy, but have you ever considered coming *inside* my office? You could have a seat. We could visit like normal people."

He stepped in and glanced out her window, his eyelid twitching.

Grace followed his gaze. Nothing but a few other buildings and trees that had exploded in buds over the weekend. She frowned at him. Maybe he was afraid of heights, though that seemed illogical given how badly he wanted her office.

Seated on the very edge of the chair nearest the door, he leaned forward and rested his elbows on his knees. "I just wanted to iron out the details for Friday night. Plus, I wasn't sure you'd still want to go since you're seeing Mr. Duncan and all."

"Of course I still want to go. Just because I'm dating someone doesn't mean I can't have friends. How about you pick me up at my place?"

"Yeah, sure." Luke jumped up. Sweat beaded on his forehead. He turned and headed out the door. Five seconds later he reappeared. "I'll be there at seven-thirty. I like to get there a little early."

"Okay. I'm looking forward to it. Should be fun." She smiled and Luke disappeared.

Her phone rang.

"Hey, Grace. Could you step into my office for a moment, please?"

"Sure. I'll be just a sec." Hanging up, she headed down the hall and knocked on Matt's office door. The irony of the situation didn't escape her. Not long ago, she'd stood there in petrified hesitation of her boss. Now, eager anticipation coiled in her belly and she smiled at Nancy.

Matt opened the door and gestured her in, his eyes warming as they skimmed down her body like a physical caress. He closed the door. She slipped her arms up around his neck and kissed him. The simple feeling of his arms wrapping around her, pulling her tight against him and his mouth on hers sent desire spiraling down to curl her toes.

He broke the kiss and smiled. "Not that I'm complaining—"

"I should hope not."

"This isn't why I asked you in here." Snagging her hand, he

pulled her to the chairs facing the windows. The scent of rich coffee filled his office and two full cups sat on the little table. The coffee in front of the chair he steered her into was the color of caramel. He'd prepared her coffee just as she liked. Another piece of her heart sheared off, one she could ill-afford to lose.

"I wanted to talk about the notes you've been getting and the guy you've seen a few times."

Grace frowned. "Why do we need to do it again? And at work?" Where she could try, or at least pretend, to forget about it.

"Because it's more important than scheduling the electrician before the drywaller. I had an idea I wanted to go over with you."

"Okay."

"The incidents seem related to your past somehow. So. . ." He hesitated and fiddled with his shirt cuffs, not meeting her gaze— very un-Matt like. Her stomach coiled tight.

Matt cleared his throat. "I contacted the Indiana Social Services and got a list of the people who fostered you. I thought we could see if we can pinpoint any likely suspects. Or at the very least discover a mobile home somewhere amongst them."

Grace sat, stunned mute. The nerve. Digging into her life, always pushing and prodding and sticking his nose where it didn't belong. His bossy domineering ways were too much.

Matt leaned forward and lifted her hand from her lap, holding it between his own. "Please don't be upset with me, Grace. We have to figure this out before it's too late. It would kill me if anything happened to you."

Some of her anger fled. Staring into his eyes, she couldn't decide if the emotion there terrified or exhilarated her. "You had no right."

"I'm sorry, sweetheart. My first concern is your safety."

The rest of her irritation dissipated on a sigh. She was being stubborn and stupid. So what if he had the entirety of her sad little childhood in a manila folder? Whoop-de-doo. "May I see them?"

"Of course." He rose and returned only a moment later with a black file folder. Inside, a modest stack of papers held the details of her youth. She flipped through them. Most of the early names meant nothing to her. She'd been too young.

"I don't suppose you have a map of Indiana? And Kentucky, apparently."

"As a matter of fact. . ." Matt again hopped up. Returning, he spread a full-sized map of Indiana across the floor. Then Kentucky. He held a yellow highlighter and glanced up at her expectantly.

"Oh." Her gaze dropped to the papers.

They spent the next hour locating every miniscule town and big city she'd ever lived in. The painstaking process only illuminated how many places she'd been shuffled through. Twelve homes in as many years, following a convoluted route from Henderson, Kentucky to LaPorte, Indiana. Grace's throat tightened painfully as she stared at the yellow circles on the map. So many.

The foster families must have found her to be an extremely difficult child. She swallowed the lump in her throat and fought the tears burning her eyes. Common sense told her the foster-care system and not the families were responsible for all the moves. Her heart remained convinced that she was unlovable.

Matt's hand covered hers. A tear escaped to trickle down her cheek, to her mortification. *No point in feeling sorry for yourself, Gracie. Suck it up.*

He wiped away her tear with his thumb. "You must have been a beautiful child. I can't imagine how difficult it was for these families to give you up. The case worker I spoke with was very friendly and helpful, right up until I asked why you were transferred so many times. She clicked away at a computer. When she came back on the line her helpfulness had died an abrupt death. According to her, the details of your case are sealed. I was lucky she'd already sent the locations, otherwise I would've gotten nothing."

Grace's brain kicked into gear. "Odd. Why would it be confidential? My parents are dead. I have no relatives. Who would care?"

"I agree." He tapped a finger to the maps. "I also find this route interesting. You traveled farther and farther away from Kentucky."

"What makes you think that isn't just coincidence?"

Matt shrugged. "Instinct. You might be able to find out more than I did from the caseworker, though I imagine she'd want some proof of your identity. In the meantime, I'm going to hand off these names and addresses to the guy who does my background checks, along with the dates. I'll put a rush on it, have him specifically search for people who lived in mobile homes at the time."

Matt lounged casually on the floor, oozing raw masculinity. She couldn't help remembering the times his arms had been wrapped around her. The way she felt when he held her so tenderly. So protectively. She glanced away and crossed her arms tightly. She stood and paced the length of the office. "May I use your phone?"

"You want to call the caseworker, I take it."

Matt stood in a fluid display of masculine power that actually made drool pool in her mouth. He brushed past and her nostrils flared. Holy cow, his cologne did things to her. Down, girl. She needed a distraction from emotional overload, but she needed to get a grip even more.

Matt spun and bent her back over his arm. A flash of intent in his brown eyes and then his mouth was on hers. Rational thought fled. She moaned into his mouth and wrapped her arms around his neck, returning every ounce of the passion he fed her.

The things he did to her, the way he made her feel. . . that couldn't be an everyday sort of thing. He was special. The connection they shared was special. Chest hot and heavy, a piece of her resistance melted.

Matt lifted her, aligning their bodies in perfection and another little piece puddled at Grace's feet. Still the kiss went on, breath mingling, desire burning hotter with each stroke of his tongue. She curled his hair around her fingers, clinging to the soft strands and the hard muscles of his shoulders, desperate for an anchor.

Dread burned, hotter than their passion, snapping her into awareness. Enrique Iglesias' "Do You Know?" played in the background. She ripped her mouth from his and stared into his rich-brown eyes. Dear God, she knew all too well. Despair flashed, followed by panic. She pulled free of his arms and paced away.

What was she thinking? Like falling in love with him would make him stay, when everyone else left. She wrapped her arms tight around her middle. Stupid, stupid little fool.

Matt's hand brushed lightly over her bottom. "You shouldn't look at me like that if you expect me to behave, sweetheart."

Acid bubbled in her stomach, curdling everything in its path. Yep, she'd screwed up big time. In love. With her boss. "Do You Know?" started playing again.

*Duh, Grace. Your phone.*

The heat of Matt's body behind her seeped through her clothes as she pulled her phone out of her pocket.

"Interesting ringtone."

She flicked her thumb across her cell to accept the call. "Grace Debry."

"Miss Debry, this is Detective Harrison. Your neighbor called in a report of an intruder. I'm standing in your condo. You need to get over here."

# CHAPTER NINETEEN

Sheriff John Sanford leaned against a big tree, enjoying the cool breeze coming off the river. He couldn't say the same for the view. The action on the third level of Grace's condominium complex held his undivided attention. CSI in their booties and hairnets had just arrived, sending the uniformed police officers scurrying out the doorway like rats before an exterminator.

He shifted against the bark. Be nice to have CSI guys back home, but small towns didn't have the budget for high-tech stuff—or the crimes to make it necessary. Handing out traffic tickets and dealing with drunks and domestic disputes about covered the extent of his job most days. There was that time a few years back when old Frank managed to accidentally shoot himself and his best hunting dog while chasing coyotes off his farm. That had been a sight, coming up on the sixty-three-year-old man sobbing over his dead dog. Never mind the blood pouring out of his leg, soaking the fertile field under him. All he'd cared about was the dog.

"Reminiscing?" Gunner rumbled from behind him, damn near stopping his heart.

"Shouldn't sneak up on me like that. You could kill me. I'm not as young as I used to be."

"You're too tough for that."

Sanford ignored his chuckle.

Gunner notched his chin at the condo. "Heard she had another break-in. There's the little lady now, love-sick boss in tow."

The curly haired beauty emerged in the open hallway on the first level and Sanford's chest tightened, barely noticing the big man hovering protectively. Pale and obviously shaken, she still carried herself with poise and confidence. There was a vast difference between knowing she resembled her mother and seeing the similarity in person. From a distance, the way she moved and flipped her hair back over her shoulder, she could have been Cassandra Sathers.

The back of his neck tingled and he tore his gaze from Grace. Matthew Duncan stood at the bottom of the stairs, his arm hooked around Grace's waist, holding her in place. She twisted around, a frown pulling at her delicate brows. Her lips moved.

Sanford would bet his bottom dollar she was giving him hell. Would've amused him, if Duncan weren't staring at him with narrowed eyes. By the set of his shoulders, he wouldn't hesitate to confront him. Sanford figured the only thing stopping him was concern for the fiery woman glaring daggers up at him.

Matt Duncan climbed a few notches in his estimation when he followed Grace up the stairs, keeping a close eye on him and Gunner all the way. He knew Duncan would be down those steps again as soon as he'd deposited her into the police department's safe keeping.

"Time to move. Nothing to see here anyway."

Around a bend in the Greenbelt, he glanced at Gunner. Damn, he was a big sucker. "Wanna explain how you missed seeing Deke get in her place?"

Gunner shrugged, as concerned as if he'd been caught pissing off the riverbank. *"It's all nature,"* he'd say with the same shrug. "Hell if I know. Must be losing my touch. I s'pose it could've been the blonde with big tits trying to bounce free and superb ass that jogged past. I was hard-pressed to remember my own name."

Gunner's eyes glazed over and he grinned, the randy old pervert. The woman was probably young enough to be his daughter. A sting of irritation hummed down Sanford's spine. He shrugged it off. Wouldn't do any good anyway.

Gunner shook his head. "If there'd been women around like that when we were young and stupid, there'd be a lot more little Gunners running around. I can't help wishing they'd dressed like that when I could've enjoyed the view without feeling like a dirty old fart."

Despite the fine thread of tension pulled taut inside his gut, Sanford snorted a laugh. What was the world coming to when he and Gunner had the same thought?

"Gunner, you are a dirty old fart."

Gunner grinned and clapped his shoulder, almost sending him face-first into the blacktop. "Yep. Deke must've gotten sly after all these years, slipping in sneaky as a ferret after a nest of eggs. Maybe he suspects he didn't do a good enough job finishing you off last week. All he'd have to do is drive by and see your Jeep's gone to know you hightailed it outta there."

"Maybe." They followed a few more curves in the path. "What's he after with all this?"

"Now you're trying to apply rational thought to a man who's never suffered that affliction." Gunner's hand landed heavily on Sanford's shoulder again. "That way lies madness, my friend. He's screwing with her, messing with her mind. Not so sure about this last move, though. Could be he's royally pissed because she spent the weekend with Lover Boy."

Yeah, made sense. Deke no doubt thought of Grace as his personal property. Her screwing around with some other guy would push him over the edge. According to Detective Harrison, with whom he'd had a long chat after Grace ID'd Gunner, this was the third incident in as many days but by far the most violent. At least he hadn't laid a hand on Grace. Yet.

They started across the park grass toward the parking lot. An engine roared to life. An old pickup idled forward. Sanford narrowed his eyes and nudged Gunner.

"I see him." Gunner whipped out a huge handgun.

The engine roared. The pickup jumped the curb and Gunner fired. The engine made an odd sound as the shot went into the truck's grill. Gunner widened his stance and steadied his arm for another shot as the truck barreled toward them.

*****

Matt's shoes hit the Greenbelt blacktop alongside Detective Harrison. He glanced back. Grace leaned against the third-floor railing, arguing with a uniformed officer.

"How long do you think she'll stay put?"

Harrison shrugged. "I doubt the guy's anywhere close. Not with so many police around. Besides, he did a pretty thorough job trashing her condo. Guy's like him are cowards at heart—"

Distant gunshots cut him off. Harrison turned, staring down the path toward Ann Morrison Park.

"Course, I could be wrong." Harrison pulled out his cell phone.

While the detective chatted on the phone, Matt ran. Around the bend and under the overpass, the park spread out before him. A beat-up old pickup, the same one that'd idled in the street outside his house days ago, tore across the grass.

In a manic version of an old spaghetti Western, two men faced off with the pickup. The bigger guy aimed the business end of a huge-ass handgun at the truck. He wished him luck shooting the freak dead and ridding them all of a nasty problem. The men would be roadkill if he didn't pull the trigger soon.

The gun jerked and a boom rolled across the grass. Glass shattered.

What the hell was he shooting, an elephant gun?

The big man leveled his gun again. The truck veered sharply to the left, minus its windshield and passed the men. Another shot shattered the back window. The truck jumped the curb and

206

careened around a corner into traffic—driver obviously alive and breathing. Guy must have the reflexes of a cat.

Tire tracks in the grass showed how close the men had come to becoming hood ornaments. They stood talking, heads together, nonchalant as could be. Two geese glided down to land. Frantic crying of frightened children from the playground contrasted with the gentle rush of the river.

He narrowed his eyes against the bright sunshine. The men were the same two who'd been standing near the river outside Grace's condo. Pay dirt.

Jumping the guard rail, he jogged across the grass. Matt's first good look at the big guy's craggy mug almost made him turn around. The elephant gun disappeared and both men crossed their arms, watching him. The wail of sirens announced the arrival of squad cars.

"You guys okay?"

"Looks that way," the shorter one said.

Near Matt's height, he had sterling gray hair cropped short. His bearing echoed that of Detective Harrison. Matt looked between the two, glanced at the police officers cautiously climbing from their cars, and abruptly ran out of patience.

"Why were you hanging around outside the condos?"

Buzz-cut cocked his head. "We know someone who lives there."

Great. Innocuous answers were the order of the day. More police cars pulled into the park and spilled uniforms across the grass. Matt focused on the bigger guy.

"Why didn't you go say hi instead of hovering in the trees?"

The guy revealed a single gold tooth amidst a startling white grin. "We weren't sure of our welcome. You know how moody women can be. 'Sides, we're kinda shy."

His gravelly voice grated over Matt's nerves nearly as much as the evasiveness. Detective Harrison jogged over and shook hands with both men.

"You okay?" Genuine concern colored his voice. Matt's eyebrows rose.

"Right as rain," the big guy said. "Sorry about the lawn."

Harrison patted his arm, a move Matt wouldn't try even if he were best buddies with the guy. "Not your fault, man."

In unison, all three looked at him. Matt crossed his arms and smiled his coldest smile. No way in hell were they excluding him. He wanted to know what was going on and who they were.

Two minutes later, Matt climbed back over the guard rail, a puppy trailing home with his tail tucked between his legs. He hadn't learned a freaking thing about those men and why they were watching Grace's condo. Harrison's reassurances didn't mean squat.

Under the bridge, he ran into Grace. Literally. He automatically closed his arms around her when she smacked into his chest then didn't let go.

"What are you doing out here alone?"

Blazing green eyes met his. "This is public property last time I checked and I'm free to roam at will. What are you doing out here?"

Okay. She was pissed.

"What kind of utter moron runs toward gunfire?" She shoved him away.

Matt eyed her cautiously.

Her hands fisted. "Anyone with half a brain avoids that kind of scene, but not you. No, you have to get up close and personal."

He bit back a smile. She was adorable furious and her concern warmed him. Even when she punched him in the upper arm. He threw out an "*Ow*" for good measure. Apparently unsatisfied, she shoved him into the fence running alongside the walkway to keep innocent executives out of the river.

"What the hell were you thinking?"

He opened his mouth, but she kept going.

"You could have been shot. A bullet could have ricocheted or. . ." She waved both hands wildly. ". . . something."

He fought it, really he did, but his lips must have twitched because her eyes narrowed dangerously.

"Sweetheart," he reached for her. "I was never in any danger."

Smacking his hands away, she stepped closer, shaking her finger in his face. "Don't touch me, you insensitive jerk. How do you know you were never in danger? You're good at predicting the possible trajectories of a bullet? Oh, let me guess. You moonlight with the FBI and you were the only man in the vicinity who had a prayer of diffusing the situation."

Matt crossed his arms, settling in to appreciate the view while she worked the fear out of her system. She stood inches away, up on her toes, voice so low and furious he could barely hear her over the spring-thaw swollen river at his back. The deep green of her eyes and the dark rose along her cheeks reminded him of how she looked right before she came.

"Not exactly." Desire roughened his voice.

"Not exactly." She spun away, stomping to the other side of the path, and his gaze dropped to admire her butt. "Yet you charged off without the slightest regard for your safety. Why, Matt?"

The wild fall of her hair was at odds with the tense set of her shoulders. Sighing, he scrubbed a hand over his face. Worry had driven her out of the safety of her police-infused condo. Fear held her lush curves rigid. As much as he loved knowing she cared so much, his intent hadn't been to upset her.

"I'm sorry I scared you. I'm desperate to stop the guy before this gets worse. Before he manages to get his hands on you or hurts you in any way."

She didn't move. "What about you?"

"Huh?"

"How am I supposed to feel if something happens to you? If you get hurt? He's already threatened you."

No longer willing to stand the separation, Matt closed the distance. He wrapped his arms around her and pressed a kiss to her temple. "Sweetheart," he whispered, "he's not after me. He's just trying to scare me off. He won't succeed. Wanna know why?"

Her breath hitched.

She ripped free of his arms. "You don't get it, do you? You're not safe around me!"

"Grace. . ." He reached for her, but she spun out of reach.

"No. Stay away from me." Tear-filled eyes gone wide and fingers covering her trembling lips, she stared at him. "Stay away from me. I don't want to see you anymore, Matt."

She turned and ran back toward her condo. Her soft, high sob echoed beneath the concrete overpass long after she'd disappeared.

After five minutes of moping and licking his wounds, Matt surrendered to the inevitable and followed Grace. Pride mingled with the sting of her rejection. Even knowing why she'd done it didn't block the hurt. Part of him expected her rejection—the pathetic part thoroughly stomped into the ground by his ex-fiancée.

The non-pathetic part celebrated the fact she cared enough to kick him to the curb. Not that he intended to let her. What kind of man cowered under his bed and let his woman face some psycho freak alone? A eunuch maybe.

When he arrived at her condo, the CSI team was clearing out. Grace stood in her bedroom, arms crossed and tension radiating from her frame. It should've taken a tornado to create such a mess. She looked so small. Isolated amidst the chaos. Tracks of tears trailed down her pale cheeks. No wonder some of the CSI guys shot him curl-up-and-die looks in passing.

Without a word, he wrapped his arms around her. She buried her face against him and sniffled into his oxford. Effortless, the way she wrapped him around her little pinky finger. A fact that should scare him spitless. And it would, just as soon as he managed to get off the high of being with her. Fifty or sixty years might do it.

"Shhh," he smoothed his hand down her silky curls. Her shoulders trembled and he wanted to kill the bastard. Fitting her curves snugly against him, he patted her bottom and cradled her head. "I'll help you salvage what you can of this."

He doubted much was left. Everything was pretty much shredded. Even her mattress was slashed. Something he resented, having spent some glorious hours buried inside Grace on top of that mattress. He rubbed her bottom, hugging her tight, longing to shelter her from her surroundings.

Detective Harrison stuck his head in the door and Matt debated doing the idiot bodily harm. The guy's gaze focused on the spot where his hand cradled her luscious bottom. A growl built at the back of his throat. Harrison had no business looking at Grace's butt.

"Excuse me." The detective lounged against the doorway.

Grace jerked away. Matt fisted his hands and stuffed them in his pockets. From the smirk on Harrison's face, he knew it too. Dislike swirled hot, growing when embarrassment pinked Grace's face.

She cleared her throat and tucked her hair behind her right ear. "What can I do for you?"

"We're done here. If you need any help with the mess—"

"No." She flashed a brief smile, her blush deepening. "I'm fine. You've done enough. Thank you."

The increased level of her discomfort raised Matt's hackles. He glared at Harrison. The detective smirked. Oh, hell no. Hands coming out of his pockets, he stepped forward.

Smirk gone, Harrison straightened. "Well, I'm off." He bolted.

Three minutes too late, by Matt's estimation. Grace picked up a scrap of light pink. Layer upon layer of strips dangled from her fingers.

"This used to be my favorite sweater."

He grimaced. "I'm sorry, sweetheart. We can buy another one. As a matter of fact, let's head out. We can pick up whatever you need for the rest of the week."

211

"But. . ." She looked around, then her shoulders sagged. "I'm pretty sure there's no point in sorting through this. It's obvious nothing is salvageable. Why do you keep saying 'we'?"

"Because it wouldn't make much sense to drive all over the place separately. Or safe, considering what this lunatic did today. We can leave your car in the garage at my place while we're gone. I don't mind parking in the driveway."

"Parking in the driveway," Grace echoed softly.

He frowned. "Yeah. I don't mind. No big deal. I know how fond you are of your car, how hard you worked to save up for it and all."

"I'm not staying at your house, Matt."

"Why not? I can protect you there. You'll be safe. And I. . ." Damn, it was hard to lay it on the line. "I want to be with you. I want you there. I really. . . care about you."

*Chicken shit.*

She snorted. "I 'care' about you too. Which is why there is no way on God's green earth I am moving into your house." She kicked a pile of clothes near her bathroom. "Bring this mess down around your ears? I don't think so."

Bending down, she hooked her finger in something. When she rose, what had been a bra swayed from her hand. The underwires were snapped and the fragile lace torn. Grace tossed the bra over her shoulder then peered around the doorframe into her bathroom and sucked in a sharp breath.

He crossed the room and looked over her shoulder.

Her toilet seat lay in pieces on the floor. Glittering shards on the porcelain tiles were all that was left of the glass shower door. The mirror over the sink hung drunkenly from one broken hook. Toiletries and broken makeup containers were scattered amidst the shattered glass and broken shards. His jaw dropped.

Across the wall, written in what looked like lipstick, were the words "TRAILER TRASH TRAMP."

The asshole was entirely too hung up on that phrase. Matt

needed to call his background guy. He'd call him when they got to his place. Grace would be staying with him, if he had to tie her up and toss her in the backseat of his truck.

## CHAPTER TWENTY

Grace winced, gently shutting and locking the door behind Matt. That was not a happy man. Once he'd realized he wouldn't be able to talk her into staying with him, his mouth had hardened into a thin line. He'd insisted on following her to The Hampton Inn.

The poor clerk who'd checked her in had cast nervous glances at Matt. When he slapped his credit card onto the counter, the young guy jumped and knocked over a stack of newspapers. Matt had glowered and cocked an eyebrow. She'd wisely kept her mouth shut.

Sighing, she walked over to the window, crossing her arms. No luggage meant nothing to unpack and put away for her indeterminate stay. A depressing thought.

She scowled at the light-mustard-yellow walls and flung herself onto the bed. Not a color she would have chosen. She tilted her head back. The deep-red accent wall was a nice touch. She'd have to remember that for her next place. Another depressing thought.

She rolled over and buried her face in the bedding with a groan. At least she still had a job. A job where she'd thrown caution to the wind and fallen in love with her Type-A, anal-retentive, bossy boss.

A loud bang woke her. Stupid motels and their thin walls. She rolled over, rubbing her eyes and smearing her makeup. Sweet dandelion blood.

Someone pounded on her door. Great. Her day wouldn't have been complete without greeting someone at the door sporting raccoon eyes.

She pressed a bleary eye to the peephole. Matt paced in the hallway. His mouth was tight. Little lines fanned out from his eyes and his hair was tousled. She sighed and flung the door open. Let him savor her messy I-was-sleeping-you-woke-me-and-now-my-makeup-is-smeared-you-big-jerk look.

Minus the barrier, a large portion of her irritation fled. He'd changed into a black V-neck tee and black jeans, both of which showed off muscles she'd licked. He also sported a sexy-as- heaven five-o'clock shadow and a frown that would've intimidated her back when he was just her boss. She was contemplating the merits of jumping him right there in the hallway when a mouth-watering smell distracted her.

He held bulging plastic bags. Surely those weren't all food?

"Can I come in?" His raspy request set off her lusting hormones all over again. If he played nice, she might let him.

Oh, who was she kidding? If he growled all sexy one more time, they'd both be coming a.s.a.p.

Twining her fingers together behind her back so she'd behave, she held the door open. A whiff of her favorite man cologne—him—as he passed, pebbled her nipples. Man, was she a sorry case.

"I brought dinner." He headed for the desk and she closed the door. "I also stopped off at the mall." His voice dropped an octave.

"That had to be the most stressful experience of my life. Including playing second fiddle to my brother's dog when he got married. I had to guess at your sizes. The women at the makeup counter must have seen me coming a mile away, because the quantity of items they insisted were absolutely necessary is mind-boggling."

One bag he sat on the desk, the rest he turned and deposited along the length of the small coffee table. A few wound up on

215

the floor. A gorgeous pale-pink confection spilled out, distracting her slavering lust-buds.

Gnawing on the inside of her cheek, she held it up. Shimmery pearl buttons and a wide cowl-neck. The sensuous softness of the cashmere sweater almost brought her to orgasm. Never in a million years could she afford something like this.

The tweed skirt beneath caught her eye. Shot with blue, green and pink on a background of soft charcoal gray, it would be beautiful with the sweater. She also found a gray-silk scarf, tights, and dark-gray low-heeled leather shoes. A pair of silver earrings with a dainty cluster of multi-colored glass beads and a long matching necklace and bracelet were wrapped in tissue paper.

Clutching the clothes to her chest, she plopped down on the couch and stared at Matt. The fine lines of tension had left his face. He leaned against the dresser, arms crossed, watching her with a slight smile playing around the corners of his lips.

Tears stung her eyes. "You didn't have to do this. They're too expensive. But so beautiful. I love them. You're so sweet." She was blubbering like an idiot. "I can't accept them. I would never be able to pay you back."

He shifted a bag aside to kneel beside her. Prying a shoe and a fistful of cashmere from her fingers, he wrapped her hand in both of his. Her stomach churned.

"Sweetheart, it's a gift. I don't want you to pay me back. If I can do anything to make this insanity even a little easier for you, I will. I don't care if that means buying you clothes or a dish of ice cream or just holding you. I'll gladly do it."

"But—"

"Grace." His fingers tightened around hers, bringing her gaze—which had strayed to the other bags—back to his. "Please. Please, allow me to do this for you."

Two pleases in a row. She reluctantly nodded.

Dropping a kiss on her lips, he rose and went to the desk,

where he started pulling out containers of delicious-smelling food. Her stomach rumbled, but the bags called.

Each bag was similar to the first, with an entire outfit inside. A bottle of her perfume was tucked in amidst the clothes of one. The last bag held piles of sheer-and-lace panties with matching bras, a half-slip and a full-slip, along with several nightgowns and a robe that would have given her old one a run for its money in indecency. Glancing at the sizes, she knew they'd fit. She also knew they suited his taste. Scarily enough, they fit her taste as well.

"I'll admit I didn't hate the lingerie store nearly as much as the others."

"No?" She smiled. "Why ever not?"

"I pictured you in each piece."

He stepped away from the desk, revealing a romantic dinner for two. A small vase held a miniature arrangement of rosebuds and two taper candles flickered in the middle of the plastic place settings. Sweet heaven, if he accepted defeat this gracefully, how did he respond to success?

He held out his hand to help her up. Carefully depositing her lapful of lingerie back in the bag, she accepted his hand. The brush of calluses across her palm made her shiver. He seated her in the office chair with a frown, then sat across from her.

"I'm sorry if my hands bother you. I know they're rough from helping out around the jobsite and must feel like a cheese grater against your soft skin. I'll start wearing gloves at work."

"Don't you dare." Her cheeks warmed. "I like your hands just the way they are."

"Are you sure?"

"Yes." *Please, please, please don't make me explain.*

"Because really, it wouldn't be a big deal to wear gloves. I don't want to hurt you."

Angelic cherubs above, he was making her explain. Cheeks heating, she met his gaze. "I like the way your hands feel against

217

my skin. I love the roughness. In college, I went on a few dates with a man whose hands were softer than mine. It was not appealing."

Matt grinned. "If you're sure."

"I'm sure."

"I wouldn't want you to—"

"Matt, I'm sure. Where did you get this food? It smells really good. Looks good too."

Chuckling, he lifted something off the floor. Her favorite wine. He was seriously observant. Knowing he not only saw but remembered so much about her affected her far more than she expected.

"I stopped at a little family-run bistro on the way here." With the flourish of an experienced waiter, he poured the wine into the tiny glasses the hotel provided. She arched her brow and he shrugged. "I waited tables at a nice restaurant during college. Helped pay my way. They closed about five years ago."

"They probably suffered a steady decline in business once the women no longer had you to drool over."

He snorted. "Yeah, I'm sure that's it."

His muscles flexed as he poured the second glass. A tiny bit of drool may have formed as she watched him. Imagining feathering kisses along his strong biceps, across his shoulders to his neck, down well-defined pecs. . . she sighed.

Color splashed across his cheeks, brown eyes glittered at her beneath heavy lids, and a muscle ticked in his jaw.

"Grace." His voice lowered, hitting the octave that never failed to make her happy parts sit up and pay attention. "If you keep looking at me like that, I promise you, not a bite of this food will pass your lips. Which would be a shame, because it's excellent."

Sucking her lower lip into her mouth, she looked from the food to Matt. Her stomach growled loudly. The corner of his mouth kicked up and his dimple made an appearance. She whimpered.

"Eat your food, sweetheart."

Her heart melted. She quickly dropped her gaze to her food. What would it be like to look at him across the table every night? To know he'd be there to cradle her in his arms as she drifted to sleep? For him to be hers and her to be his, forever and forever, till death parted them?

She tried to shake the foolish fantasy.

Brush it aside.

Shrug it off.

The images clung with relentless tenacity.

Grace closed the bathroom door, one of the sheer nightgowns Matt bought draped over her arm. Back pressed to the door, she dropped her head back and stared at the ceiling. The noose tightened every time she was with him. She slid to the floor and rested her forehead on her bent knees.

It was going to kill her when he left. Her foster mother's death had been the worst to date, but Matt's absence. . . Just thinking about it closed her throat and made her hurt. Everywhere. A hot tear dripped off the tip of her nose. She needed time to compose herself before she facing him.

Halfway through dinner she had noticed the black duffle bag sitting in the middle of the white comforter. Matt explained that if she was staying there, he'd stay with her. His calmness had killed any argument before she even voiced it. Drat the man. Sharing a space with him like they were a real couple made it impossible to keep any portion of her heart safe—if she hadn't already surrendered every nook and cranny.

A hot bath would help. Lots of steam to clear her mind and heat to relax her muscles. Then she'd climb into bed with all the romantic sweetness wrapped in sinew and bulging muscle and let him sweep her away. Just the thought sent a shiver of desire racing down her belly.

"Matt, I'm going to take a bath."

"Take your time, babe," was his muffled response.

Fifteen steamy minutes later she couldn't take it. The steam had cleared nothing and the heat had relaxed nothing. Everything was wound tight in anticipation.

She dried off and dropped the filmy nightgown over her head, then freed her hair from the towel. The outline of her hard nipples was clear as day through the black fabric. Quietly opening the door, she took a deep breath and walked around the corner. Matt had the blankets folded back and lay sprawled on his back in the center of the bed watching the news. Naked. With an impressive hard-on throbbing and twitching. She shot her gaze up and met Matt's eyes.

"I like the nightgown," he rumbled in his midnight voice.

Already perky nipples tightened to an aching throb.

"Take it off."

The nightgown fluttered to the floor. She straddled his feet, dropped to her hands and knees on the mattress, then paused. The TV announcer rattled on behind her. She wanted his undivided attention.

His mind-reading mojo worked in her favor for once and he clicked off the TV.

She smiled and ran her fingertips down the length of one thickly muscled leg. His hair tickled her palm. She dropped a kiss to his knee, the center of his thigh, the top of his thigh, his hip. He shifted beneath her and she looked at him from beneath her lashes.

"Something wrong?"

"No." He stilled.

Moving a little higher, intentionally brushing her breast across his erection, she dropped kisses along the bottom of his ribcage. Then she used her tongue, lapping along his skin like a cat. Finding every sensitive spot that made him twitch. Brushing her breasts and nipples back and forth.

Shifting down slightly, she settled her pelvis over his knee and blew a breath across the head of his dick. It jumped. Holding his gaze, she eased the head into her mouth. A sweep of her tongue pulled a groan from him. She sucked and he swore. With an audible pop, she released him.

His leg shifted beneath her, the rough hair scraping across her swollen clit and she gasped. He lifted his knee again and she rubbed against him with a moan. But this wasn't his show. Settling more firmly over his knee, her inner muscles clenching rhythmically with need, she took him into her mouth again. Deeper, hitting her throat. Backing off a little, she sucked and wriggled her hips.

"Grace, come here."

Well, okay.

But first. . . she swiped her tongue from the base to the tip. He groaned and fisted the bed sheets. She rose onto her hands and knees and crawled up until she straddled his hips. Raising up on her knees, she reached down and wrapped her fingers around him. The swollen head of his erection rubbed across her clit when she moved to guide him inside her, sparking the fire higher in her belly.

She paused. Did it again. Back and forth, then in a circle. Her eyes closed and she circled her hips on the head, spreading her liquid arousal. Pushing herself closer to orgasm.

Matt's hands tightened on her hips to the point of almost pain, but he didn't try to take over. Abruptly, she couldn't take anymore and sank onto his thick erection. Her head fell forward and she couldn't breathe. So close. She was so close, but her muscles clamped down and she couldn't move.

"Matt," she whimpered.

Big, gentle hands swept her hair from her face and lifted her chin. She met his tender gaze.

"What, sweetheart? What do you need?"

"Please. I can't. . ." Move. Talk. Breathe. Her heart might stop in two more seconds. So very close. So much pleasure.

He pulled her down to his chest and reversed their positions, never leaving her body. One thrust, two, three and her climax rolled over her with the force of a tidal wave. She arched up and cried out as he pounded into her and found his release. Heat spilled inside her.

Matt dropped his head and whispered in her ear. "I love you, Grace."

The emotions she'd held tight all day burst free in a rush of tears. She wrapped her arms and legs around him. "I love you too," she whispered. "And it terrifies me."

"Why, sweetheart?"

A laugh choked out. Rhododendron blooms. She was out of control. Matt lifted up on his elbows. He cradled her face. His thumbs swept the tears away, but more ran down to replace them.

"Everybo. . . body leaves ev. . . eventual. . . ly," she sobbed.

"Baby, please stop. You're killing me. I'm not going anywhere. I promise. The only way I'm leaving you is if I'm dead. Please, stop crying."

Oh, sweet heaven. Laughter bubbled, dangerously close to hysteria. Tipping her head back, she gulped air and tried to calm down. Nice. Really. So romantic, sobbing out her first declaration of love. The snotty nose was probably driving him wild with lust.

"I'm s-s-sorry."

"No." He wrapped his arms around her and pulled her tight against him. "Don't be sorry. If you'd just stop crying, I'd be the happiest man on the planet. The woman I love loves me back. What could be better? Except maybe no crying." His warm chuckle did more to calm her than all of her deep breaths combined. The room swam. Then again, too many deep breaths might be a bad thing.

Pressed against him, she inhaled the combination of phero-mones that made up Matt. Her belly tightened and deep inner muscles spasmed. His cock's answering twitch startled her.

Matt lifted his head and met her gaze. "I find declarations of love arousing. And tears. Tears are a guaranteed turn-on."

Laughing, she rubbed her palms down his sides and squeezed his butt. Nipping his shoulder, she arched her hips. He sank deeper. "Have I told you how much I love your butt?"

"No. I'm pretty sure I'd remember that." Leisurely strokes in and out rubbed all the right places. He bent his head and sucked her nipple into his mouth.

She gasped. "And your arms."

All the way back until just the tip teased her entrance, then his hips lunged forward. He did it again, and again. His tongue traced slow circles around her nipple. Coherent thought fled.

Hours or days later, she didn't much care, she lay snuggled against him with her head pillowed on his chest. Pillowed might not be the right word. She had yet to find a soft spot on him. There was, however, a very pleasant niche beneath his shoulder, where she fit nicely.

Warm blankets covered them and the only lights came from the city outside. As the heater hummed, she drifted. Matt's hand rested on her hip and their fingers lay intertwined on top of his stomach.

"What was it like when you were little, changing homes and families so often?"

Languid from making love and half asleep, Grace didn't tense as she otherwise might have. "It was hard. I have a very vague memory of the first time. I must have been three or four. My foster mother was crying and I kept patting her cheeks, trying to make her feel better, I think, even though I was crying too. The caseworker had to pull me from her arms. She kept asking why. There were tears the next few times, but eventually I stopped crying and so did they. Maybe they told them I wouldn't be staying. Maybe as I grew out of my toddler years I was no longer so lovable. I don't know. Once I hit my elementary years, I distanced myself from the families. Even from the teachers and other kids at my school. I didn't have many friends." She shrugged. "I didn't feel sorry for myself or anything, so don't think that. It's just the way it was."

223

The muscles on his abdomen tensed as he pressed a kiss to the top of her head. "I'm sorry you didn't have a normal family life growing up."

"Well, a lot of the kids at school had divorced parents. Living in two different homes, getting new fathers and mothers whenever their parents remarried. I didn't suffer a broken home in that sense. Sometimes, I think my situation was preferable to theirs."

"Hmm, I suppose that's true."

"Must be nice that your brother lives here."

"Mmm."

She rubbed her cheek against him. "That's a very noncommittal sound."

"My brother has issues."

"What do you mean?"

"He's only cares about himself—like our father—unreliable, believes the world owes him something. And when things don't go his way, he expects his family to bail him out. And we have. . . a lot."

"That's gotta be tough. What did you mean when you said you played second fiddle to your brother's dog in his wedding?"

Matt's chest lifted in a sigh. "He got married six or seven years ago. The marriage didn't last. Anyway, in the ceremony he had his dog play best man. I did nothing. Sat in the audience like I was nobody."

"Oh, Matt. I'm so sorry. That's awful."

"I'll admit, it hurt my feelings. Maybe it should have been a clue that all wasn't right with our relationship, but then again, it's never been exactly normal. No, that's not true. Growing up we were totally normal."

"You must feel a bit like you've lost your brother, then."

"You're very perceptive."

She tipped her head back and met his gaze. She couldn't believe he loved her and wanted to be with her. He was so handsome. So sweet and caring. Nothing at all like he appeared at work.

"Why are you so hard on your employees? Even people who've worked there for years. You're a very demanding boss, which I guess is okay, but you're not very nice."

His eyebrow rose. "I didn't know you had to be nice in the business world. Competitors would walk all over me."

"What does that have to do with your employees?"

"Being hard-nosed and tough has always gotten the most out of people. I guess I want to be careful to keep personal and profession lines clear."

Laughing, she shifted to drape herself across his chest and rested her chin on her hands over his breastbone. "Really?"

"Yeah, really. You were the exception from the start, smarty pants." He smacked her on the butt, then soothed the sting with his palm. Shifting his leg, he pulled her the rest of the way on top of him and cupped her bare bottom in both hands. "I want you to know I didn't hire you because I was attracted to you, but you really threw me. I wasn't sure if I should even hire you because I was so attracted to you."

"I never knew. You treated me the same as everyone else."

"The boss asking out an employee is a pretty sticky situation. I gave serious thought to firing you first."

Rising up on her elbows, she gaped at him. "You what? Like I would have gone out with you after you fired me, you big jerk."

"I didn't."

Still. . . "The nerve."

"What? I didn't realize at the time that you had a thing for bosses."

She gasped in mock offense.

He wriggled his eyebrows and rocked his pelvis against her.

Sweet angelic cherubs above, he was hard again. "You're insatiable. You're going to kill me."

"It's been two years. I'm making up for lost time." He pulled her head down to smother any objections with his lips. Though, honestly, she didn't have any.

225

# CHAPTER TWENTY-ONE

"Hey. How's Mom doing today?" Matt leaned back in his office chair. "That's good. So the doctor thinks he got all the cancer?" Some of the tension of the last few weeks eased. "That's excellent. . . Yeah. . . We should celebrate once she's feeling better. Speaking of celebrating, I have news." He grinned. "I'm going to ask Grace to marry me. I know it hasn't been long, but there's no doubt in my mind."

As soon as he hung up, the phone rang again.

"Duncan."

"Hey, Matt. I wanted to let you know Luke is taking me to lunch."

Frowning, he drummed his fingers on the desk. "Are you sure that's a good idea?"

"Sure I'm sure. What the big deal?"

"We don't know who the SOB stalking you is."

"You did a background check on Luke, right?"

"Yes. Doesn't mean I like him taking my girl out."

Grace laughed. "Oh, so this is about jealousy, not safety."

He groaned.

"You're being silly. It's just lunch. I should be back in the office by one. How about I give you a call when I get in?"

"Yes." Being patted on the head sharpened his temper, but he kept a lid on it. "Where are you going?"

She named a popular restaurant a few streets away then hung up. Matt wandered his office restlessly. Following them to lunch appealed, but he figured that leaned too close to stalking.

His phone beeped. "Mr. Duncan? There's a Detective Harrison here looking for Miss Debry."

He snatched up the phone. Harrison made an excellent source to take out his irritation on, especially considering the times he'd caught him leering at Grace. "Send him in, please."

Quickly crossing the room, he snatched open the door in time to catch Harrison mid-knock. "Come on in, Detective. You're just the man I wanted to see."

A hitch in the guy's step was the only indication of any surprise. "I live to serve."

Matt sat behind his desk while Harrison settled into one of the—according to Grace—intentionally uncomfortable chairs across from him. At the moment, he appreciated that they were uncomfortable. He'd enjoy watching the detective squirm.

"Good. I want to know who those men were." He tilted his chair back. "When Grace and I arrived at her condo, they were standing by the river watching the complex. Then they just happen to get involved in an incident with the same guy who's been bothering Grace? That's not coincidence."

"I'm not at liberty to discuss that, Mr. Duncan."

"Really? Men just happen to be popping up in convenient places while Grace is enduring cruel and destructive harassment and you can't discuss it?" He narrowed his eyes and leaned forward. "I can and will go over your head if I feel you're suffering a conflict of interest, Detective Harrison."

"I know those men." Harrison lost the relaxed and controlled pose, to Matt's satisfaction. "Trust me, they have absolutely no intention of harming Miss Debry. The only thing they're doing is helping. Trying to catch this guy and prevent him from getting a hold of her."

Matt rolled a pen between his fingers, watching the detective in his peripheral vision. "I'm supposed to take your word for it?"

Tension leapt and snapped from Harrison's posture. "That's right. This is an on-going investigation, Duncan."

227

Harrison had dropped the Mister. He was pissed. He stood and headed for the door. Matt watched the sunlight glint off the sterling pen as he twirled it. Just as Harrison's hand grasped the doorknob, he spoke.

"You'd better pray nothing happens to Grace, Detective. Or I promise, I will personally see that you lose your badge."

Harrison turned. "Is that a threat?"

"Not at all. It's a simple statement. Have a good day."

Harrison slammed the door behind him. Matt couldn't care less. He would do exactly as he said if anything happened to Grace. As far as he was concerned, it would be dereliction of duty on the part of Detective Harrison.

*****

Grace sat at her desk on Friday afternoon, counting estimates and sorting them into separate piles. Ah, the excitement. At least the monotony allowed her mind to wander. Her entire thought process pretty much did its own thing lately.

Stress did that to her. Her body and heart were out of control around Matt. Then there was the psychopath stalker freak terrorizing her. She didn't know which was worse. Being forced from her home really ticked her off. Then again, the way her hormones sat up and begged every time she was within the same vicinity as Matt was just shameful.

Along with her heart. Dropping her head to the desk, she fought a wave of panic. Stupid idiotic hormones. If only she'd been able to display a fraction more self-control, she wouldn't be in this mess. Matt might swear to Doomsday and back that he wouldn't leave her, but life had a way of making other plans. Something as fragile as love couldn't be trusted.

She covered her face with her hands. What the flip was she gonna do?

Groaning, she stared at the surface of her desk. The number for the Indiana Foster Care and Adoption Association and the caseworker's name stared back. Okay. Hint taken. She punched the numbers into her phone. The phone rang while her stomach wrapped into knots.

*Riiiing.* What if she found out something awful? *Riiiing.* What if some mastermind had been orchestrating her life with Machiavellian intent? *Riiiing.* What if all those foster homes hadn't wanted her, because she really was unlovable?

She pulled the phone away and started to press END CALL.

"Indiana Foster Care and Adoption Association, Missy Lyons speaking."

*Gulp.* "Hi. I'm looking into my foster care background and would like some information."

"Of course. I'd be happy to help you with that. Can I get your name and date of birth, please?"

"Grace Debry. October nine, nineteen eighty-three."

Grace drew in a breath, drumming her fingers on the desk as the static on the line droned uninterrupted.

"Hello?"

"Uh, right. Someone called to request a copy of your records a few days ago, Miss Debry."

"Yes, I know. Matthew Duncan. He said when he asked about the reason behind the multiple foster homes, you told him you were unable to release information to anyone other than me. Which is why I'm calling." Her hand tightened around the phone.

"Um-hmm." *Click clack* came through the phone as the case-worker typed away on her computer. "Would you please verify your social security number?"

Grace did. More typing.

"Thank you."

More typing. Was she writing a book?

"Miss Debry? If you could send me a copy of your driver's

229

license and social security card, along with your contact information, I'll get a full copy of your records to you."

"My social security card?" Great. One more delay. "I don't carry that with me. It's. . ."

Oh, no. Blood-sucking mosquitos, masochistic marigolds and vicious vines.

She balled her free hand into a fist, heart in her throat, struggling to resist a full-blown temper tantrum. Why, why, why had she ever vowed to stop swearing? Dread swept through her.

*Crap, crap, crap.* Grace closed her eyes and accepted the inevitable. "Would you prefer that faxed or scanned in and sent through email?"

"Whichever is easiest."

"Perfect. I'll get that emailed as soon as possible." *I hope.* "Will you be sending the file in the email as well?"

"Well. . . it's a very large file. Perhaps it would be best if I mailed it."

"Ms. Lyons, it's imperative I get the information as soon as possible. The size won't make any difference to my system, I promise."

"Okay. As soon as I receive verification of your identity, I'll email the file. I'm sorry for any inconvenience, but we have to be careful about the information we release."

"I understand. Good-bye."

Stinkin' bloody dandelions. She stared out the window and gnawed on her fingernail. Fluffy white clouds drifted across the deep-blue sky.

The box with her personal files was in her trashed condo. She hadn't even thought to check and make sure it was still intact.

It was near quitting time. If she hurried, she could beat the rush, grab what she needed from the condo, come back to the office to scan it in and email, and still be on time to meet Luke for the Celtic Women concert. She'd have to really fly.

Five minutes later, she screeched to a stop in her parking space at the condominium complex. Thank heaven she lived so close. Fumbling her keys, she jogged up the steps. She unlocked the door and her heart clutched. The passage of time had done nothing to lessen the impact. Her heart and soul had gone into making the condo her home.

She dropped her purse and keys on the little table by the door and dodged an overturned chair on the way to the bedroom. Stay focused, she reminded herself, blinking back tears. Tucked into the far corner of the closet sat her storage box.

She hugged it to her chest like a long-lost child as she carefully maneuvered the mess, tears blurring her vision.

Her foot caught and the box slipped from her grasp. She flung her hands out. The floor rushed toward her and she slammed into it with a gasp of pain. Hip and wrist throbbing, she whimpered and sat up.

"Oh, man."

The contents of the box were spilled across the floor, mixing with broken glass, CDs, DVDs, and who knew what else. Grace rubbed her aching wrist.

One folder was mostly intact. Pretty sure it held her important papers, she reached for it. A movement caught her eye and she glanced toward the balcony. Time slowed, her heartbeat thudding loudly.

A man with shaggy blonde hair leaned against the sliding door, handsome in an aged Robert Redford way, arms crossed, blue eyes cold and hard as he stared at her. He looked to be in his mid to late fifties. He also looked exactly like a man she'd seen before, jumping out of an old pickup in front of Matt's house to give chase.

*Oh, God.*

Heart in her throat, she glanced at the door. No way could she jump to her feet and make it there before he did, but staying flash-frozen to the floor wasn't going to help.

"Finally." Straightening from his lounging position against the door, he strolled toward her.

Grace shoved to her feet and backed up. Her side hit the breakfast island. *The kitchen. Knives.* Gaze glued to him, she sidled around the counter.

"No need to make this difficult, angel." His smooth, deep voice shouldn't have sent a shiver of fear down her spine.

She spun into the kitchen and almost tripped again. The contents of the room were scattered everywhere. The back of her neck tightened. There! The light glinted dully off the serrated edge of one of her knives.

A movement fanned the back of her hair as she dove for the knife, and strands of hair ripped free of her scalp.

The man laughed. "Damn, you always were a spirited little thing."

Her skin crawled. He didn't know her. Almost sobbing, Grace closed her hand around the hilt of the long blade and twisted to face him.

"Stay back." She scooted back on her butt until she came up against a cupboard. "Stay away from me."

He laughed again and shook his head. "You think I'm scared of a little knife? I'm not gonna let that come between us. Not after I've come so far for you."

His accent grated, shifting something inside her mind. Memories old and faded as a weathered photograph twisted and spun just out of reach.

Grace shook her head. She didn't know this guy any more than he knew her.

A pan screeched across the tiles and she jerked her head up. Half the distance between them was gone. Crap. Tears blurred her vision. She quickly scrubbed them away.

*Great. Bawl like a baby when some psycho is trying to kill you. Good plan, Grace.*

"You belong to me, angel." His low voice was almost hypnotic.

In another lifetime, by some other female, maybe through thick metal bars, he might be considered handsome. "We'll be together again. Forever, this time."

"There will be no forever, you freak." Grace slashed the knife through the air between them. "I don't know who you think I am, but I don't belong to anyone. Now get back unless you want to lose a few fingers."

He didn't move.

"I swear I'll do it, buddy." Her voice rose an octave. "I keep my knives sharp enough to split hairs and I will not hesitate to slice off anything that gets close."

A slow smile creased his cheeks. Sheer force of will kept back her violent shudder. He backed up. One step. Two. He stopped in the doorway to the living room.

Grace scrambled to her feet, knife gripped tight. "Keep going. All the way out the door."

His wrinkles grew more pronounced as his smile grew. He backed across her disaster of a living room with uncanny grace.

"You won't get away from me, you know."

"I know nothing of the kind."

He stopped by the front door.

She gestured with the knife. "Open the door and get out."

*Beep beep beeeep.*

Grace glanced over her shoulder into the kitchen and he rushed her.

Her peripheral vision caught the movement and she spun, slashing out with the knife. He easily dodged it and slammed her to the floor.

*BOOM!* A blast of searing heat roared over her.

His oppressive weight smothered her. Her vision blurred. The air was so hot, it hurt to breathe. With a grunt, he lifted up. Grace rolled to her side, coughing, ears ringing.

"Come on."

He tossed her over his shoulder like a sack of dog food.

233

She forced her head up. Flames licked the black hole where her kitchen used to be and thick smoke curled along the ceiling. What had he done? The smoke pouring out of the condo blinded her as they cleared the front door.

"*Cher*? What—"

Flesh smacked into flesh, followed by a thud. Vomit climbed up Grace's throat. She blinked hard, trying to clear her vision, and struggled against his hold. Through a haze, she saw Lisie sprawled across the hallway. She wasn't moving. Grace struggled harder and tried to scream. She managed a squeak. Her throat was on fire.

Lisie disappeared from view as he quickly jogged down the stairs and onto the Greenbelt. Tears clogged her vision. The wail of sirens joined the ringing in her ears. At least Lisie would get help.

Grace whimpered, tried to swallow and threw up.

The monster ran faster, bouncing her on his hard shoulder. Pain spread. Her fingers and toes tingled.

Finally, mercifully, he came to a stop. He flipped her up and tossed her onto a bench seat. She twisted and recognized the old pickup.

"No!" She lurched forward.

He backhanded her. Her eye popped and pain exploded across her face. "You need to learn obedience, angel. We'll have plenty of time to renew old lessons, but for the time being. . ."

Struggling to get upright again, she glimpsed his fist flying toward her. Night descended abruptly.

# CHAPTER TWENTY-TWO

Matt paced the hotel lobby. People gave him a wide berth and the desk clerk watched him warily, one hand on the telephone. He didn't care.

Where the hell was Grace?

He glanced at his watch and fought the desire to slam his fist into something. Anything. His gut clenched. Nancy said Grace had bolted out of the building at 4:20. Almost two hours ago.

The lobby doors whooshed open and Luke strolled in, hands in the pockets of his tan slacks. Matt narrowed his eyes and prowled forward.

Luke stumbled to a stop. "Mr. Duncan."

Matt didn't stop until he was close enough to watch Luke's pupils expand.

Luke licked his lips. "Uh, I'm here to pick up Grace for the concert. I imagine she told you?"

"Grace isn't here," he growled. "I don't suppose you know anything about that?"

"Wh-what do you mean?" He shifted to the side.

Matt followed. Luke glanced around the lobby. He didn't know if he was looking for help or checking to see if he was joking and Grace was really behind him. He wished.

"Why would I know where she is? She's supposed to be here." Luke frowned and met his eyes.

Maybe he really didn't know. Damn. Matt shoved a hand through his hair. "Grace left the office a couple of hours ago.

Nancy said she seemed to be in a hurry, but no one knows where she went."

"Huh." Luke smoothed his hair, visibly relaxing. "Not like her to miss an appointment, dude. We've had these plans for a while."

"Yes, I know." Dude? Matt clenched his jaw.

"You don't suppose. . ." He paused. "It sounds kinda stupid considering everything that's gone down, but you don't suppose she went to her condo?"

Matt's gut clenched. His cell rang and he snatched it out of his pocket. Not Grace. "Duncan."

"This is Detective Harrison. There was an explosion at Miss Debry's condo."

Sweat broke out on his forehead. Spinning away from Luke, he braced his fist against a pillar. "When? Is she hurt?"

"I was hoping she was with you. When did you last see her?"

"Two hours ago." Matt fisted his free hand, hating the frustration. The helplessness. "You're sure she's not there?"

"We've searched the condo. There's no sign of her."

"I'll be there as fast as I can."

He ended the call and stuffed the phone in his pocket with hands that shook.

"What's up, dude?"

Matt glared at Luke. One more *"dude"*, and he'd plant a fist in his face. To hell with the consequences.

"Nothing. Is. Up." He shoved past him. If he drove ninety and broke every traffic law in the book, he could be there in sixty seconds.

"Come on, man!" Luke called after him. "Don't hold out on me. She's my friend too."

Flattening Luke would take valuable time he couldn't spare. The diesel engine of his truck rumbled to life. He roared out of the parking garage, taking out the wooden arm at the toll booth. The guy jumped out of his box, screaming and shaking his fist.

*Too damn bad, buddy.*

A minute and a half later, he jumped down from the truck and shoved through the crowd outside the condos. Two cop cars screamed into the parking lot. He took the stairs two at a time. Firemen, paramedics and police jostled for position in the hallway. Matt blew by them all, ignoring their shouts and grabbing hands.

He kept picturing Grace. Laughing in the park, moaning on his Harley, sharing a bite of her food, writhing beneath him as an orgasm swept her away, confessing her love. His heart clutched and he hit the third floor at breakneck speed, almost mowing over Detective Harrison.

"Whoa, man." Harrison grabbed his arms. "Calm down. I told you, she's not in there."

"You're sure?"

"Positive. We swept the whole condo. Although. . ." Matt followed the direction of Harrison's hand gesture. "That's her purse. She was here."

Wispy tendrils of smoke drifted out of Grace's door. "What the hell happened?"

Harrison's expression tightened Matt's gut further. "There was a kitchen knife lying in the middle of the living room. The handle wasn't blackened from the blast, so my guess is Grace tried to use it for self-defense."

Matt shook his head. No way the psychotic asshole had her. No. He stared at her purse, smudges of smoke marring the smooth ivory leather. Clenching his hands into fists, he faced Harrison.

"Those men you know, the ones you said were watching out for her. Where are they?"

Harrison looked beyond him and Matt turned. The big one was stoic as ever, but the other guy was pale, sweaty and green around the gills.

Matt stalked toward them. "Why didn't you stop him? What the hell happened?"

"I'm sorry." The WWF guy's gravelly voice was oddly humble.

Blood trailed down the side of his face. "He snuck up on me and whacked me over the head."

"Fuck." Matt wanted to punch something. "Any idea where he took her?"

The two men exchanged a look. The green color on the one guy dialed up a few notches. "I haven't a clue." His Adam's apple bobbed. "God have mercy. I should have taken care of him years ago."

Matt stepped forward, vision hazing red. The big guy blocked him. Harrison put his hand on his shoulder. The other guy just stood there, defeat oozing from him.

"I think it's time we made introductions." Harrison gestured between them. "Matt Duncan, meet Sheriff John Sanford of Sebree, Kentucky. And this is Gunner. He's a local private investigator. Gentlemen, Matt Duncan."

Matt stared at the green-tinged sheriff. "What's a sheriff from Kentucky doing in Idaho? I find the coincidence fascinating, since Grace and I recently traced her foster-care route to a town in Kentucky."

Sanford sighed and rubbed the back of his neck. "Henderson, Kentucky."

His focus sharpened. Sanford knew a lot more than any of them combined. "What the hell is going on?"

Harrison stepped between them. "Why don't we head down to the station. See if we can come up with a plan for locating Grace."

Grace licked her lips and pried her eyelids open to. . . nothing. Solid black met her gaze. She clenched her hands, took a breath and blinked the haze away. Little details emerged. The interior of the pickup, the faint outline of trees, something high and wide—a big, solid fence.

"Good of you to join me, angel."

She gingerly rolled her head to the side. A large male shape slouched behind the steering wheel, his square jaw outlined against the window. Nausea rolled through her.

"Who are you?"

He shook his head. "You know damn well who I am."

*Uh, no.* "Let's pretend I don't."

"Fine, I'll play your little game. Name's Deke Sathers. Pleased to meet you." His eyes gleamed in the darkness. She shivered. "And you are the conniving snake bitch I married thirty-three years ago."

Grace blinked, her sluggish brain a little slow on the uptake. "What? I'm only twenty-seven. That's not possible."

"In your dreams, angel. Tell me." He leaned close.

She leaned back.

"How many rich old farts did you have to fuck to get all that plastic surgery?"

She gasped. He laughed.

"Course, I'm not complaining. You look damn good. Good enough for me to overlook how many men you've screwed."

He grabbed her hair quick as a striking snake and pulled her close enough to heat her skin with his breath. "Especially if you can still give me babies. You owe me."

Her jaw dropped. "What?"

Fist buried in her hair, he hauled her across the seat and out of the truck. Her bare feet hit hard dirt—where were her shoes? He dragged her along behind him. The guy was certifiable. Never in a million years would she marry a raving lunatic.

Just her luck, some escaped psycho patient decided she was his missing wife. Awesome. He'd probably killed his real wife.

Her knees went weak and she stumbled. Not a good train of thought.

A cold breeze ruffled her hair and blew the clouds away from the moon. Grace looked up. Then up some more. They stood in front of a huge stone wall.

"Uh. . ."

Deke yanked her against him. For an old guy, he wasn't real soft. "You and I are gonna make us some pretty little baby girls to replace the ones you stole from me, bitch."

Bile rose. His mouth pressed down on hers, grinding her lips against her teeth. His fingers dug into the side of her jaw and forced her mouth open. His tongue darted in. Grace wrenched back, but he held her too tight to escape. She whimpered, gagged, and stomped on his foot.

He pushed her away, to her undying relief.

"With all the fucking, you'd think you'd have learned how to kiss by now." He turned and fumbled in the shadows beneath the wall.

Nobody could accuse her of being a fool. She ran. Small rocks dug into the tender soles of her feet. She could barely make out the outline of the foothills and large outbuildings. Deke cursed, his feet thudding heavily against the ground in pursuit.

*Come on. Faster. You jog all the time. Dig!*

A rock sliced into her foot. Grace cried out. Stumbled. Caught her balance and ran harder. Instinct told her she'd lost valuable distance.

*Doesn't matter. I'm younger, I'm in great shape. . . .*

His heavy weight slammed into her. They went down, hard-packed dirt tearing across her knees and palms. Pain shot up her arm.

"Stupid bitch," he growled, panting in her ear. He ground his hips against her bottom. His erection poked her and her muscles seized. She tasted dirt and copper.

"Please," she whispered. "Please. Don't."

Above her, he stilled. His hold on her hair didn't relax, but his hips stopped thrusting. "Now that's real nice. I knew you'd remember all those lessons."

*Oh, God. Please. Somebody help me.*

Grace's belly quivered. How had someone this sick and twisted been allowed to roam free for so long? Something was seriously wrong with society.

He rolled off and dragged her to her feet by her hair. She cried out in pain.

"Don't worry, angel. We'll have our fun. I'm getting old though. I'd rather have a bed to use while I fill your belly with my seed."

Acid climbed up her throat. She began to shake. They were isolated. No lights shone nearby. No chance of rescue.

His grip on her hair tightened and he headed back the way they'd come. Her whole body hurt. She stumbled behind him, straining to distinguish the shadows. A shovel would be a real blessing about now. One solid whack should be enough. If not, she'd be happy to repeat the gesture as many times as necessary.

"Up." He shoved her into a ladder. "Nothing funny either."

"I'm not in much of a joking mood."

*Smack.*

Her lips stung, her ears rang and her vision swam.

"Your smart mouth can be put to better use, angel."

His hot breath feathered across her ear. She shuddered. Up the ladder she went, with him right behind her. On top of her. Instead of dropping down below her, where she could have—and would have—kicked him in the face, he stayed a few rungs down with his arms around her.

At the top, she climbed onto some sort of floating wood walkway. The boards sagged with each step. The whole city spread out below. She looked down and her stomach dropped.

They were inside an old prison, various sizes of buildings dotting the interior. The Old Idaho Penitentiary. Her mouth went dry.

"Come on."

Deke straddled the wall, one hand on the stones and the other still firmly entwined in her hair. She could shove him, but no doubt he'd take her along for the ride. And she really didn't want to die. Matt's face swam across her mind.

"I said, come on." Deke yanked her off her feet and halfway over the wall. She scrambled for purchase. Her foot touched a ladder rung. She hugged the ladder on the other side of the wall and her stomach landed back in her belly.

"It won't accomplish a whole lot if we both go splat on the ground," she mumbled.

"What'd you say?"

"Nothing."

"That's what I thought."

Smug bas. . . Grace bit her lip hard enough to draw blood. Laura deserved better than to have her memory soured because of the psycho freak behind her. She thought of Laura's husband. "Why did you kill Darrell Wells?"

She felt more than saw his shrug. "I knew he'd fucked you. Any man who screws my wife deserves to die, far as I'm concerned."

Her fingers tightened on the ladder. Matt. He was going to go after Matt.

"Move."

She moved. Down the ladder, fast as she could with him on top of her. She needed a plan. Now more than ever. Eyes peeled to spot even the smallest opening, the smallest weapon, she bit into her lower lip.

At the bottom, he headed toward a squat building sitting in shadow like a monster crouched low in the dirt, waiting to devour her whole. She stumbled. Deke jerked her against him.

"I have a special room all picked out for you."

His grin gleamed in the moonlight. Deke stepped inside. She tripped on the high threshold and he dragged her in, scraping skin off her leg.

She gasped.

"Shut up."

Too many emotions collided and rational thought fled. "You could have warned me to step up. But no, you decided I don't need any skin on my legs and let me trip so you could drag me across raw metal instead."

*SLAP*

Blessed numbness blocked the pain for one. . . two. . . three. . . Agony shot from her cheek to the back of her head and radiated down her spine. She fisted her hands and held her breath against a cry of pain.

Deke shoved her through a narrow doorway. She landed on cold concrete and instinctively curled into a ball. The slam of the door echoed eerily. A metallic click followed.

He was locking her in this shivering hellhole.

"Now, angel." His velvety voice came through the blackest black she'd ever experienced.

Shaking with more than cold, she edged into a corner. Warm blood oozed down her shin-bone.

"I'm leaving you here for the night, safe and sound. I have a few. . . chores to take care of. I didn't expect to catch you today. No worries, though. I'll be back bright and early to spring you before the groundskeepers arrive."

*Matt.* She lunged forward, scrabbling against the unforgiving door, screaming. "No!"

Laughter floated back and mixed sickly with her scream. She sank to the floor, sobbing. All her life, in the deepest corner of her heart, she'd just wanted to belong to somebody. Now that an incredible man loved her, some lunatic was going to take it away. If only she'd shoved him off the ladder when she'd had the chance. She would have died along with him, but what did that matter?

A hard shiver woke Grace. The tiny room had lightened enough to reveal scribbling on the walls. Goosebumps marched across her skin. Never had she been so cold. Curled into a ball, the chill seeped through the floor and into her bones.

Something scraped. Her head shot up. A pant leg faintly showed through the bar-covered opening at the base of the door. Was he worse than the cold? Difficult decision, that. Her jaw ached from clenching to prevent her teeth from chattering.

"Mornin', angel. Up and at 'em."

His silky voice shriveled her insides. She buried her face against her knees. Maybe he'd think she was dead and go away.

"Come on now. No dawdling. Things to do, places to go." He'd walked into her cell. "A bit chilly this morning."

He grabbed her hair and yanked her head up.

So cold. Her head should have snapped off in his hand. So cold her emotions were frozen.

"I'm not in the best of moods, this morning, angel. I suggest you get your ass in gear."

Unable to summon interest, she noted new bags beneath his blue eyes. "Bad night?"

Using her hair as leverage, he pulled her to her feet. She swayed, locked muscles unable to support her weight, and stared at the monster hidden behind the aging movie-star façade.

"Yes," he hissed. "I couldn't track down your lily-livered boyfriend."

Joy leapt. He jerked her across the small room, snapping hair free of her scalp.

"Hello, Deke."

The new voice came from outside the room. Deke released her and she collapsed.

"John." He braced a shoulder in the doorway. "I remember when you called me Hoss, like everyone else. But I guess you always were too clever for your own good."

"Hoss was the town hero. Heroes don't beat their wives and children. I'm just sorry I didn't figure out what was going on till too late. Sandra deserved better."

"Don't talk about my wife," Deke growled. "You don't have the right." He glanced down at her. "Don't you worry, angel. I won't let him touch you."

"Wait. You think. . . You think she's your wife?"

Finally, a voice of reason.

"I didn't realize. . . Deke, that girl is your daughter. Your wife

244

is dead. She's been dead for twenty-five years. Grace is your youngest daughter."

Her dad was dead. No way this escapee from the looney bin was her father.

"So you're telling me. . ."

Grace glanced up.

Deke stared at her, nothing remotely paternal in his expression. "This woman with the same curly black hair, green eyes and perfect body as my wife is not my wife. My little girl had blue eyes."

"Oh, I'll admit she's the spitting image of Cassandra. Kind of freaked me out when I first saw her. And Grace's eyes were blue. Until she turned three and they changed to green."

He'd seen her? Knew her mother? She wriggled a little, trying to sit up, but her muscles wouldn't cooperate.

"That's Grace. Not Sandra. Not your wife. Deke. . . you can't take her."

"The hell I can't." His roar echoed off the walls.

Grace wrapped her arms around her head.

"Even if I believed she's my daughter, which I don't, she still belongs to me. Just like the girls she stole. They were mine. My property."

Spittle peppered her arms. She shook her head. No. There was no way this twist of nature was her father. Her father was dead. He died alongside her mother.

"Do you know everything I went through to make sure she was mine and mine alone?" Deke's voice became eerily calm. "You remember the fire that killed her parents the night of the Homecoming dance, Sandra's senior year? She'd gotten a scholarship to some fancy college and was gonna move away. She wouldn't give me the time of day. 'Course, she wasn't giving any guy the time of day, so I didn't mind so much. 'Cept I knew time was running out. So I killed 'em and used the fire to cover it up."

Heaven above.

245

"You killed her parents?" Raw pain splintered the man's voice. "Deke, that tore her apart."

"Yeah, but she leaned on me from then on. Taught her I was the only important thing in her life. The one constant."

Even with her arms covering her head, Grace sensed his gaze on her. Revulsion increased her shivering.

"Didn't it, angel? You and me, we're meant to be."

"Deke, you can't have her."

"Like hell. After all the trouble I've gone to? She's mine. She's going to give back what she took from me."

"I won't let you take her."

"You don't have a choice."

A metallic click echoed off the concrete, like a round being chambered.

"You gonna shoot me?" The man—John?—sounded strangely calm.

Oh, no. Please, please, please no. No way was she going anywhere with this psycho freak.

"I'll give you one chance," Deke said. "You can turn and walk away, or you can die."

The man sighed. "I really wish it hadn't come to this, Deke. We grew up together. I guarded your backside all through high school. I believed in you when Sandra came to me with her stories of abuse."

"Of course you did." Deke sounded offended. "What else would you do?"

"Believe her. Protect her. Save her."

"From me?"

"Yes."

A gun boomed, so loud in the tiny room her ear drums throbbed. The following silence was as loud as the shot. Grace peeked out under her elbow. Deke slid down the metal door, leaving a dark streak behind.

He stared at his blood-soaked shirt. "You shot me."

"You left me no choice."

Deke raised his gun. "Then I'll take you with me. You can't have her either."

*BOOM*

Another shot echoed in the too-small space. Grace gasped and too late shielded her eyes. Far too late. The image of blood bursting from the center of Deke Sathers' forehead burned her eyelids.

A gentle hand settled on her back. "Grace?" The stranger's voice. "It's okay. You're safe now."

Quick footsteps rushed toward them. "Dad?"

Grace's eyes flew open. She knew that voice.

"Dad?" High-pitched with distress. "Oh, God. What did you do?"

The man near her rose. "Luke? What are you doing here?"

The stranger knew Luke?

"You did this?" Luke wailed. The pain in his voice wrenched at Grace. "You killed my father?"

"I had no choice. He was going to hurt Grace. He was going to shoot me."

"You had a choice." Luke's screech pulsed through her tender ears. "Grace deserves whatever he gives her."

*What?*

"She's a stupid bitch who belongs to him. In every way. His daughter or his wife, what difference does it make? She's his." Steps shuffled closer. "What did you do, Dad? You were supposed to wait. Why didn't you wait? We had it all planned out. I pick her up for that stupid concert and bring her to you. It would've been safe. Why couldn't you just wait?"

Grace forced herself to move, to lift her arm and look at the man kneeling beside Deke's still form. Luke smoothed his hand down Deke's arm and tears streamed over his cheeks.

"Luke," the man said quietly.

"I hope you're happy, Sheriff." Snot dribbled from Luke's nose, over his lips and onto Deke. "You killed the only father I ever had."

"Deke was your step-dad. I doubt he was that good a father, Son."

Luke lurched to his feet, his hand fisted. His other hand. . . Oh, no.

"Sheriff," Grace whispered.

He turned toward her. Luke pointed the trembling gun and pulled the trigger. Surprise blanked the sheriff's face. He slid to the floor.

Another shot reverberated, followed by a muffled thud. Grace flinched.

"Grace?"

Matt. He darted around Detective Harrison, who barely had time to lower his gun. Worry lines were sharply etched around Matt's mouth and his eyes were dark with fatigue, but she didn't care. Her heart welled with emotion.

Sharp sobs wracked her, fierce and sudden. He'd come. She was safe.

# CHAPTER TWENTY-THREE

"Sandra was a beautiful woman, married to a monster, who beat her and abused their little girls." Sheriff Sanford clenched his hospital blanket. "She came to me once. I was so young and stupid, I told her husband what she'd said and we shared a good laugh. We didn't see a whole lot of Sandra and the girls after that. A few years later, I was driving the country roads, patrolling the outskirts of the county. Came upon a sight I'll never forget." He stared out the window. "The train engine twisted the big car into a mess. The engineer was sitting on the tracks, sobbing. Can't say as I blame him."

Grace sat so still she could have been made of marble if it weren't for the brilliant bruises. Forty-eight hours had passed since they'd found her. Matt rubbed her back, his need to be in constant contact a living, breathing thing. The night he'd spent trying to figure out where she could be, wondering if she was okay, had been a hell he had no desire to revisit. Ever.

"Your mom and sisters died on impact." Sheriff Sanford sighed. "Hard to believe it was so many years ago. I'm sorry, Grace. Maybe I should have done things differently. It was such a miracle you survived. You were sitting there in your car seat, covered in blood, sucking your thumb and never made a sound. I remembered what your mother had told me about Deke. After seeing what she'd done to herself and her children, I knew everything she'd said was true. The coroner was able to verify the abuse, due to the extent of old injuries on Sandra and the little girls. And your arm. . ."

He hesitated. Grace rubbed her arm, something Matt had noticed she often did when upset. She'd mentioned once how it ached when the weather turned stormy.

"Your little arm was badly broken. The doctor said it was at least a day-old injury, so it had happened before the accident. I had to get you as far away as possible. A friend helped me place you in foster care. Then I kept making them move you, just to be safe."

She stared at the faded photograph the sheriff had given her. Matt wrapped his arm around her shoulders, wishing he could do more.

"I found Deke later," Sanford continued. "Lying in a pool of blood on the floor of their mobile home. I thought for sure he was dead until I discovered a pulse. I really struggled not to leave him there to die. He deserved that, and more. In the end, my training kicked in. I called an ambulance. He recovered. Used his time in the hospital to romance one of the nurses. They got married as soon as Deke got out of rehab. She had a little boy, only two years old at the time. Luke. I spent quite a few years flat-out terrified he'd treat her the way he did your mom. Or that they'd have children. They never did, thank God."

Matt glanced at Grace. Her green eyes lifted from the photograph to the sheriff.

The guy had to be uncomfortable after his recent surgery to remove the bullet that had grazed his lung and lodged next to his spine. Luke had been shaking too hard to get off a good shot, even at point-blank range. Even so, the sheriff wasn't young and his recovery would be long.

The sheriff took a deep breath and winced. "I suppose you're wondering how Deke found out about you after so many years. My mother's to blame, I'm afraid. About a year and a half ago, my wife had a stroke that left her disabled. My mother moved in with us to help out. After my wife passed, she kept helping out by sorting through her personal things. Thought it would be too painful a process for me. Maybe she was right. Regardless, she found an album my wife had made over the years. My wife shared my pain and guilt over what had happened to your mother and you girls. She kept track of you, with my help, and created an album of all your accomplishments. She was proud as could be of you."

Grace leaned forward, her tension radiating straight to Matt. She needed to hear this. To know people had actually cared about her all those years.

"When my mother found that album, she figured out who you were. Who you belonged to." Sanford sighed and shook his head. "You have to understand. There's a different generation of thought there. She figured your father had a right to know you were alive and well. There was no way she could've known he'd flip his lid like he did. Nor did she know the history. Even if she had, I don't know that it would have mattered. All I can do is say I'm sorry, Grace. Whatever you need, I'll do everything I can for you."

Grace sighed, some of the tension leaving her muscles. "I'm sorry about your wife. It must be a terrible loss after so many years together."

Sanford stared at her blankly. Matt was sure as hell surprised. Impressed too. Sanford had essentially ripped Grace's life apart. Matt didn't know if he'd be able to offer any degree of empathy in her shoes.

"Thank you." Sanford's eyes looked suspiciously wet.

"I would prefer to have gone through my life without this drama. Discovering the truth cost a lot of lives, but I've learned a great deal in the process, Sheriff." Grace reached up and covered Matt's hand with hers. "Most importantly, I realized sometimes people come into your life to stay."

Sanford's gaze shifted from Grace to Matt. A satisfied smile curved Sanford's lips and he relaxed against the bed, crossing his hands over his belly.

Grace rose and limped to the side of Sanford's bed. Placing her slender hand atop his, she leaned down and whispered in his ear. Sanford's grin grew. She kissed his cheek, patted his hand and straightened.

"You do good by her, Matt." Sanford ruined his stern tone by winking. "I suspect she'll be a handful, but I think you're up to the task."

"I like to think so."

Grace rolled her eyes. "Get over yourselves already."

Sanford chuckled then groaned. "Damn. Get out of here. You two have better things to do on a fine spring day."

"Yes, sir." Grace snapped a mock salute, but she was smiling. "You behave now. We'll be by tomorrow to see you. The nurses will tell me if you've been difficult."

Matt wrapped his arm around her waist, accepting some of her weight as he helped her from the room. The cuts on the bottom of her feet and her shin had to be agony, but she was stubborn. Her bruises had turned slightly less enthusiastic shades of purple and blue overnight. The cuts and scrapes would take longer to heal. He was confident she could handle any damage to her psyche. Grace had more strength inside than she knew.

"You don't have to help me so much," she said for the hundredth time. "I'm perfectly capable—"

"Of managing on your own. Yes, I know. There's no harm in accepting help. Your doctor wasn't exactly thrilled when you insisted on being on your feet, if you remember."

She snorted. "Yeah, he would've stuck me in a wheelchair. Over a few cuts and bumps."

"I think you're underestimating the damage. You know, I'm more than happy to carry you wherever you want to go."

"Oh, I can just see that." Grace chuckled, the sound so precious he couldn't help smiling. Even if she was being obstinate. "You walking through the grocery store with me in your arms."

"Maybe I'd just toss you over my shoulder."

She laughed and leaned more of her weight onto him. Some of the lingering anxiety eased. He really would be only too happy to carry her—if she'd cooperate.

"I'm so glad Lisie was able to leave the hospital yesterday."

"What was she mumbling about?"

Grace laughed. "Apparently, one of the doctors was giving her a tough time about going home to an empty house. She told him she didn't need a babysitter, and things escalated from there. All the nurses were talking about it."

"She is a fiery little thing." He gently squeezed her waist. "Almost as much as you."

"I'm sure that's why we became fast friends."

"No doubt."

In the parking lot, he ignored her objections and lifted her into the truck. She stuck her tongue out—a tease he couldn't ignore. Anchoring her with his fingers in her hair, he fused their lips. Her hands skated down his sides. Then back up and around to knead the muscles in his back. Matt groaned and pulled her closer. Tucking her head against his shoulder, he deepened the kiss.

Someone cleared their throat. Reluctantly, he released her. Grace sank back against the leather upholstery and licked her lower lip. Muscles clenching, he almost said to hell with whoever stood behind him and went back for more. From the curve of her lips, she knew it too. His expression when he turned probably wasn't too welcoming.

He bit back a frustrated groan. "Detective Harrison."

"Mr. Duncan. Miss Debry." Harrison nodded at Grace. At least he managed to keep his expression from sinking into puppy love. "How are you?"

"Good."

"I want to reiterate my suggestion that you see a counselor. As a preventative measure, if nothing else."

"I appreciate your concern, Detective. I assure you. . ." Grace linked her fingers through Matt's. "I have everything I need to recuperate from my experience."

His heart warmed, and no doubt his grin was sappy as hell.

"If you're sure," Harrison hesitated.

Matt almost felt sorry for him. Must be tough to want something you couldn't have. Since there was no way in hell he was letting Grace slip through his fingers, Harrison definitely couldn't have her.

"Well, I wish you the best of luck." Harrison glanced at him. "Both of you."

"Thank you." Grace smiled. "For everything."

Matt stretched his hand toward Harrison. Really, he wasn't a bad guy. "Thank you, Detective."

The detective left and Matt cocked his head. "I kinda feel bad for the guy."

"Why?"

He turned. Corny as it sounded, she took his breath away. She was so beautiful, inside and out. And she loved him. That sort of thing could go to a guy's head.

"Because he's in love with you."

Her eyes widened. "He is not."

He shrugged, shut the door and walked around.

"I'm serious, Matt." Grace frowned as he climbed in. "Detective Harrison is not in love with me. He doesn't even know me. That's silly."

Resting his left arm on the steering wheel, he leaned over the console.

She blinked and her pink tongue emerged to sweep across her pouty lower lip.

"Grace, sweetheart, you're a stunning woman. You're intelligent, sweet, gracious, and damn sexy. All a man has to do is stare into your beautiful green eyes and he's lost."

Light-pink color washed her cheekbones and he grinned. Man, he loved her. Then she did the most astonishing thing. She winked, leaned forward and kissed him. The need he tasted on her tongue just about did him in.

He sucked in a ragged breath and started the truck. "How fast do you suppose we can make it back to my place?"

Grace reclined in the lounger, enjoying the warm spring weather. Birds chirped and the scent of jasmine floated on the cool breeze. Tranquility and renewed life. Closing her eyes, she allowed the hazy, fragmented memories to wash over her.

Sheriff Sanford had stopped by last week on his way out of town. He was heading back to Kentucky, but he'd said he couldn't leave without giving her something—a worn brown-leather album recovered from Deke's meager possessions. Inside were numerous newspaper articles, pictures, school papers, and drawings. They spanned her entire life, starting at two years old.

In the very back was a newspaper clipping telling the story of a beautiful twenty-seven-year-old mother killed at a railroad crossing. Her five little girls had been in the car with her. They'd died on impact with a large freight train. She didn't realize she was crying until Matt knelt in front of her and gently wiped the tears from her cheeks.

Four sisters. She'd had a family. Not only was the album a rough trajectory of her life after Kentucky, it also included snap-shots of a life long gone. Dark-haired sisters, inspiring dreamy thoughts of them hushing her when she took a tumble, sharing their ragged little dolls and cuddling her in their little laps from a monster in the dark. Common sense—and experience after meeting the man—told her the monster was none other than their father. Best of all were the hazy memories of her mother. Soft black hair tangled in her fingers; an impression of comfort and warmth snuggled against her.

Darker images were there too. Soft sobs, raised voices, thumps and thuds she instinctively knew were bad. Her mother flinching away when Grace touched a dark bruise, then pulling her close and smothering her in kisses until she giggled and forgot about the pain in her mother's green eyes.

The one memory she stubbornly believed with every fiber of her being, the one she chose to focus on now, was of her momma singing to her. They were sitting outside. Under the star-filled night sky. Little Grace clutched a black-haired, green-eyed dolly. Momma held her close on her lap and rocked her back and forth. Her soft, sweet voice rose and fell with the melody of "Amazing Grace."

Matt's familiar hand smoothed her hair from her face.

Smiling, she opened her eyes. "You're home early."

"How can I resist when there's a beautiful woman waiting?" He came around to the front of her chair and knelt down. "Besides, I couldn't wait." Holding her gaze, he gathered both of her hands in his. "Grace, I love you so much. I hope you know that."

She nodded, her stomach tightening.

He played with her fingers. "The first time you walked into my office I knew you were special. Maybe that's why I held off for so long on getting to know you. Although there is that whole sexual-harassment issue." His dimpled smile still bowled her over. "When my mom got sick, I realized I was letting life slip by me. I'd become afraid of getting hurt."

Grace squeezed his hands. She was well acquainted with that fear. He had overcome it with much more determination and charm than she had, just one of the many things she loved and respected about him.

"The more I got to know you, the incredible woman you are, the more I fell in love. You awed me at every turn."

His hands were clammy. Grace's stomach rolled. He wasn't breaking up with her, was he?

He cleared his throat. "I can't imagine my life without you. I know you moving in is a temporary thing, but I don't want it to be. I want you here every day. I want to know that when I come home, you'll be here. When I go to sleep at night, it will be with you in my arms." He cleared his throat again. "What I'm getting at, in a roundabout kind of way, is. . ." He took a deep breath. "Grace, will you marry me?"

Holy.

Cow.

For a second, Grace couldn't breathe. He wanted to marry her? To be together forever? And ever? She launched off the chair into his arms.

"Yes." She wrapped her arms around his neck and kissed his jaw. "Yes." Kissed his chin. "Yes." Kissed his cheek. "Yes." Kissed him on the mouth and whispered, "Yes, please."

Matt laughed, settling her bottom on his upraised knee. "Is that a yes?"

"Yes." Just in case he wasn't sure or she was speaking gibberish, she nodded emphatically. Then she kissed him again. He mumbled something into her mouth.

"Hmmm?"

He pulled back. "I have an engagement ring for you. And a wedding ring. We won't be doing a long engagement."

"We can go to Las Vegas tomorrow for all I care. Or tonight." She tried to tug his mouth back to hers, but he resisted. "Matt."

He chuckled. "Don't you want it?"

"What?"

"Your ring."

"Matt." She grabbed hold of his hair on either side of his head and looked him in the eyes. "If you do not take me inside right this instant and make wild passionate love with me, I'm going to hurt you."

"Now?"

She nodded. "Now."

He sighed. "If I have to."

Her jaw dropped. *As if.*

Laughing, he scooped her up and strode into the house. He dropped her on the big bed. Then he covered her with his body. "Whatever the soon-to-be-married lady wants," he whispered against her lips.

# EPILOGUE

*Three years later*

Matt's arms wrapped around her from behind and he rested his chin on the top of her head. Contentment hummed. Grace leaned back. The waves outside the big windows beat against the dark-gray sand. She liked the fact that the walls and insulation didn't keep the sound of the ocean out.

"How are you doing, sweetheart?"

"Hmmm." Practically purring, she sank a little deeper into him. "Tired, but good."

His hands smoothed down over her swollen belly. A little foot kicked against his palm. He chuckled. "This one's going to be as sassy as her momma."

"You won't think it's funny when our son is as ornery as you."

"That's okay. I've got years of experience on him. I'm pretty sure I can handle him."

Laughing, she turned. "So cocky. I can't wait to see how confident you are two weeks into having twins at home."

Matt grinned. "I don't see the problem here."

Laughter and running feet thundered down the stairs of their vacation rental. Sarah, Charles and Terrance tore into the room. Little tornadoes of mass destruction, but she adored them nonetheless.

"See? I've had these terrors to prepare me. Nothing could be as bad as these three."

"Hey," Terrance shouted. He'd learned to talk and gone straight to yelling everything. "That's not nice, Matt."

With a final pat to the ginormous belly preceding her these days, he released her. "I dare you to deny you're a terror to my face."

Never one to back down from a challenge, four-year-old Terrance marched right up to him. Grace groaned. So much for the five minutes of peace she'd enjoyed.

"I am not a terror. She," he pointed toward Sarah, "is the terror."

Matt snatched Terrance and, in a blink, had him hanging upside down. "Now, Terrance. We've talked about this."

Terrance shrieked with laughter, intimidated beyond belief, obviously.

"That is not the way you talk about girls. They are sweet, precious, delicate little creatures—"

"What?" Jane placed her hands on her hips.

". . . and us men," Matt continued, "need to be respectful of their more fragile temperaments."

"As if." Grace rolled her eyes.

"Yeah. As if," Sarah echoed.

The first child they'd taken in, the seven-year-old little girl had quickly become a regular mini-me of Grace. At nine, she'd decided to put her own spin on things. She did so by placing her fists on her hips and flipping her long-blonde hair over her shoulders.

Grace couldn't decide if her spunky attitude was a good or bad thing.

Taking in foster children had been an easy decision. Letting go when and if their parents got their acts together. . . not so much. Except for Charles, the youngest of the group, none of them were orphans. Sarah's parents weren't married, her dad was in jail for armed robbery and her mom was in jail for criminal neglect of her child. The bright little girl sashayed out of the room with another hair flip. A comment about her dolls being better company than a bunch of boys drifted over her shoulder.

Matt met Grace's eyes over Terrance's tennis-shoe-clad feet and raised an eyebrow, as if to say, *"What was that all about?"*

Grace shook her head. Despite their commonality of an X-chromosome, Sarah was often beyond her grasp.

There was a tug on her pant leg. Charles stood beside her. The look of patented longing in his big blue eyes spoke volumes. Dismissing the half second thought of sitting on the floor like she used to—she couldn't even see her feet anymore, let alone get off the floor—she gingerly lowered herself into a chair. Halfway down, Matt's arms came around her.

"There are two of them, so it only seems right I help." His brown eyes twinkled. She was really hoping at least one of the babies would have his eyes. "After all, two against one is hardly fair."

"Ha-ha." She'd married a regular comedian.

Once she was settled, Matt scooped Charles off the floor and placed him on the narrow wedge of what was left of her lap. With a toothy grin, Charles fisted her blouse in one hand and reached for her hair with the other while scrambling up the mountain of her belly.

Matt intervened with a gentle *"No"* and parked his diapered bottom back on her leg.

Another attempt had them both chuckling, but Matt persisted. Only this time, he put Charles on the armrest of the chair within the circle of her arm. The closer proximity to her face seemed to relax the fifteen-month-old. He dropped his blond head onto her belly and stuck his thumb in his mouth.

Matt rubbed the baby's curly hair. "He adores you."

"That's only fair, since I fell in love on sight."

"Kind of like with me."

"Uh. . . yeah. Exactly like that."

Matt narrowed his eyes and leaned down until their noses were an inch apart. "What's that supposed to mean?"

Fluttering her lashes, she widened her eyes and made her smile as guileless as possible. "Nothing, honey. All those months before we began dating. . . Why, I could barely restrain myself from jumping you during those dry board meetings."

"I think you're confused. I was the one tormented with lust for months. I know darn well you never noticed me."

"Oh, I noticed you."

"Not like a man. A man you'd like to get naked with," he whispered to avoid the children hearing.

"Well, I think it's pretty obvious that changed."

Someone knocked at the door.

He patted her belly. "You stay put, sweetheart. That's the rest of the family."

The scent of the ocean swept in through the open door, along with Matt's mom and step-dad, his brother and his girlfriend, an aunt, a couple of uncles and too many cousins to count. The irony of her life since marrying Matt was not lost on her. For a woman who'd spent her whole life alone, isolated from relationships and lacking a family, she now had more relatives than she could count on both hands *and* feet. Permanent relationships were coming out of her ears. Not the least of which were the foster children they cared for.

Grace snuggled Charles closer. He was such a somber toddler, as if on some level he sensed what he'd lost so early in life. Her dearest hope was that she and Matt could restore some part of these children's faith in humanity by providing a stable and happy home.

Oh, man. She had to pee again. That'd be like the fourth time in less than an hour. "You babies are really taking up more than your fair share of room." She squirmed enough to ease a dozing Charles onto the seat cushion—he showed his displeasure by frowning and sucking harder on his thumb—then heaved herself up and waddled to the nearest bathroom.

In about three weeks, according to her doctor, she would be

able to walk like a normal female again. Not only that, she might actually *feel* like a normal female again. Not to mention sex. Holy cow, did she miss sex. She'd become so uncomfortable in the past month that making love was an impossibility.

Halfway across the kitchen pain arced through her back. Her belly tightened, stealing her breath. She gasped and planted her palms on the counter.

"Matt?" Her voice came out a whisper. She gathered herself to try again.

Before she could, Matt was there. He wrapped himself around her. "You okay, sweetheart?"

*Really not a good time, kiddos.* They didn't care. A fact demonstrated with clarity when liquid trickled down the inside of her thighs.

"Um, not really." She winced and pressed a hand to her swollen belly. "The babies have decided to put in an early appearance."

"What?" He snapped straight, like someone had used a cattle prod on his butt. Then he flew into action. An admiral commanding his troops, that was her husband.

Grandparents were assigned babysitting duty. Everyone promised to stick around and help entertain the children. He swept her up in his arms, despite her protests. She flushed. Another contraction hit and she stopped caring that she weighed as much as a walrus.

By the time they reached the Ilwaco hospital, the contractions were only two minutes apart. Matt rushed inside for a wheelchair. Giving birth to premature twins in a tiny coastal hospital hadn't been on her agenda.

She focused on not hyperventilating or worrying about things she couldn't control. Like when and where her obstinate children decided to be born. They were going to be just like their father, that much was obvious.

Four hours, one emergency helicopter ride to a better-equipped

263

hospital, and more screaming and agonizing pain than she cared to recall later, Grace cradled her newborn babies. Their tiny fists waved in the air. Little Cassandra sucked on one of her fingers. Christopher curled his teeny fingers around Matt's finger and her eyes misted over.

"Just a few more minutes, Mrs. Duncan. Then we need to get them to the neonatal unit."

Matt's head snapped up. "Why? What's wrong?"

"They're doing really well, but they're five and a half weeks early and we want to keep a close eye on them. If they're still doing as well in a few hours, we'll bring them back and your wife can try nursing."

Matt nodded, but she could see he was still worried. So was she. Astoria's hospital was much larger, but it wasn't state of the art, by any stretch. Portland would have been preferable. Unfortunately, her labor had progressed at lightning-fast speed. No way would she have lasted for that trip.

Grace dropped a kiss on the top of Christopher and Cassandra's little heads and reluctantly handed them to the nurse. She and Matt watched in tense silence as the nurse placed their little swaddled bodies in a warming cubicle together.

The woman tossed a perky smile over her shoulder when she reached the door with the wheeled cubicle. "They're doing great. Try not to worry. You need to relax and get some rest while you can, Mrs. Duncan."

The nurse disappeared. Grace chomped down hard on her lower lip to hold her tears at bay. It didn't work.

"Shhh, sweetheart. They'll be fine."

She nodded, but the tears kept coming. Matt gently scooted her over on the hospital bed and lay down beside her. Curled around him, she cried into his shirt until physical exhaustion dragged her into sleep.

Three days later, Grace heaved a sigh of utter relief. The mobile munchkins darted past, Charles doing his best to keep up. Matt followed her in. His arms were full, so she shut the door.

"Home," she moaned.

Collapsing on the couch, she closed her eyes and waited while her body's aches sorted themselves out. Wasn't easy pushing out two babies then traveling across an entire state with twin newborns and three older children. Matt settled a fussing Christopher in her arms. He quickly latched onto her breast and settled down. Both babies had been able to leave the hospital with her—no small miracle.

Matt rocked Cassandra, enthralled. He had yet to look up from their daughter. When he did, the wealth of emotion in his dark eyes made her heart pinch.

"How did I ever get so lucky?" he whispered.

Grace smiled, looking at the baby boy suckling her breast. "I beg to differ. You didn't get lucky. I did."

### THE END

Printed in Australia by Griffin Press
an Accredited ISO AS/NZS 14001:2004
Environmental Management System printer.